KrafT

Nicholas Oyoo

First Edition January 2012

Edited by Charles Phebih-Agyekum
Cover Design Concept: Abel Murumba
Cover Design: Danielle Pitt
Layout Design: Kemunto Matunda

Published by Nsemia Inc. Publishers
www.nsemia.com

Note for Librarians:
A cataloguing record for this book is available
from Library and Archives Canada

ISBN: 978-1-926906-13-3 paperback

In memory of Lucy Nyambura Mugwandia

ABOUT THE AUTHOR

Nicholas Oyoo discovered his passion for writing early in life. He remembers his first manuscript called the *Daltons* which he co-authored with one of his friends while in primary school. Unfortunately, *Daltons* was never published. *Kraft*, his first novel has been a work in progress starting back in his days in secondary school. The novel developed as he prolifically contributed on topical issues in local dailies. He admits to 'straying away from the box', a feature that will come out through the pages of the *Kraft*.

Nicholas was born in 1974. Nicholas holds a degree on Journalism and Media – Development Communication option, from the University of Nairobi. This is in addition to a Political Science Diploma from Kampala University.

Nicholas is actively involved in a number of initiatives aimed at the welfare of Kenyans. In this respect he has trained in Leadership Development under a programme called Political Leadership Development Program (PLDP). Partly through this program, and working with other program alumni, they registered the trust Pioneers For Change (P4C) in which he holds the positions of Trustee and Administration Secretary. In addition, Nicholas has held a number of key leadership positions in various organizations, including that of Vice-Chairman of a promising political party, Twaweza Party of Kenya.

'Lord, protect me from my friends; I can take care of my enemies.' - F. Voltaire, French Philosopher

ACKNOWLEDGEMENTS

To my mum, I remember you pulled my ears when you discovered I was so engrossed what would have been in my first novel and was ignoring my standard 8 upcoming exams...but you were my biggest anchor in the latter days when I embarked on this novel in those early days of the typewriters and hand writing of scripts.

To my siblings - Your interest in this novel made the dream remain alive.

To my friends at Aga Khan High school...You inspired the seed that developed into this. To my university colleges in Kampala International University, Kampala University, and the University of Nairobi...unknowingly you were a source of motivation in moments when this book was stalling.

A special mention about Naftal Nyabuto and Tony Moturi - The two of you literally facilitated my final push with your support and advice every way since we met.

I will not forget my readers - Jackline Maina, Elizabeth Ombati, Peter Mbuthia, Ben Indimuli, Masiwo Willis O. Omanya...It is when your views about Kraft came back that I realized in deed this was a worthy writing.

Jed Odero Omorit...your forward was an eye opener.

Finally, to my publishers - *Kraft* was ready for first submission some 10 years back but I would not find publishers willing to look at the novel until you came along.

FOREWORD

The Kraft is a very complex tale, spanning several scenarios woven simply from daily occurrences to become stunningly believable. Nicholas Oyoo has proven that, despite the youth being engrossed with careers, family...and attendant challenges, they are observant and keen about issues and happenings around them; happenings that impact their lives over generations. Loyalty, consistence, betrayals, corruption, impunity, indiscretions and many other ills underpin *Kraft;* attributes that are so prevalent in modern day society that they have become the norm, and hence "acceptable" by many in society. Oyoo interrogates those beliefs sensitively, leaving the reader in no doubt about the higher ideals that he espouses and expects of society. For long we have decried the dearth of writings by Kenyan authors, *Kraft* puts paid to that lie. True, many publishers have avoided publishing works of fiction citing lack of market. Now young authors are here talking to their peers, in a language comprehensible to most across generational divides.

Jed Odero Omorit
Social scientist working with local communities

BOOK ONE - THE ALPHA

PROLOGUE

The disappearance of multi millionaire Juve Teluve was more than newsworthy. The Voice of Kenya reported it the day the millionaire had absconded a high court order by not appearing before the judge as was expected, prompting the judge to issue a warrant of arrest. The judge must have regretted his earlier decision to grant Mr. Juve and his co-defendants bail when the case had come up before him a few months earlier. He had simply presented the chance for the millionaire to run.

Following the issuance of the warrant decision, the next morning was a big day for the media, like every other day the millionaire's story was the chief item in the press.

Mark Lubevu and two others, who had been accused with them, had all charges against them dropped, as the police could not find any thing leading directly to them. Juve was facing charges as the owner of the lodging. The prosecutor had in fact written a note and presented it to Mark, hoping that it might make up for any wrongdoing on his part. It was unwise to start a fight with someone who was rich if you could not finish that person off, an important safeguard in the context of how the Kenyan society operated.

The tribulations of the millionaire on the run started when a local daily published an investigative report in linking him to the ownership of a brothel, which was also allegedly a safe haven for drugs and other contraband. His signatures, through a third party on ownership deals done under-carpet, had been undoubtedly proven by the bold report.

The report alleged that Juve Teluve paid off law enforcement agents to keep the ownership under-carpet and operations at the brothel away from the eyes of law enforcers, monthly cheques had been going to some police officers at several police stations. These cheques were traced back to the millionaire. In response to the damning report by the newspaper, the Wenjuve official spokesperson issued a statement to distance the organization from ownership of the lodging in question. The police reacted quickly and raided the lodging. However, it turned out that there was nothing against the law. It was an ordinary run down lodging in downtown Nairobi.

Why would the millionaire, president of the Wenjuve group of companies, want to own an ordinary lodging in the city? And why would he dispute its ownership with his signatures all over the ownership documents? Maybe Mr. Juve had something to hide that would be scandalous. But one thing the police force knew was that disputing ownership is not a crime. It could be some political tactic the millionaire was using as a springboard to enter politics. That had to be it. Mr. Juve Teluve had always refused to join politics and had always kept a distance between himself and the practice. May be it was just a matter of timing. But whatever the newspapers kept printing, the issue ended up being resolved. No laws broken.

The police promised to keep looking and all was quiet for a few months. Then like a flash of lightening falling from the skies, the hammer struck the nail unexpectedly, and with great repercussions as this time around, the millionaire could not escape.

An anonymous tip-off led an elite squad of the police back to the lodging, this time just when they needed to be there and exactly where they had to look - a secret basement. No one was found at the lodging at the time that the police raided.

The raid yielded over five thousand kilograms of cocaine and three hundred kilograms of heroine. Also confiscated were rhino horns, ivory, some leopard and cheetah skins, some forged vehicle documentations and fake currency in local and foreign denominations. The top four Wenjuve executives were taken in for questioning but 3 of them were released.

There was overwhelming evidence, but Juve was granted bail and the case was set for hearing a few months later. The police had stumbled into a gold-mine of evidence. A witness had agreed to testify against Juve about the acquisition of the lodging and the illegal activities conducted in the building.

Juve exhibited surprise at the developments and insisted somebody wanted to see the last of him and the Wenjuves, no matter how far they had to go to achieve this goal.

Mark described the situation as outrageous, devilish and malicious. He insisted he knew Juve and the other two executives well, and nobody amongst them was capable of the crimes being pinned on them. "The bastards will pay for this." He retorted angrily to the local and international media.

A sea of journalists from all over the globe swarmed the Jomo Kenyatta International and Wilson Airports, hungry for information. Nobody was going to miss the unfolding story. It was another millionaire going down the drain and another juicy story to be covered for the whole world to see, read and pay heavily for. The fully booked hotels around the city of Nairobi said it all.

In the weeks leading up to the trial the Wenjuve executive seemed to shun publicity, even when follow-up reports were creatively done by the various section of the media, ensuring the public was kept abreast with the 'Wenjuve Crime Investigations' as it came to be referred.

And so when the shocking turn of events that cumulated to the death of the main suspect, Millionaire Juve Teluve, were taking place, the media was alive to record the tragic but astounding on goings. It was alleged that a pensive

Juve took his car keys, drove into the countryside 'to clear his mind' two days before the trial began, and drove to his disappearance and subsequent death.

Mark Lubevu stood in front of the huge audience as he delivered the eulogy at Jamuhuri Park.

"Personally, I have lost a friend, a brother, a father, and my whole family in one stroke. I shall not just stand back and watch as those who brought harm against an innocent man get away with it. They are the very persons responsible for this turn of events. Ladies and gentlemen, six feet under goes the one exceptional man who built a very positive image for Kenya, slain by the invisible bullets of allegations and outrageous accusations."

"Let them for one single minute not think it is over. I will not rest until I prove to the world that the man sinking into the ground here was a harmless person if it is the last thing I do on this earth."

Suddenly he could not continue: He broke into tears. He had to be helped off the dais.

And that was how the late millionaire's remains made the last journey to the magnificent 25 storey Wenjuve Towers to be laid to rest next to his beloved wife, Wendy.

A special executive meeting held several days later unanimously backed Mark on the presidency of the company, though the will clearly stated that the estates were to go to Kate Teluve – who was yet to be found. After all Juve had formed the habit to refer to him as his son. In fact, very few people were aware that Mark was not Juve's son.

ONE

The fugitive, Juve Teluve, looked at the blue skies above him. He looked at the caves that had become his home, behind him. Then his eyes wandered to the wildlife, peacefully grazing at a distance. That was his source of food. He had gone into the caves three years earlier to escape being arrested. But he knew that soon he would have to come out and the fight would have to continue.

Usually several hours before the sun disappeared into the horizons, he would creep out of the caves to meet his closest friend, who worked at the colonial intelligence office. Then he would learn what the administration was planning to do next. He would make a move when most appropriate. His friend, Mark Lubevu, was his informant for the past one and a half years. He would overhear as plans were laid down, or he would come across messages which were potentially harmful to the fighters in the forest, and he would pass these messages to the men in the caves who would in turn relay them to all the others in the forest.

On several occasions, the administration planned fool proof traps that they hoped would lure the fighter, one of the most sought after, into the open, where they would mount an arrest and charge him with the murder of a British general.

But thanks to the very reliable information, he always found a way to fool them.

The latest wave of events was a very exciting one. The British were finally caving in. Freedom was surely inevitable. But his case was a different one. He was to be charged with the killing of a British general. He intended to wait until the British had left, then he would quietly creep out of hiding and settle down to a quiet life. Most African states were getting independence. That meant hope. Mark was a good informer.

His mind slipped back to the bitter past. The colonial motorcade consisting of two huge trucks had suddenly appeared in the village. At least seventy men were loaded into the gigantic automobiles to be ferried back to Nairobi to face charges of disturbances in the capital, where several dozen policemen had been slain. The troublemakers had fled to their ancestral homes to avoid the swoop. The administration insisted that at least a hundred of them were from the Tuve community.

His father was one of the most sought after figures in the "campaign to root out the bad seeds," as the general had referred to the exercise. When they finally arrested him in his hut, he refused to accompany them to the lorry and so they opened fire on him and the whole family as an example to the rest of the community, just to make sure they did not even think of resisting.

Juve had been out fishing at the time. On returning to the village, the gravity of the sad events hit him hard as he was met by the lifeless bodies of what had been his family. A seemingly dark shadow had enveloped the world the moment he walked into the village and into the screams and shrieks of the people as they moaned their losses. But it was nothing compared to what he found in the hut.

In a rushed ritual, he quickly performed the final rites for his family, and consumed with vengeance, he gathered fifteen daring young men, mostly his age mates in their mid-twenties and went into hot pursuit behind the colonial administrators.

Their chase led them to a heavily equipped prison camp, where they attacked without warning.

Taken by surprise, the sophisticated prisons security system was overwhelmed by the spirited invaders.

The attacks, on achieving some degree of success in their bid, set free the prisoners held in the camp.

The brutal prison attack left a heavy loss of life on both sides, with the government loosing a respected war general in the fierce battle.

The colonial authorities responded to the loss by mass arrests and had taken as many prisoners as they could handle and employing torture routines to gain valuable information about the ringleaders of the attack.

This process yielded the information about the kind of protagonists that the government had to face in the prison attack and the identity of their leader.

The authorities went into a manhunt for Juve Teluve, blaming him for the *'cold blooded'* murder of the general.

On learning about the new developments, Juve went into hiding in the Mabonde caves in the suburbs of Nairobi.

Mark, one of the young men who escaped unidentified, offered to spy on the colonial administration for him. He sought a job at the colonial intelligence office and landed it. His role always kept Juve afloat.

Then like an erupting volcano without warning, Mark's cover was blown sky-high. The unsuspecting Mark walked right into the waiting hands of the colonial police.

"Do you think he could lead us to Juve?" an intelligence man inquired.

"He obviously knows where the man is," another answered.

"Then let's release him, and tail him day and night. Somehow he would have to see the man."

"No, I think we should get Juve when we get the chance. Who knows, maybe he is aware that we've got his friend. That would put our situation with him in a delicate position. He would sink into his hiding even more if he knows. And we both know how this man can surely vanish. I think some 'deadly torture' will make him talk." the senior man said.

"But do you people realize that the moment Juve

learns about this arrest he would shift every thing and the information would be out dated and even misleading," one of the members of the intelligence team meeting chipped in.

"But you bet he won't leave his friend to rot in custody. That's where we will get him," the most senior man smiled at the thought.

When Mark did not show up where they were supposed to meet, Juve had the ill feeling something was not right. He waited for another day before going into the forest where he would know if something was indeed wrong.

Everything was wrong. The caged cock in the forest had fainted for lack of food and water. That was the sign they had agreed upon. Mark was in trouble, in fact deep trouble.

Juve looked into the clothes box Mark had filled up with both male and female clothing as he had instructed. He looked for a pair of scissors and cut off his dreadlocks and then completely shaved off his beard and moustache using a razor.

He put on earrings, wore a well folded hair scarf to cover his head, then wore a long dress that went way down to cover his legs, which were wrapped in stockings and shod in high heeled stylish ladies shoes. Under the brassiere, he put in soft clothing to look like breasts. An early thirties plain looking lady was the result.

The newspaper headlines screamed 'Judge Haddock Henry to handle informer's case.' *She* bought a copy of each of the dailies and read them thoroughly. Thank God again *she* had attended school and excelled especially in language. *She* now knew where to get the information.

She travelled into the city centre and then to the high courts. *She* walked into a court- room. A case was in progress. A petty thief was answering to the case. That wasn't of much interest to him. However, the black court clerk caught his attention. That was the man who was going to inform her. *She* decided subconsciously.

Once the sentence had been read, and the session had ended, *she* followed the clerk to an office room. He was arranging his things in readiness to leave the building.

She looked around the corridors and on seeing no one *she* walked into the room and closed the door lightly behind her.

"Hey lady, can I be of assistance to you?"

"Of course you can help me." The feminine reply surprised even Juve himself. "Are you free for lunch?" *she* posed after a hesitant moment.

That was the very first time the clerk raised his eyes, his face registering surprise. His eye's leveled on *hers*, momentarily, before wandering downwards. "You think you can just walk in here and book me for lunch, what are you, the queen or somebody?"

"No need for that Mr....." *She* did not know his name.

"Stephenson," replied the clerk.

"Mr. Stephenson, right."

"How can I help you Miss Gracie?" Stephenson finally said once they were seated at the cozy Labona restaurant.

She opted to go straight to the point. "I want you to tell me about judge Haddock. I want to meet him."

"What was that? You want meet who? Stephenson could not hold back his surprise.

"The judge, didn't I just say so?"

"You are probably crazy. That is my boss and if I'm busy, he is busier. What is it you want to see him about?"

"I'll tell you a little womanish secret, Mr. Stephenson. When a woman's dreams are filled with a man, we women know the only way to get him out of our systems is to make sure we've crossed paths with him."

"You are really crazy, aren't you? The judge has a 20 year old daughter, you are black and he is white, and this is 1961 in Kenya, and you must already know how much he despises black people. He won't even notice you. Let alone reject you," Stephenson said as a matter of fact.

"That is exactly what I'm bargaining for, to get him out of my system."

"You know something; there are those things I'm not supposed to discuss at all. My boss is at the top of that list," Stephenson said.

"Not a word leaves this table," *she* promised, persuasively.

"That's my boss and I might lose my job just like that," Stephenson insisted.

"It can never get to that Mr. Stephenson."

"What do you want to know?" Stephenson finally gave in, with his voice dropping to a whisper.

"Every thing, his wife, what he likes, what he hates, and what kind of a man he is."

"He is a very difficult person. He lost his wife when his daughter was only ten. Since then, he has closed his romantic side completely. His love is towards one direction - his daughter. The man cares about nothing and nobody. His daughter lives like a prisoner, completely surrounded by his riches and protection. Police escorts, chauffeurs, and too much money all around her."

"About him?" *she* urged him on.

"Anyway, why am I telling you this? Listen, if you want to know about the judge, talk to him yourself. Bye bye Miss Gracie. And remember this meeting never took place." Stephenson stood up suddenly and walked hurriedly out of the restaurant.

He looked helplessly behind Stephenson as he walked out of the restaurant.

No worries, Stephenson had performed well enough with the information on the judge. Besides, the disguise was getting into his skin. The information was good enough to be useful.

****

"You're soon going to be Mrs. Willis Jr.," Judge Haddock announced in a firm confident voice.

Wendy Henry, the daughter of Judge Haddock, had had more than enough. She was not going to let herself into this. She had always been under inspection, in the name of protection. To the judge, she was just an asset to be used as a tool for gambles. The world had to believe how much his daughter mattered to him.

She was not ready to take more of the punishments such as no lunch, no dinner, the senseless beatings and canings. Now she had to deal with the big blow that she was going to be married to a certain Willis Jr.

"Over my dead body!" she promised herself. All she knew about this Willis character was that he was the son of a judge. "It's time to get up and fight back, young lady," she told herself as she soothed herself to sleep.

That night she dreamed of a prince who would appear and save her from her prison home. It was not the first time she had had that dream. It was only that every morning when she got up, she could not make up the face of the prince.

Every living soul could easily have believed that judge Haddock was a compassionate and loving father, and a good man. But the truth was that he loved no one at all. He was actually a beast of a person, and especially so when he had taken doses of those powerful concoctions he used.

It was in between one of those overdose sessions when his wife resisted his attempts to undress her, he slapped her so hard across her face that she went rolling down the stairs like a log and died instantly of multiple injuries.

On realizing what he had done, he went outside into his own compound and broke into his own house. When the police came to investigate, he insisted that his wife had rolled down the stairs after a wrong footing, as she fled from the burglars.

Afterwards, the judge openly boasted good riddance to a group of friends in a bar over drinks, saying he had only married her because of a bet against a rival gambler on who would conquer the 'Virgin Mary,' as they referred to her then. His only motivation was the large sums of money he had received on the wedding night from the rival for the conquest. Had the lady allowed him to sleep with her without the marriage bullshit, he would not have gone through with the bloody wedding. It was only because the rules in his kind of profession were too tight against its non-upright members. That is what compelled him to keep the 'whore' and 'her bastard.' It was all in order to qualify for some favours from the judges' league.

Somebody reported the case to the police and the judge was taken in for questioning. He was however released due to lack of enough evidence. Not long after that the judge was again involved in another scandal, this time accused of fixing cases for the bad guys. The judiciary could not get rid of him due to lack of solid evidence, and had only one realistic alternative - send him to one of the colonies where his wrong doings would not matter very much unless they were very severe.

In the Kenyan colony he was thus trying to win back some reputation and the limelight he had lost.

On the sixteenth birthday of his daughter, he threw a huge party and took so much booze that he ran out of control and cornered her in one of the rooms and ordered her to undress. She knew exactly what this routine entailed. He had always done it on her mother every other night when he came home drunk and proceeded to beat her half dead before thrusting himself into her.

He proceeded to undress himself shamelessly in front of her. Wendy stared in disbelief. Silently within herself, she swore he was not going to rape her. Not as long as she was alive.

With one hand hidden behind her, she grabbed a bottle of scotch from the crate behind her and waited as he moved closer. With one decided thrust, she swung the deadly bottle for his head. He stepped aside abruptly, and she missed terribly.

It was over. She had no chance. He grabbed her like a hungry monster. She tried all she could to resist. He was too strong. He obviously had the training from doing it to her mother every other night.

And the process began, first the senseless beating, then the ultimate of all, sex.

A maid in the house had always known the judge's tendencies, especially when drunk. She dashed out quickly, having read the signs and sensed the danger. She abruptly abandoned her trays in the noisy merry making party hall and shot upstairs. The commotion was unmistakable. The second process was about to begin.

"Let her go. Take me instead, or I'll let the whole party know who you really are."

"What, are you threatening me? I do what I want any time and no bloody maid can threaten me! I'll give you the honours of watching the operation on the V.I.P stand."

"Oh, no you don't. The police have a file that has all the information about you. Every bloody rotten thing you've ever done in this world, word for word. I only added the murder of your wife. She compiled the rest. I have strict instructions that it should be looked inside the moment my life is near anything called threatened."

The judge walked over to the maid. He raised his hand to administer a blow. He could not bring himself to it. Even in his drunken, closed state he knew when he was beaten flat. "How can I tell that you are not lying to me?"

"Look inside your drawer. There are copies of the documents. I wanted to give them to you tonight, but it seems necessity prevailed."

The judge grabbed for the drawer like a mad man. He removed the blue spring file from inside the bedside drawer. It was one he had never seen before.

He started looking at the pages inside. It was there, everything. The drugs, the murder attempts on the government minister, the fixing of the cases, the molestation of his family, word by word. It was like a personal diary. Everything inside there enough to build a strong case that could earn him a long time behind bars. In fact the only thing that was missing about him in the file was a visit to the doctor who informed him of his inability to father. Wendy wasn't his daughter. He was determined to make her pay for the sins of her mother.

"What do you want, money?" the judge asked coldly.

"No, I want you to keep your pants on, around your daughter. Anything suspicious happening around her and that will be opened."

The judge didn't like being pushed around. He will finally find a way to deal with this maid, he promised himself. For now she had won. Any bad move and he was dead meat.

The only way he could vent his anger on Wendy after that incident was by enforcing maximum punishments at the slightest opportunity.

"Toe the line or you will follow your 'whore' mother to the grave," he was fond of telling her.

TWO

The police force didn't keep any secrets. The arrest of Mark Lubevu was not unheard of anywhere in the capital. Judge Haddock, who was to handle the case, had a reputation. Everybody was giving their opinion on the matter.

"He'll probably try his antics again," an intelligence officer said during a meeting to discuss how best to handle Juve in case he tried anything.

"Or maybe we should get a bit careless with the prisoner. That way we can easily tell when he would strike and we can mount an ambush."

"Good thinking. No worries, we'll catch our man," the most senior man said.

"What if he does not appear before or during the proceedings?" somebody was concerned.

"There's still time. I think he'll come for his friend sooner or later."

"We will not make it look as if we are expecting him. Once Juve knows the prison in which we are holding his friend, you can be sure he will try something."

"Anything else somebody wants to add?" the senior man said. Nobody answered. "Okay, I want you all to have your best sleep tonight. We don't want people sleeping on the job. Tomorrow we will report here at exactly seven," he said after a moment's pause.

The next day, was going to be the end of a manhunt that had taken them years. The hunt for the man they believed had to pay a heavy penalty for going against the colonial administration, or so the police believed.

****

The intruder arrived at Judge Haddock's servant quarters chauffeur residence, at 6.30 that evening and stayed well hidden out of sight. He could smell the aroma of the nice meal cooking. He was in luck that there was a drizzle beginning. He knew the wife of the judge's chauffeur would have to come out of the house to collect the dry clothes from the line. He readied himself, his poisonous powder in the ready. The blend was just enough to send anyone to the hospital. When she came out he found his opportunity to add the powder in the stew. He cursed that he did not have time to steal a few pieces of meat before adding the powder. It looked tasty. By the time she was returning, the rain now a shower, he had already left the kitchen and had found his way out of the house.

Judge Haddock's official chauffeur dropped the judge at his doorstep, parked the car, and washed it in readiness for the next day. He then walked the few metres to his servants' quarter residence.

It was eight already. Food must be on the table by that time. His beloved wife was never usually late in the cooking. He adored that punctuality in her. He was a voracious eater, especially when the meal was one of his favourite dishes.

His wife opened the door smiling. "Food's on the table, dear."

"That's one reason why I picked you for my lifelong partner. You are the best by far." A peck of thanks was exchanged.

He caught the familiar aroma of rice and stew. That multiplied his appetite tenfold.

"Your favourite, eh."

"Wrong. You are my favourite of everything. That's just my favourite dish."

"Very flattering."

"Wrong again. That's the plain truth."

"You are sentenced to a hug. But first, food's on the table."

And so the happy couple settled to a hearty meal, not aware that an intruder had helped mix the stew. The next morning, both stomachs were in great pain and agony.

The chauffeur therefore, could not perform his daily chores that morning. The gardener notified the judge and handed him the car keys.

"What does that chauffeur think I am? A charity organization or what? I don't pay him to be getting sick on me."

"I don't think he is in a position to think at the moment, sir. The ambulance should be on its way here to take them to hospital, sir," the gardener answered.

"Damn!" the judge cursed under his breath. He realized the implications. He would have to drive himself to work that morning.

He had barely driven half the route to the courthouse when a hard, cold, rod like object touched the back of his head. He tried to turn and see what it was, then the smell so near his nostrils instructed him otherwise. The familiar scent of gunpowder registered its overpowering frightful smell through his nostrils, down his spine, and into every nerve of his body. He lost the vehicle's control, momentarily, before recovering. The car danced on both lanes of the road for that one moment, dangerously. The roadside was free of pedestrians, and there were no other vehicles in sight. Otherwise it would have gone down as a fatal accident.

"Good morning your honour, scared?" It was a thick accented and frightening voice coming from the rear seat of the car. The judge almost lost control again. He tried to look into the rear view mirror inside the car, but the mirror was poorly angled. He could not yet bring himself to adjust it just yet. Anything unusual at that time could easily prove suicidal, so he kept his shaking hands firmly on the steering wheel.

"Take a look at this, pal," the voice said. This time a piece of paper was passed over from the gunman. He threw a quick glance at the paper. The familiar drawing of Juve stared back at him. The cold shiver went through him.

"Now, adjust the mirror to certify if those two look alike."

He did as was instructed. There was no doubt. The dreadlocks may have been shaven. But he was still the very same Juve. Not a question about that.

The judge didn't need to be told it was going to be a long bad day, maybe the worst day of his entire life.

"So Judge, or shall I say your honour, I hope you won't forget for even a fraction of a second, who you are dealing with. It would obviously be fatal if you did."

Shit, why should he repeat those words? The judge did not need to be reminded that forgetting whom he was dealing with would be suicidal.

"Pull up the car."

He slowed down, chose a suitable place to park the car, and switched off the engine. Sweat was quickly making him wet. He could choose to reach for his gun, which was in his briefcase on the next seat, but he decided against such a move. At least not yet, as this man they called Juve was an ice cold no nonsense kind of a troublemaker. He would waste a life at the slightest of excuses.

"Now listen carefully, I want you to undo the combination of that briefcase you have at your side, and don't think of opening it. Then pass it slowly to me at the back. Remember that it's your life we are bargaining on here."

This guy is a professional. The judge knew he was beaten. Anything stupid would surely be fatal. He did exactly as ordered. The angry, life stopping tool did not at any moment leave the back of his head.

"What have we here? Wow, if I give the Judge a chance he would shoot me, eh," Juve said amusingly the moment he opened the briefcase. He emptied the gun and put it back where it had been then passed the briefcase back to the Judge after inspecting it, making sure there was nothing of significance to him. "Now we are off to Ngong. You know the geography. Lets get moving." Ngong urban centre was some 20 kilometres north of Nairobi.

"Ngong, where in particular?" His voice trembled with fright and desperation.

"I'll let you know where, when we get there. Drive." The judge did the necessary turns and was soon on the Ngong road. After about thirty minutes of driving, Juve ordered him to stop. The road was lonely with no vehicles in sight and it was covered with trees and shrubs on both sides. The judge's fright increased three fold. Was this man going to waste him anyway?

"Drive on." The icy order cut through him like a knife. If this maniac was going to do that, he wasn't going to be murdered without a fight, he decided as he started the car.

"Stop," the voice came five minutes later.

The judge wanted to scream. He wasn't used to being ordered around, and especially not by this black maniac. Who was he to order him around? His answer came when the rod struck his head – the man with the gun...nay, the ruthless man with the gun.

With the butt of the gun he knocked the judge unconscious. He then pulled the judge into a hut he had earlier selected. He carefully tied the judge up then took a bucket of cold water and poured its contents over him.

It took some more buckets full of water before the judge jerked into consciousness wondering where he was. The fright registered on his face when he realized what the situation in which he was - at the mercy of the ruthless man with the gun.

"Now, this is what I want you to do." Juve calmly told the judge as he handed him the receiver of the phone.

"How can I do anything when I'm in this state?"

"No need to worry about that, your honour. I already solved that part. Keep your mouth shut and listen. I won't repeat anything. Thanks to those missionaries who had the idea to bring civilization to remote places like this. Imagine a telephone in perfect working order in this place. You are going to call your residence and ask them to bring your daughter to Ngong. The number please?" He pressed the rod of the gun over the judge's forehead to break any thought of resistance.

Once the Judge had given him his residence numbers, he dialed and waited. When it was picked up, he put it conveniently to the judge's use.

"Please be convincing, because if you don't, those will be the last words you'll ever speak in this world."

Once the Judge had relayed the message Juve grabbed the receiver and proceeded to reinforce the order.

"Did you hear what the judge said?"

A precise feminine voice answered positive "Who's that?" She asked.

"Stephenson." The judge was surprised when he heard the name. "Now be in Ngong in the next two hours."

"I'm the house-keeper Nellie. Don't you recognize me?"

"Tell her to be at the Bulbul Lodge within the next two hours. Her father has already left towards Bulbul." Bulbul was a popular entertainment spot in Ngong Urban centre.

"Alright, but you sound a bit different today."

"Next time I'll be my usual self. Sorry, I have to go now." He hung up before she could start another line of inquiry.

It was now time to proceed to the most vital part of the plan.

"You listen very carefully, your honour. They've got Mark Lubevu in custody. Mark is my man. You are to try him tomorrow. I want Mark to walk out of there a free man. If not, you'll receive your daughter in pieces, you understand me?"

"What makes you think my daughter is at your disposal or that you can dictate terms to me?" the judge almost burst out laughing. His only fear was what that bitch Wendy could tell this son of a bitch once she realized the tight spot she would be in and about to be butchered. But there was one consolation. The maniac would not believe her. These were the kind of men who thought they were very smart and would reason that Wendy was just trying to sweet talk her way into freedom. The only other thing the judge would lose would be that lucrative five figure deal Mr. William Willis was offering for Wendy's hand in marriage to his son, Willis Junior. There was only one catch to that deal on his part, the issue of giving Wendy to someone else where he could not monitor her. But he already had an answer to that. He would take the Willis' fortune, then go round their back and kill Wendy – the act styled like an accident, of course. Then he would blame the death of his beloved 'daughter' on the Willises and maybe get out of it with another multi figure deal as compensation for the life of his daughter. That way he would have killed two birds with one stone. Finally, he would get rid of the errant maid. That would be the wonderful world of the judge, with thousands of pounds around, no bastard Wendy to worry about, no spoiling bloody Nellie of a maid, and no worries in the world. He would even call it quits with the judges' league, start his new life, and live it his own way and by his own rules.

Now the maniac Juve would do the dirty job for him. Juve would kill the bitch for him, and he would take care of the maid personally. The Willises thousands can stay. Now all he needed to do was juice up the maniacs thoughts, then things would start rolling. He almost smiled at the thought. If this world had that group of people who could be called the lucky few, he was convinced he would make it to that list.

"Do I have to chew it for you, your honour? You'll only see your daughter alive again if Mark gets out of prison. I'll be there to see what happens at the courtroom. I'll only release your daughter several hours after the case has been finalized. That will give me time to assess the situation. Anything fishy and she dies. Oh, and don't try looking for me at the courtroom because you wont find me." Juve said.

He left the hut and walked back to the road. He drove the Mercedes for ten minutes towards the city centre, before stopping and parking the vehicle hidden from sight. He waited patiently for the white Morris to appear, sipping his fruit juice slowly.

He saw the Morris after some thirty minutes of waiting. He quickly engaged the gears of the judge's car and started the engine as the Morris passed by the bushes where he had parked, hidden from sight.

He eventually caught up with it a few minutes later. He pressed in the accelerator, sending it to its fullest. The Mercedes started rolling past the Morris and its unsuspecting occupants. He was soon to put his plan into action.

Inside the Morris, there was dead silence. Everybody had their own thoughts to think about.

The driver of the Morris looked at his speedometre. He was a foreman at the residence neighbouring that of the judge and doubled up as a replacement for the judge's chauffeur, when his regular chauffeur was not available. He was out when the judge called that particular morning asking him to cover for his sick driver. He was doing seventy kilometres an hour! Too fast. He began to release the accelerator pedal, just as the grey Mercedes started rolling past the Morris. It looked familiar. *It was familiar.* Then it hit him. Judge Haddock's Mercedes! Suddenly, it was blocking his path. It was too close. He swerved to avoid ramming into it. The Morris drifted onto the uneven roadside. The left side of the vehicle rammed into the roadside bushes and vegetation. His head hit the steering wheel and he lost consciousness. The car stopped abruptly.

Frank Bandy, the blond haired former hit man from England, was a rough and cold blooded no nonsense character, which is what influenced the judge's decision to pick him as the personal bodyguard for Wendy.

The judge saw the necessity of hiring a personal bodyguard for Wendy, when she contemplated escape and made the mistake of relaying her plans to the then chauffeur, thinking he would support her. The chauffeur had instead gone to the judge with the story.

Frank Bandy had carried his gun everywhere he went for the past two years. He had to accompany the judge's daughter everywhere she went. Of course, none of her destinations were ever her choice.

He did not notice the grey Mercedes rolling past the Morris. He was half dozing. The previous night, he had taken in the laundry girl and had ended up sleeping for just two hours in the morning. His drowsiness was enhanced by the fact that he found long drives in cars very boring.

When the car suddenly started behaving like it had run into an earthquake, his sharpness quickly returned to him. He reached for his gun automatically, and lost an opportunity to shield his face from hitting the back of the front passenger's seat, hard. He got dazed for a moment and drifted to the floor of the car.

Wendy Henry was, as usual, buried deep in her own world. Coming out of the house with all these people under orders from her father was nothing unusual. This was just another of those 'meet my daughter' meetings, as she had come to know them. That morning she could not decide what to wear. She almost wore black to symbolize her life in prison under her father, but she decided on white. Her final attire was a long white dress. She knew the kind of punishment she would earn for not being dressed to satisfaction. She hated every bit of it but had no recourse.

Her thoughts were suddenly incursioned by braking, an uneven road surface, confusion then suddenly a halt. Instinctively, she grabbed the seat directly in front of her and pushed hard against the impact, not knowing that that had saved her from taking a hard knock on her forehead. She did not pass out, but almost vomited due to the impact.

Juve did not waste time. Immediately after he had charged the Morris off the road, he moved in for the final catch. He ran to the Morris and opened both the right hand doors, then stepped back a metre away from the vehicle and ordered everyone to step out. The doors were not locked and those on the left were jammed by the roadside trees and could not open.

The driver and his two passengers stepped out as ordered. When the bodyguard hesitated, Juve pressed the trigger and the shot missed him by the narrowest of inches. He knew this type, the kind who thought they always had something up their sleeves, even when squarely beaten.

The bodyguard dropped the pistol he had been trying to conceal. Juve decided the driver wasn't armed from reading his body language. He ordered them to move away from the car, slowly.

He grabbed the girl and put the gun against her neck. She was beautiful, unexpectedly. More than he could even have imagined. He pushed that line of thought out of his head.

The cold murderous rod on Wendy's neck was causing sensations of fear in her. She gave a brief scream of surprise. Frank moved for attack, but then stopped. He could not stand seeing this. The boss would kill him with his bare hands. However, he realized there was nothing he could do. They were dealing with a professional and a lunatic, to make matters worse.

"What do you want?" Frank asked. He wanted to add –"you bloody fucking bastard," but he opted to swallow that. You can never tell with these unfeeling natives.

"You don't ask any questions and I swear it will keep you alive. Now young lady, I'm sure you know how to make strong knots. I want you to tie these two men together, with their faces facing opposite directions of each other and their backs to one another. His left hand should be tied to his friend's right hand and vice versa. Got me?"

She was too frightened to say yes. She nodded instead.

"Remember, you don't want to test my patience. I would sure hate to see an angel like you getting hurt. Stick to my instructions and you'll live to tell the story," he said handing her the strong synthetic ropes he had carried for the job.

As she was doing what he had ordered, he took the chance to look at her well. She was of an ineffable rare beauty, in the form of a magnificent curvy body. If the judge did not cooperate...he pushed the thought out of his mind.

He checked to make sure the knots were strong enough and found that they were.

"Now young lady, I hope you know how to drive, 'cause if you do not, you will have to drive anyway," he said firmly.

"She doesn't," the bodyguard and the driver said in unison.

"Doesn't mean she can't learn," Juve cut in icily.

"I do," Wendy spoke for the very first time.

"No Wendy! You do not know what you are getting into. This guy is a lunatic," Frank said in panic.

"I'm perfectly grown up, Frank." She never once liked Frank.

"Good, full marks on that answer, angel. I hope you are grown up enough to realize that I do not buy into cheap tricks. I will shoot to kill if I see anything suspicious. I sure would hate to waste such beauty through bullets."

"You won't have to. I'll be a good girl." To her it did not matter if she was being kidnapped. To both her captor and her father, she was just a prisoner, a puppet, to be used as a tool for manipulation. It was just like being moved from one prison to another. It may be even better, as there was the chance that her captor might not be as harsh as her father.

"Let's hope so. Now, get into the Mercedes and let's get out of here. I'll tell you where to once we are off. Gentlemen, at least I left you with the option of being able to wander around. There is a hut in the woods that has a working telephone box. Can you imagine that?"

He walked into the Mercedes and took the back seat. "Nairobi. Remember, I'm sitting just behind you. I'd sure hate to blow those beautiful brains to kingdom come."

"That won't be necessary, tough guy. I'll be a good girl. Remember I already promised."

"I surely hope so."

The Mercedes changed directions and rolled back onto the road, towards Nairobi.

THREE

Frank Bandy and Simon Komba watched as Wendy expertly handled the vehicle. Frank was stunned but Simon was not. He had helped Wendy learn how to drive, though he did not expect such expertise on her part. Immediately the Mercedes disappeared into the horizon, Frank and Simon agreed on one thing; for mobility, they had to move sideways. They had waited along the roadsides for several minutes, but no vehicles had passed. Or maybe it was just their impatience and discomfort that had magnified the time.

Their only other chance was to try to locate what the lunatic was talking about. The roadside vegetation was making it hard to spot any building structures. Thankfully Komba noticed a hut in the bush. That had to be it. The crazy one wasn't just imagining things. There actually was a hut.

Using one body and two brains was not actually the easiest of things. The lunatic is a professional. The style of bondage he had preferred on them was a testimony. They had to agree on where to turn, how to do it, which way is right and which is left, which way is forwards and which is backwards. Finally, they managed to get to the hut, somehow.

They were surprised to find the door ajar. They clumsily pushed it open and struggled in. Except for a dusty telephone box on the floor, there wasn't any furniture in the hut. That shattered any hope within them. The hut must have fallen into disuse quite some time back. Nobody was going to find them here. It must have been just a deception employed by their captor to give himself some time to get away. He had outwitted them and made off with Wendy.

"Maybe he was right, Komba. Look at the receiver. He must have used it himself." Frank said referring to the clear outline of a handprint on the receiver.

"But how do you suppose we are going to make any use of it. Remember we are a person with four legs and no hands." Komba reasoned.

They both heard the thin groan coming from somewhere within the hut.

"Who's there? Get me out of here. Help!" a familiar voice cried out.

They started for the direction of the hut where the voice had come from, but realized they had to agree on how to get there. They were soon looking down at the messed up and bonded figure of judge Haddock.

"Judge! What could you be doing here? What's going on? Do you know that some lunatic has taken your daughter captive and is using your Mercedes?" Komba said, the surprise in his tone unmasked.

"Am I glad to see you guys? Not that it's a surprise. That guy is a pro and a maniac," the judge said.

"He knocked us off the road and took off with your daughter as we watched helplessly," Frank said, dejectedly.

"Okay. Now what do we do?" the judge asked. They looked at him like a drowning man would, at a passing straw, with hope yet realizing that hope itself was helplessness. When they heard his voice earlier, they hopefully thought it was rescue, somehow. They were now disappointed.

"Judge, you got your fingers free. We'll just sit down and you unfasten these knots your daughter tied on us," Frank suggested after a few moments of pensiveness.

"Great idea. Now let's get ourselves out of this mess," the judge said enthusiastically, once he understood the concept.

It took several minutes for the judge to work on their knots, before they in turn freed him.

"That guy is using Wendy to shield a friend of his from

facing the wrath of the law. That bullet hole was meant for my head. I just have to comply with his wishes. Otherwise, as he says, he will send my daughter to me part by part."

Not that the judge would mind, especially since his biggest of worries would be eliminated, but what this bastard Wendy would tell this lunatic just to stay alive worried him sick.

The lunatic had promised to take good care of the bastard, as long as all rules were obeyed. Wendy would not open her mouth to speak against him, as long as she knew she was going to be back in his house eventually. She knew she would face his full wrath.

"Sorry judge. So, what's your first move," Frank asked.

"I'll find a reputable lawyer for Mark. I know the case very well and I know the loopholes it may have. We'll have to see that Mark gets his freedom alright. Somehow, this Juve and Mark will both pay for meddling with the wrong person. Not a word about this to any soul, living or dead. Let's find our way back to town."

"I believe the Morris will manage," Komba said hopefully.

They pushed the vehicle back to the road and soon were on their way to the city centre.

FOUR

Wendy Henry expertly handled the vehicle for about ten minutes before she was ordered to stop and get the car off the road into some roadside bushes where it would be hidden from sight.

A rape? The thought suddenly cropped into her mind. She wondered why it was always her. She realized she had to keep her cool. She would only make a move when she was sure enough that she could carry it out all the way. Otherwise, she had to win the trust of her captor. Somewhere along the line he might get careless. That would accord her the chance of escape.

"Step out of the car and walk slowly to the front. Remember my promise of not intending to cause you any harm. Of course that is only true as long as you keep your end of the bargain."

What would rape constitute? She wanted to ask aloud. Men are always idiots of the first order. She will play along and the moment his guards are down and the murderous rod is safely and conveniently positioned, she will strike and make her escape.

"Now, I want you to walk slowly towards that thicket. I hope you have enough wisdom in that beautiful skull of yours to know that anything stupid would finish off your existence on this planet." His voice was as cold as ice.

He had just confirmed it. She was going to have her first sexual escapade in the form of a rape. The elevation of fear in her multiplied a hundred folds. She could no longer contain the fear within her.

The panic and fright were immediately printed on her mannerism and gait. She realized her only chance was to keep her calm until she could handle him. Maybe she could even grab the gun or shoot him in the legs. The realization kept her moving.

"Get into the car and lets proceed with our journey, angel," he said as soon as they were in clear view of the well-hidden red Ford Cortina in the thicket. He had read and realized what she was thinking. He almost burst out laughing. But he smiled when she was still looking away and quickly composed himself. Showing your prisoner your humane side could constitute a huge mistake, lest he or she took full advantage of it.

She was overwhelmed by relief and could not help letting out a sigh. She could not thank the Lord enough in a mini brief prayer for being wrong on that suspicion.

Once they were back on the road and on their way to Thika, some 45 kilometres east of Nairobi, in the red Ford, she smiled on reminiscence of her interpretation about his intentions at that instance.

"What kind of captive would smile in the middle of a kidnapping? Or maybe you are so confident that your daddy will get you out of this." He had seen the smile.

"I thought you were going to-to...." She could not bring herself to complete the sentence. She felt stupid.

"Rape you?" She nodded to mean yes.

"No, I won't do that. It would make me not any different from you whites who rape Africa of its resources. Then again it all depends on your father, angel."

"I believe I can understand your bitterness."

"You drive real well eh," Juve said, changing the subject.

"Thanks. My father does not know that I know how to drive. It's the only thing that the driver and I ever agreed on. My father would kill me if he knew about it."

"Oh, so we continue playing 'I don't really love my daddy' and his company poker game eh," Juve said sarcastically. He was not at all amused. Ladies have always thought they could always charm their way out of any situation, especially where it involved men. This one was in for a rude shock. He had decided he was not going to allow her beauty to cloud his mind and lead him to lower his guard.

"I want to tell you the real story of my life. You just appeared from the blue and got me out of prison, plus you broke my wedding to a certain Mr. Willis Jr., whom I know exactly nothing about."

"Wow. What a nice story. You know something. I already like you for your creativity and innovativeness. You could rival the likes of Newton, Galileo, and Daimler Benz in that field I bet" The sarcasm in his voice was unmistakable.

"I don't expect you to believe me, really. You'll probably think I am playing. But I will not be going back there and I will always be in debt to you for freeing me."

"Save your breath angel. Tomorrow you will be dinning at the same table with your father, as long as he sticks to his end of the bargain."

"What bargain? Are you in someway linked to this Willis Jr. character?"

"No. I'm not supposed to be telling you this, but what's the harm in letting you know?" He took a deep breath as if to make up his mind before beginning. "They've got my friend Mark Lubevu in custody. He is supposed to face trial tomorrow, and the judge happens to be your father. Going by his reputation, Mark could get a long time behind bars, if not a life sentence."

"You bet. That man known as my father cares about nobody. Especially not you people," she noted.

There was pain in her voice that Juve did not expect. She must be a real good actor, he concluded. "Don't start with that line. He obviously cares about his only daughter and child. Why should he go through with this if he doesn't give a damn at all?"

"I can confidently tell you I would be the least surprised if your friend lands himself a death sentence tomorrow."

"You are obviously trying to tell me how confident you are of them catching up with me before the trial begins tomorrow, eh."

"I'm trying to tell you that my father cares not an inch if you shot me. In fact you will be doing him a favour to a point that he will even drop his full wrath of hatred on your friend to ensure that you are compelled to carry out whatever threat you uttered. I'm one of the three people alive who have evidence that he killed my mother." The bitterness was unexpectedly real.

She was a real professional liar, he thought. "I can see you got brains enough to help you create fictitious stories."

"I'll tell you something. You scribble somewhere that you know about my mother and the drugs and that you will sell the story if he crosses you. Otherwise I don't see him keeping his end of the bargain. Unless he is greedy enough to only see the cash he will receive from my arranged marriage and not see his chances of saving himself."

"Keep your beautiful mouth shut."

"But I'm trying to..."

"I don't need your help. Next time you are going to be suggesting that I should write on a piece of paper about where I am holding you hostage."

"I'm perfectly happier here, Mr...." She realized she didn't even know his name. She didn't expect him to tell her. "At least do me a favour and let him know you know a lot about him."

"Lady, don't you ever give up? Don't you ever realize when you are beaten square?"

"You sure are a difficult one." The soft voice exhibited more concern than anger. This lady would sure make a good movie star. Or was she not acting?

"Turn left."

She turned left as ordered, into an uneven, murram road.

"Take a right." He said after about a kilometre's drive.

She obeyed and turned into a small pathway, overgrown by grass, evidently from disuse.

"Stop," he directed a few seconds later.

She braked, disengaged the gears to neutral, killed the engine, and tried to engage the handbrakes (which were not working), before re-engaging the first gear to keep the vehicle from rolling off its parking spot.

"We are using the right hand side, please," he announced, once he had pocketed the car's keys.

She opened the door and stepped out. Right in front of them stood a battered cottage.

"After you, remember ladies first? And I hope I don't have to remind you, I will not hesitate to use this death-awarding instrument. We are all by ourselves for miles, so you'll be committing suicide."

"I wouldn't want to ruin such a romantic night for us, would I?" There was not the hint of sarcasm in that tone that answered. It surprised him.

"Call it what you want, but I want you to know something, I'm a good host if you are cooperative. This is going to be your home for the night. I realize you are used to the lavishness of your father's residence but for today, you will have to do with this frugality. I would not have put you through this, if I had a choice, sorry about that."

"Honestly, I am glad you didn't have a choice. You may choose not to believe me, but your decision made my day."

"Please don't hope sweet talk will get you out of this. Only your dad's sensibility will."

"Somebody ought to have put some sense in his head, obviously."

She had to be acting. He decided to ignore her. "Get yourself in there. We should be having some coffee about now."

She pushed the door open and walked into the cottage. The single roomed structure was well arranged, with a bed at the farthest end. There was a kitchenette, which consisted of a stove, a tray, two cups, two plates, two spoons, a thermos flask and a cooking pan. A wooden table separated the *kitchen* and the *bedroom*. There was a chair next to the door.

"If you want relieve yourself, just say the word. We have a latrine at our disposal."

"Great place. I would love living here."

"Now, you see that chain?"

One end of the chain was padlocked to the hind end of the bed. The other end of the chain was lose. On the bed, there was a padlock and some keys.

"I guess I know what you want me to do." She walked to the bed, took the keys and chained her leg to the bed, then tossed the keys to him.

"I had hoped you would be cooperative, but this level of it is bizarre. Maybe it's because in the back of your mind you hope that they will catch up with us, and your dad will be triumphant in the end."

"You need me to get your friend out of trouble. What you don't want to believe is that I also need you to get me away from the man they call my father. You've already done just that. Except now you want to send me back to him."

"I will fix us some coffee. You must be the kind of people that do not forgive. You intend to keep lashing at me, and you think that this treacherous approach of pretence of friendship will work."

"Good coffee," she said immediately after she took a sip.

"I entirely depend on myself for everything. Did I tell you my name? I'm called Juve Teluve."

"Wonderful name. I'm Wendy, Wendy Henry."

"You see, I can't get myself a wife and start a family, because your kind is chasing me around in our own land."

"I would also hate it. I know you won't believe me, but I understand, and I hate what they are doing to you and your people." It was again the sorrowful, concerned echoed in her voice and tone that surprised him.

"You can't possibly understand how it feels like if somebody came from a distant land and started dictating terms to you over your own things."

"I know, I can never tell exactly how it feels, but I can imagine. If I had the capacity, I would change all these, believe me."

"Wow. That's a great page," he said, teasingly.

"It's not just a page, its straight from the heart and I don't care if you believe me or not. Why don't you tell me more about yourself? We have all night, remember."

"I'll talk about myself when I choose to. You obviously want me to give you some information to use against me once you are free," he was trying unsuccessfully to disguise the bitterness in him.

"Sorry," she said when she sensed the bitterness hidden beneath his accusation of her real intentions. Himself was obviously a topic he would rather not be reminded of. Obviously, there was pain in his past he was not willing to confront yet.

Suddenly, the memories he had long kept away started returning to him. The killings, the funerals, the pursuit, the prison attack, everything, as it happened. What he did not realize was that his lips were letting it all out as he remembered.

She just sat there, not interrupting him, nor urging him on or even commenting. And when the monologue was over, he looked down in shame. He almost lost the battle against his tears.

She wanted to walk over to him and console him with an embrace, but she could not. She was in chains. She said sorry, instead, from deep within her.

It was then that he realized what had happened.

"I'm going to get us something to eat." And he stormed out of the cottage, knowing very well what he had done. He had just broken a basic rule of survival. He had exposed his sensitive and tender side to the enemy. He returned a few hours later with meat that he roasted and they had a quiet supper.

That night, when she was in bed, Wendy stared into empty space in deep thought. She could not believe that this fortuitous occurrence would end with her being sent back to her prison, back to the monster called her father. She could not stomach the thought. She had never known anyone who had had such an effect on her as her captor had, all her 20 years of existence. Her abhorrence for men was of a high degree. Maybe that had clouded her chances as years went by. But even if she had found someone she had feelings for, nothing would have happened with them, for her father would have seen to that. Ironically, her captor was the first man to make her feel something. Maybe it was simply because he had taken her out of her prison, just for one night. It was far better being chained to the bed rather than being Haddock Henry's daughter. As she drifted into sleep, she made up her mind. She was not going back to that house.

Juve revisited the day's events. A successful day it had been. It was also a day on which he had laid eyes on the most beautiful person he had ever seen. That had almost ruined his plans, but he had learned how to deal with it. He had just pushed it off his mind. He looked at her as she slept. He could not believe how beautiful she turned out to be. A delicate exotic beauty. That was the daughter of Judge Haddock. That man did not deserve such a person for a daughter. He would keep this girl if the judge did not do as planned. He cursed the circumstances of their meeting. Then he wondered what was there to curse about, anyway. This was a lady way beyond his league. She would not look at him twice.

He wondered how she could be so beautiful and yet so manipulative, since every word she uttered about her father was pure fabrication meant to lead him to disaster, in his opinion. He did not believe that anybody could have such an angel for a daughter and not enjoy a great relationship with her.

Kenya in the 1960s wasn't a place to fall in love with a white woman. That was the most fatal mistake a black man could commit. It would more often than not translate into deadly consequences for the two lovers.

He decided he would take her advice and write her story on a piece of paper. Not that he believed her, but he was not ready to risk losing to the judge. He did not think there could be something untoward in writing some words on a piece of paper and passing them to the judge, unless it was a code of some sort between a loving daughter and father. He tried seeing through the words but decided it would be unlikely that a coded message would help her father track them down, especially when he selected the words himself.

He sank onto the chair to catch some sleep. He wondered what Mark had been through in the hands of the authorities. Mark was truly a friend. Had he talked, they would have caught up with him. He was not going to lose Mark without a fight.

FIVE

Juve Teluve drove into Nairobi on the morning of the trial. He wanted to get the news of the acquittal immediately. He did not expect the judge to let him down. But he wanted to make sure. He would have eight hours to act after the judgement, before releasing the girl.

Wendy Henry was safe under the padlock. He realized that the longer he kept the girl with him, the more his chances of succeeding improved. To guarantee Mark's release, he needed to play the Wendy Henry card on the judge. He knew the offices of the judge, but he realized it would be stupid to try walking into the building. There was normally tight security in and around the building.

He walked over to a security guard and handed him the envelope he was carrying with him. It was addressed to Judge Haddock Henry.

"Urgent delivery for Judge Haddock, please."

"Who is it from?" the guard looked puzzled.

"Willis Senior." He answered, walking away to avoid further questioning. He was thankful on that occasion that the guard did not suspect a thing. Had the guard suspected something fishy, his plan would have blown up right in his face. Inside the envelope was a note written by Wendy. He had instructed her to write: *'Do as he says father, or I'll let him know about the past, my mum for instance.'*

****

Wendy moved into action immediately. She had seen where Juve had placed the keys. He must have forgotten to carry them with him. She could not believe the chance that was before her. However, she could not access the keys, with the chains restricting her to the bed.

Suddenly, it struck her that she could pull the bed with her. She tried that, but the bed would not budge. It must have been fastened to the walls. She lifted one end of the mattress to see if her fears would be confirmed. The leg of the bed was placed between a huge stone and the wall. When she lifted the other end of the mattress, there was another huge stone there. No wonder the bed would not move.

She was a woman all right, but that did not mean she could not move stones, especially if it meant freedom. She started pulling the bed again, this time with renewed energy. It didn't move.

She stopped to catch her breath, and then started again.

The bed started moving, slowly. She tried stretching towards the keys. Still too far. She pulled again and stretched again, but still she could not touch them. She pulled again and tried once more to reach the keys. This time her fingers reached the keys and freedom – finally.

She was not sure she could remember the way to the main road from the cottage. The red Ford was no where in sight. But there were fresh tracks leading away from the cottage. She followed them.

After about forty-five minutes of walking under the morning sunshine, she could finally see the road just ahead of her. She crossed the road and waited.

A vehicle appeared. She waved it to stop, but it sped past. Another did the same. The third vehicle, a tiny Toyota, rolled to a stop when she waved. A white man in all black attire with a brief white band on his full-buttoned black shirt and a rosary hanging around his neck was behind the steering wheels.

"Where to, young lady?"

"Nairobi."

"Get in."

It was never a good idea to get lifts from strangers. But in the circumstances it was the most reasonable thing she could do.

"Where from, young lady, you look messed up."

"I went to visit a friend but she was not there so I had to walk some considerable distance to and from the main road."

"Any problem I can help you with?"

"You did enough with the lift already, thanks."

"I'm Father Augustini a missionary from Italy."

"I'm Sally."

They arrived in Nairobi after almost an hour's drive.

"Listen daughter, if you need to talk to someone or if you are going through any difficulty, you can come and see me," he said, handing her a card. "And pray to God for assistance of any sort."

"Be sure I will, Father. And thanks a lot for your help," she said as she watched the car pull out of the parking spot and disappear in the corner. She then dropped the card. Such a thing could be a lead to being traced.

She crossed the few streets to the bus stop. She boarded the Kenya Bus Service bus headed to the destination she wanted. She alighted at the stage near her father's house after 30 minutes. The few coins she always carried with her came in handy to pay the bus fare.

****

Judge Haddock managed to get hold of a reputable defence team. He secretly paid them, the agreed half amount. The other half was to be paid once the case was done with. Everybody must have been wondering how Mark could manage to put together such a defence team, when he was just a poorly paid labourer. 'Maybe the churches had footed the bill,' they must have thought.

Judge Haddock had something up his sleeve. He smiled

at the thought. The Willises' money can go. He had to get rid of Wendy. She could ruin him. The lunatic had vowed to do it for him. How convenient.

When he walked into the office that morning, a courthouse guard gave him an envelope. It was from the Willises. The Judge almost threw it into the waste paper bin, had it not been for curiosity. What were they offering this time around?

He tore open the envelope then the bomb dropped. He simply could not believe what was in there. The bitch Wendy was now threatening to tell the lunatic all about him! He was sure that even that lunatic Juve would not be stupid enough to harm her if she had anything concrete on him. He would surely kill that bitch with his bare hands.

His hatred for blacks had prompted him to pass heavy penalties on them whenever they appeared in his courtroom. No black suspects ever passed through his courtroom without winning themselves heavy sentences.

When it was reported that Judge Haddock was to handle the case, everybody knew the verdict. Mark had no chance. To Judge Haddock, every black person was guilty even before trial – without a second thought. It was just a matter of how harsh the punishment would be.

That lunatic Juve had taken a personally obnoxious action against him. Until he opened the Willises letter, that morning he was going to enjoy himself in the courtroom. Now he had to save himself from ruin. He had to get his daughter back. Then he would settle scores with both her and the black pair.

****

Mark Lubevu was surprised at how popular his trial had become. He was shocked at the concern shown by a defence team he didn't even hire. He decided he would not at any time cooperate with them. It was probably another colonial propaganda tactic. They wanted the world to think that there was justice in Kenya. Yet, they would throw him in the prison anyway. All he wanted to do was to know how long he was going to serve. He would not be surprised if the judge ordered he be hanged even if his defence team managed to successfully argue that he was innocent and succeeded in putting some reasonable doubt in the prosecution's case.

That morning Judge Haddock was in a jolly mood. The trial had lasted two months and on the day that he was going to give the sentence, he would enjoy his court performance. His plan was excellent. He had secured the services of the best defence he could so that when he read his verdict it would go completely opposite of justice based on the proceedings of the case in order to make Juve mad enough to act on his threat. However all that was quickly overtaken by a simple piece of paper written by his daughter that he received the moment he walked into his chambers. But of course Mark did not know about the on goings outside his jail-room. He was not expecting to escape hard labour and at least ten years or more. Judge Haddock was predictable. Or so he thought.

****

The defence team did enough work and took the prosecution through some desperate moments the last two months. Both the defence and the prosecution knew there existed reasonable doubt.

But the prosecutor also knew that as long as it was Judge Haddock on the bench, the case was won not matter what the defence team would do. He smiled at the reassuring thoughts.

And so when the deliberations were over, everybody sat attentively as the judge's voice echoed through the room.

> *"...after listening to the deliberations from both sides and after looking through the bulk of evidence, including the witnesses brought forward, I have decided that the prosecution has not managed to convince this court, beyond any reasonable doubt, that the defendant committed the crime leveled against him. I feel that the defence has managed to create enough doubt to the prosecutions case. I am therefore, left with no option but to acquit the defendant...."*

There was a marked murmur of surprise at what the judge had said. The prosecutor could not believe what he was hearing. Not with Judge Haddock. He had always been reliable. Suddenly his breathing became laboured, and his legs could not hold his weight. He collapsed and fainted. It could not be happening. Mark remained transfixed in the dock, not knowing what to do with his surprise freedom.

He looked around at the audience. There was not a single face he could recognize. His eyes picked a woman with very familiar attire on, from the audience. That must be it. He wondered how Juve could have succeeded in pulling off such an unexpected victory against judge Haddock. Immediately, he remembered their secret location in town, which was the obvious place they would link up once he was finished with the formalities of his release. He made a secret gesture to the *woman. She* responded positively. He couldn't wait to meet Juve again and hear all the details of how he had been helped to escape the death sentence. Juve told Mark everything on their way to the cottage.

Mark was stunned. It could not be true. How could he have survived Judge Haddocks wrath? Once at the cottage Juve opened the door majestically, hoping to show off Wendy, the judge's daughter.

He was shocked at the sight that greeted him. The room

was in a mess and Wendy was no where in sight. "She has escaped, Mark. We can't stay here any longer. I bet the police are just around the corner by now."

"You don't have to, prince," came the gentle soft feminine voice from behind them. They both turned to see who it was, though they already knew.

The seraphic figure of Wendy was standing behind them! A sweet satisfied smile was printed on her face. Under one arm was a medium sized travelling bag that seemed to be packed beyond capacity.

It was over. Never joke with the judge. Hanging sentence applicable. End of the road. "I am all by myself if that's what you are worried about, gentlemen." The smile did not go away. They stared at each other in disbelief. They would be crazy to listen to this crap. The sixth sense warned them not to fall for it. Yet a seventh was telling them she was genuine.

SIX

"You still don't believe me, do you? I said I am not going back to that prison of a house and I meant it. This bag contains all I need for the time being and here is a copy of the letter the judge is going to read once he enters his study," she said, reaching for her shirt pocket and handing Mark the handwritten piece of paper. "You must be Mark Lubevu."

"I see no need in denying. And you must be Wendy Henry."

"Well, I knew we would meet soon. Nice to meet you."

"I haven't decided if it is nice meeting you yet. Sorry about that."

"Careful too, just as your friend Juve, I understand though. Survival is all about knowing who to trust and who not to trust."

"You said it angel, let's see what you claim to have written to your loving papa," Juve said looking directly at her to see if he could trace any guilt in her eyes. All he found was piteous desperation.

Mark perused the note carefully, his senses trying to pick up something that could tell them she was faking. Nothing turned up. Could she be that good an actress? The note read as follows:

To Judge Haddock,

If I were a magician, I would perform to change the circumstances of my birth so as to be born to a different person. I know I can't change that. But I know I can change my life.

51

I always thought there was a reasonable person underneath the wicked person you are. My mother complained about this and that but you never made any effort to change.

Instead you moved from bad to worse, which resulted in that fatal slap on my mother that sent her tumbling down the stairs to her death. You opted to make it look like a burglary, and to you, her death was nothing other than the death of a fly. I realized that was you. You will never change.

I would long ago have killed myself, but I had hope one day a miracle would happen. Thanks to the black pair of Juve and Mark for the chance they accorded to me. I only wish they realized how much they have positively influenced me, and a life destined for doom. I have not an iota of regret in me in taking this decision of running away from you.

And don't go around looking for those two guys, Juve and Mark. They don't have an idea of where I am. I will not be found, since I know exactly what you will do to me if you find me - kill me.

Wendy.

"Believe me guys. You are my tickets to freedom."

"Damn, why should we be the ones to wind up with such a problem?" Juve queried.

"Should I then kill myself to demonstrate that am telling the truth? You people needed me to get Mark out of prison. Now I need your help to get me away from my father."

"Maybe if you did that kill myself trick convincingly then we could believe you and without any *reasonable* doubt," Mark said jokingly.

"I want to go to England and start afresh there. I can't try make a life out here with the judge combing all over for me."

"You really got the guts, pretty. What makes you think I cannot amuse myself with that exotic body of yours, kill you and get away with it?" Juve said bluntly.

"If you had intended to do that I should think you would have done so by now."

"I could be taking my time and waiting for the right moment."

"I guess I just have to take my chances and hope for the best."

"Do you just trust any one you come across?" Mark asked seriously.

"Not really. I have this overwhelming confidence that I am in safer hands." She meant it.

"Maybe we should give you the benefit of the doubt and see what happens," Juve said finally

"Believe me, if I am to choose between staying with him or my captors, I've already made my choice."

"We don't intend to rape anyone." Juve tried to portray sarcasm.

"Thanks. I needed such a promise for once in my life," she said, grabbing a quick embrace, her brown eyes sparkling thankfully. Coupled with her curvy body, she was mesmerizingly gorgeous.

Juve was caught by surprise. It was the first time someone had ever given him such an embrace, since the slaying of his family.

Their eyes locked for a split second. Each looked away, unwillingly, to avoid giving themselves away.

"Okay, you just earned yourself a pair of helpers. But we are watching you closely. Anything suspicious and you won't know what hit you," Juve said, at last.

"Agreed," she said, and then announced that it was lunch time. "I got us some food in my bag."

The two men looked at each other in surprise. This could not be happening. Was she in some way just trying to gain their trust then strike at the most appropriate moment? Was the food containing some lethal ingredient? Couldn't she even wait for them to relax their guards?

The two men cautiously waited until Wendy swallowed the first bite of the food. Once she had taken a spoonful, Juve changed the plates with hers, as a precaution. Once convinced of the food's safety, they spooned through the delicious meal of rice and beef stew. Whatever was left made the menu for supper with some coffee.

"How do you expect your father to react to this?" Juve asked over breakfast as they took coffee and sweet potatoes, which they had taken from the fields.

"By now he must have gotten every cop to believe that you two are holding me captive and they are in a massive manhunt for you guys. His biggest motivation is revenge."

"He is not badly off the mark. We actually are holding you. Or aren't we?" Mark commented.

"I had already made an escape then I came back, don't you remember. He must suspect I may try to get out of the country. By now all the outlets are swarming with police."

"It would be hard to get the police to believe that we are holding you captive and you are actually trying to get out of the country," Juve reasoned.

"It would be very easy for him to say something like, 'my daughter called me and I heard a rough voice interrupt and her screaming, as the phone was banged. But she said something like 'border'.'"

"Yeah, that could get them blocking the outlets, especially with all the respect he commands," Juve said.

"They would even reach the conclusion that I got my acquittal because we had you captive." Mark added.

"It would be much easier if you could stay in the country," Juve said hopefully.

"I have to get out as soon as possible, cops or no cops."

"Getting out would be quite risky," Mark said.

"Maybe we could just outwit them. Mombasa is the very place they expect us to try and make our exit. The place will be sealed off, then they will not expect us to stick to our plans, especially if we let in information that we know they will be sealing it off. All we need to do is manipulate that piece of knowledge to our advantage. We could make an anonymous call and give the police a tip off just as a third party would. We could wait a few days then head for the coast, or we could let them into our secret that we know they know about the plan to the coast and proceed there immediately. When they realize that we have the knowledge that they are aware of our plan, they will not expect us to dare go through with it," Juve observed. Mombasa is a port town 400 kilometres south of Nairobi.

"Sir, you never cease to amaze me." Mark complimented.

Wendy had to agree, it was a brilliant idea, though risky in its very nature.

England was far, but it was the only place she could pick her way through. When Wendy looked at Juve's eyes, she could see something his pride did not want to let him say what he felt. She made the decision. Once this independence wave was over, she would come back to face her feelings for him. That could take a long time, but she would wait and if it looked like things are not going to get better, she would just come anyway. He was the first man who had made her feel something special.

"Time for work...Give me an hour. I'll get us a vehicle," Juve said.

"I'll take an hour too. We might need two," Mark observed. She did not see them wink at each other. She still had to pass another test. They would leave her all by herself and see what happens.

"Don't open the door until we are back," Juve gave the simple instruction. But they would know if she had opened when they came back. A weak elastic band tied both to the door and the doorposts would break. She would not know it was there, but they would know she had disobeyed the instruction and that would help them decide whether she was genuine or not. Once they had agreed on a knocking code, the two men left for their destinations.

"You got yourself an hour Wendy, me and my father have to make the plans," Mark had said as they walked out.

"What? You two are father and son?" she asked, genuinely surprised.

"Well, you could say that. Mark lost his family and I lost mine, too. We were drawn together by need. I came to refer to him as son, and he to me as father," Juve elaborated.

His mind drifted back to the time he met Mark.

He had just chosen his men and had ordered them to take an oath. They were all in their early twenties as he was. The hurriedly taken oath was almost complete when a young teenager of barely fifteen years came to take the oath.

Juve could not remember choosing him. He was too young for the task they were out to perform. He had enlisted only experienced warriors.

"Back off, youngster," Juve ordered.

"No, master, I'm part of the team and I am going with you, no matter what," the teenager answered back tenaciously.

"No, you aren't. You need to grow up and make a family. We'll need you here more than in the battlefield." Juve tried to be firm, but the stubborn teenager went on and took the oath, with Juve protesting.

"Hey kid, it's your life you are throwing in the dust bin here. Can't you understand that?"

"I do understand sir, but my mind is made up."

The voice was more than firm.

"Who are you, kid?"

"I am Mark Lubevu Taboni. The white men killed

my parents, the Tabonis. I don't have a home to go to anymore."

"Do you realize what you are getting into?" Juve tried again.

"I am in a perfect state of mind as I make this decision, sir."

"I want you to take sometime and think this through. You'll eventually see the sense in not joining us at this stage."

"I don't need anytime, sir, I'm decided."

And on that raid on the prison camp, he came out a hero. Juve did not regret having allowed Mark join them. He decided he would take care of Mark personally.

****

Wendy lay in bed looking at the empty space when a coded knock jolted her back to reality. It was exactly as they had agreed. One of the men must have returned. Mark reported success. Another similar knock and Juve stepped in – success, again.

She did not realize that she had passed a test with flying colours. It was time to move on to the other stages of the exodus.

SEVEN

They walked towards the Bigview hotel under the blazing sun. The rough, uneven terrain inflicted its toll on the unshaken companions.

When finally the Bigview hotel came into view, standing prestigiously on a hill, they stopped a few paces from the gate. Juve walked into the parking lot and looked around, as if to find a specific car.

The red Mercedes was parked exactly where he had earlier instructed his men to have it parked. They were a reliable bunch.

Except for honeymooning couples, the place was devoid of humanity, which was the reason he had chosen it in the first place. Satisfied, he walked back to the others. Everybody took their position, as had been pre-planned.

She took hers, in front of Juve, wearing a shaken, shocked and frightened face. Juve stood there behind her, holding an angry, glittering, sharp blade by her neck. Mark walked next to them.

Once they were at the hotel compound, she started sobbing. When they were a few steps from the Mercedes, she slipped from his grip and made for the run, screaming for help fiercely, attracting enormous attention. He quickly cut her off, with a hard slap across her cheek, before grabbing her roughly and pushing her into the back seat of the vehicle. Mark did the doors.

Before anyone had the chance to react, Mark had already reversed the vehicle and drove off in a huff.

An informer quickly grabbed the telephone to report the incident. He cursed the operator for being slow.

"Everybody, relax, the show is over," Mark said.

"Sorry if I hit you hard," Juve apologized.

"You sure know how to hit hard, eh."

Everybody roared with laughter. The Mercedes' speedometre needle was pointing at eighty miles an hour. After a few turns, Mark's foot rested on the brake pedal. He disengaged the gears. The car came to a smooth stop next to a white Mini Minor. He hopped out and opened the luggage compartment with another set of keys he had.

"The two of you are all set for your trip to the coast," he said when he saw Wendy's bag was still where he had left it. "I just hope we had enough time to throw you a farewell party, Wendy. Now all I can manage is just to let you off with prayers. Have a fine trip to England and God bless you, farewell Wendy," he said, handing Juve the keys and kissing Wendy's hand.

"Farewell, Mark. Here is a little something you will need for our little surprise, Ouch!" she exclaimed as she pulled out some strands of her hair and gave them to Mark.

"Hey, son, don't over do anything. Do only what is necessary. Losing you is not part of the plan."

"I'll be the most careful, father," Mark said as he walked to the Mercedes. "Take care, father."

"I'll be back before you even know it."

"I'll be waiting for you, father."

Juve and Wendy slipped into the white Mini and both drivers engaged their gears, released the handbrakes, switched on the engines, and drove off hooting a final goodbye for the time being, before proceeding in the opposite directions - the Mini towards the coast, and the Mercedes for Nakuru.

Mark slowed down once he reached the spot he thought was suitable for the execution of the plan. He parked the car hidden in a bush and forced the hair strands from Wendy to stick on a protruding metal plate. He took the lamb he had in the luggage compartment and slit its neck, letting blood ooze on the places he wanted it seen, in the vehicle.

He got into the car and engaged the gears, switched on

the engine, and got it back onto the road. Once the vehicle had gathered enough speed up the steep hill, he opened the door and readied himself for a jump. He jumped off just as the vehicle started downhill, swinging the steering wheel in the process to the left.

The vehicle plunged into the valley, about fifty metres deep, from the dangerously winding road, turning several times before coming to a rest at the bottom.

****

The Mini Minor, midway through its journey to the coast, stopped in the bushes and its occupants changed into disguises they had carried with them. She put on the long black veil, which covered her whole body, including her face, where she had on tinted glasses to hide the brown eyes. He changed into a long white robe and tied a turban on his head. They had some snacks and were back on the road.

****

About five hours later, the wreckage of the red Mercedes was spotted about ten kilometres south of Nakuru, totally battered. There were traces of blood, but not a sign of life. Not a dead body or even an injured one for that matter was found.

The dark jet hair strands found belonged to Wendy as investigations revealed. They were identified by the judge himself, among others.

There was an escalation of excitement that Wendy may have taken advantage of the accident and escaped from her captors. She may soon resurface.

The police combed every quarter that offered any form of medical attention. Every herbalist's hut, every witch doctor's den, and all hospitals and dispensaries were checked.

Any person thought to be sympathetic to the freedom fighting cause in the vicinity was arrested for questioning, lest they were hiding the fugitives.

After a few days of intensive investigations, that proved fruitless, the police were left with not much of an option but to wait.

****

Three days after the wreckage of the Mercedes was recovered, a veiled lady walked to the docks where a French bound liner, *'Monsieur,'* was being prepared to sail off.

She walked straight up the gangway and bumped right into a crewman.

"Hey girlie, you ain't a passenger on this liner, eh, everybody is already in their cabins," the thick accented voice challenged her.

"I've got a problem. I have to be in Paris as soon as possible and I don't have airfare. So I came here to try and get some help. My mum is seriously ill at a hotel there," the piteous voice responded.

"No space lady. The *'Monsieur'* is fully booked." And the crewman started off.

"I've got myself some vote, I mean if that's what it's going to take to get me on board," she said hopefully, her voice trailing off.

The sailor stopped as if unsure of what he had heard.

"I see I got your attention finally," she said triumphantly.

"What have you got, Missy," the crewman questioned, ignoring the victorious tone that wrapped her previous statement.

"Three hundred pounds, sir."

"Make it five hundred, take it or leave it."

"Deal." She paid her *fare*, picked her bag, walked up the gangplank into the *'Monsieur'* ready to begin her journey to France and ultimately to England.

Juve watched behind her for a long time after she had disappeared into the ship. Those same feelings of loneliness and emptiness, as he could remember them during just one occasion, the day he had returned home and found his family butchered, returned to him.

He could still feel her lips on his and the promise she had whispered after that long, passionate kiss they had exchanged.

"I'll be back for you, no matter how long it takes. Will you wait for me?" It was not the words, but how they were said that moved him. The nakedness of the passion between them was very apparent.

"I'll be right here waiting for you," he had answered thoughtlessly.

"You are the first man I have ever felt anything for. I love you."

"I love you, too." He could not stop his heart, which had taken over from his brains. His tone betrayed him the more.

Then they looked at each other for a long time, not saying anything, before she walked away, not looking back, as if, if she did, she would not get into the ship. He had just watched as the seraphic body disappeared into the ship.

Theirs had just ended, even before it had started. To him, she was gone forever. They would have made a good couple. As he boarded the bus back to Nairobi, he wondered why good things never lasted.

EIGHT

There was only one other person who believed he knew exactly what had happened. Wendy could have escaped from her captors and returned home before taking off to some other destination, where they had caught up with her again. She had taken advantage of the accident to make her second escape. She was not going to resurface. Judge Haddock knew that only too well. He wished he had killed her together with her mother when he had the chance.

He called in Nellie, the unwilling partner during his frustrating moments. He had a hard on. He had to take care of that.

She responded immediately. She knew what to expect. He grabbed her like a hungry beast. She allowed him to do what he wanted, as long as he kept away from Wendy. That was the agreement. But to her, those moments were just time for work. She had the experience. She had been a call girl in England, before Wendy's mother hired her to work in the house. She had given her a letter one day and told her not to open it, but rather send it directly to the lawyers. However, Nellie became curious and opened the envelope whose contents startled her.

So the judge was a drug trafficker, and a corrupt case-fixing wizard. Mrs. Henry wanted to ensure the judge would not harm her daughter. She feared for her life and what would happen to Wendy, in the event of her death.

Before Nellie could get the letter to the lawyers, the worst happened. The judge slapped Mrs. Henry to her death. He then covered up the incident and promised to pay Nellie an extra hundred shillings for her silence. "Anything to keep herself in the house to protect Wendy." She had told herself and accepted the settlement.

She had taken the file and added to its contents the fact

that Mrs. Henry's death was not an accident. In fact, her husband killed her.

She could not forget what Mrs. Henry had told her, "take care of my daughter in case anything should happen to me." She also told her about the secret account she wanted her daughter to inherit. Two days after that she was dead!

From then on, everything had been smooth until the attempted rape on Wendy, though the judge usually beat his daughter senseless, almost every other day.

With Wendy missing, the Judge was in a really dangerous rage. She had learnt to read his moods. He normally had the strongest drives when angry and frustrated, and a lousy one when in the mood for just sex itself. This was one day he had the toughest of drives that she could remember. It was not safe, even for her. She looked around and saw the kitchen knife on the table; he had been using it to carve out his fishing rod. In case anything went out of control, she would turn to that.

He tore through the apron and the garments she had on and forced himself into her with some quick, angry and rough thrusts. She was used to such treatment, although today it was angrier, rougher and tougher. She expected him to come soon and cool off as he always did. When he finally came, he grabbed her neck and started squeezing. The more she cried out and struggled, the more his deadly grip on her delicate neck tightened.

She could feel precious air stopping short of reaching her lungs and life moving further and further away. She stretched out and grabbed the kitchen knife, but only on the third try. His grip had tightened, and now every bone under his pressure, felt as if it was holding the whole earth upon it with life moving away, more rapidly. Thoughtlessly, she plunged the knife into his ribcage, with a decided thrust.

The knife sunk deep into his body. His eyes almost

popped off their sockets from surprise and pain. His body bolted as he fell over her, his member finding its way back into her.

She gasped for precious air then held on as precious life came back to her. Then she pushed him over with one decided push. He landed on the carpeted floor face first.

She reached for the telephone and called the police, still choking and coughing more life back into her.

She was arrested and charged with murder. She pleaded not guilty, citing self-defence. The high-profile trial, especially due to the stature of the slain victim, commenced in earnest. The court returned a verdict of man slaughter and she was given a year in jail. The court had also directed that the jail term begins the moment she had been arrested which knocked off some three months from the sentence.

After serving eight months and a few days, she was released. She had been through it all. She would fly to England and face a peaceful transition into her forties. The secret account would be her capital once she was there.

NINE

The momentum towards Kenya's independence was a fast one. The militant Mau-Mau was a thorn in the flesh of the colonial government. In the year 1952 a state of emergency was declared to suppress this shadowy outfit. Senseless arrests and killings marked this period, as both the colonial administration and the Mau-Mau battled for supremacy. Both sides reported heavy losses of lives and took high numbers of casualties. Regular Africans and white settlers were not spared of the chaos and disturbances, as they were caught in the middle of the battles.

It was during this period that Jomo Kenyatta and other prominent Kenyans were arrested and charged with managing the Mau-Mau. But armed resistance continued.

In 1954, the principle of multi-racial society was accepted in the Littleton constitution. Ministers from all races were appointed to cabinet in Kenya for the first time. There was one African minister in the six member unofficial council of ministers.

The colonial administration continued to resist changes and arrested many African freedom fighters as they continued with the crackdown that had begun in 1952 when a state of emergency was declared. During that time, instruments like the *kipande system* were advanced methods that the colonial government employed to ensure African intentions of becoming independent were suppressed. The arbitrary arrest of Africans continued as the killings by both sides of the conflict intensified.

The harder the militant Mau-Mau struggled, the more the colonial administration cracked down on them to stop the uprising.

The colonial government tried to sell a picture of a happy colony of Kenya to the western world, but the probing western dailies started unveiling the image of a conflict ridden Kenya full of disturbances and unrest. Juve had avenged his family's Killing on them and now it was time to cool off the tempo, and let the dust settle.

They were using his prison attack to discredit the Mau-Mau. They likened Juve to the likes of Kenyatta and Dedan Kimathi, who they accused of leading the Mau-Mau.

Faced with mounting pressure by the western world, countries like the USA, having played a major role in giving victory to the allies in the Second World War and therefore in close association with Britain, being a major source of such demands, the colonial administration had to admit that colonialism had failed. That was one huge step, and independence for Kenya was just around the corner.

By 1956, there were two Africans in the council of ministers. By 1957, the Africans could now send their representatives to the legislative council by direct election.

It was in 1958 when Juve went underground after disturbances in the capital Nairobi and the police trailed hordes of Africans to their ancestral homes in order to quench any militancy remaining. Heavy penalties were meted out by the partisan judicial system and murder remained the order of the day. For Africans, oath taking was used and they targeted white settlers, while the settlers brought in arms and killed on sight any black skinned person who they thought was a threat to them. The total number at the legislative council was thirty six, with 14 Africans and 14 Europeans and the rest of the seats being shared out among Asians and Arabs.

The first Lancaster House Conference of 1960 assured Africans the majority in the unofficial side of the 2 chamber Legislative Council, with twenty of the fifty-three seats reserved for the minority communities in the order of ten Europeans, eight Asians and two Arabs. The Council of ministers was to have twelve ministers with four official members and eight unofficial members. This would be distributed with four seats for Africans, Europeans getting three seats and Asians occupying the last one seat of the unofficial ministry slots. Africans and Europeans shared 2 seats each in the four official ministry slots.

The National Legislative Council members consisting of four Africans, four Europeans, three Asians and one Arab were to be elected by members of the legislative council.

1961 was an eventful year. It saw Mark's arrest that culminated in the flight of Wendy Henry from Kenya and an election between the two African parties, Kanu and Kadu. Kanu won a majority but refused to form the government until Kenyatta was released.

In 1962, the year of the second Lancaster House Conference, Kenyatta was released and became president of Kenya African National Union (KANU), and a coalition government came into being to work out the constitution.

Fresh elections were held and Kanu won the majority in the 1963 exercise.

On the 1st of June 1963, Kenya gained internal self-government with Jomo Kenyatta as Prime Minister.

It was time to celebrate. Juve and Mark were among the mammoth crowd that converged at Uhuru Gardens to watch the beginning of a new dawn. They both wept tears of joy as the Kenyan flag was hoisted up and the Union Jack flag came down. It was Uhuru, finally.

On the 12th of December 1964, Kenya became a republic and Jomo Kenyatta became its first president. It was time to build a new nation. Elation and jubilation climbed to high levels within the eight million Kenyans all over the country, as the Kenya National anthem hit the airwaves. They could not believe it was real.

****

Wendy Henry stepped on the soil in London exactly three months after she left Mombasa. It looked completely like being in another world.

While Kenya was warm with sunlight rays filtering though the tropical air, in England sunshine was distant wherever it occurred. In Kenya they wore light clothing while in London everybody seemed to be having their raincoats on, every other time. She felt lost here the moment she stepped out of the ferry. Heavy traffic, huge highways, huge buildings, and at night it looked like stars had suddenly fallen on London with so many lights illuminating the skyline. It was hard to imagine Nairobi could look like that one day. London was full of mobility and life as hordes of people moved about their business. The noise was unbearable with hoots and engine din filling the air, especially during the rush hour. It was like nothing she was used to, especially after so many years in captivity in the name of a home under her father's watchful eyes.

From the two-thousand-six hundred pounds she had picked from her fathers safe for her escape, she had left five hundred pounds on the table for Mark and Juve. She had ended up paying the crew member a hefty one thousand eight hundred pounds through-out the journey.

It all started when the crew member sneaked into her cabin, the bulge under his tight fitting sailor's uniform very apparent.

"What brings you here this fine afternoon, anchor boy?" she asked sarcastically, the bells of suspicion ringing within her.

Fine afternoon I guess it is, and should continue to be, harbour girl," he answered in a similar sarcastic reference to her.

"What are you implying, anchor boy."

"Don't pretend this is some new thing, harbour girl. A beautiful girl like you should figure out when a handsome man like me suggests. It is as simple as that," he was saying, moving dangerously close. "We are going to have a good time, harbour girl."

Suddenly, he was close enough and she could smell the unmistakable odor of sweat and booze. She could recall what Nellie had told her all too well on the night the judge almost raped her.

"Anything foolish and the ship's captain will learn first hand why I refer to you as harbour girl," he said sensing some resistance.

"I don't think so, Mr. Anchor. Remember that it was a transaction and we both participated. I'll simply tell him you took my money and let me into the ship, and I'll insist I don't know the rules."

"Captains are people who stick with their crew members. You'll just end up paying a real hefty fare. In addition, with such beauty, I don't think he would mind laying you. Remember, you will be at his mercy. Once he is finished with you, we will all get a share of it. I guess you have no choice but play me a good game to erase my mind of such thoughts as talking to the boss. And don't forget if his moods are not good enough, you'll land yourself some real long time behind bars."

"Who said we'll let it go that far. I guess I could do with some good sea games myself. Besides, you look very able to me," she said, referring to the bulge under his trousers.

"That's my girl. You'll love it I promise you." He moved closer to her, his excitement comparable to that of a seventeen-year-old getting his first lay.

She waited until he was within range. Then she released the knee missile. He jumped with a start, grabbing his groins as if a bullet had just hit him, screaming like a goat that had just learned of its eminent slaughter. He was breathing out curses and threats as he wriggled in pain on the floor. She reached for her purse, got fifty pounds, and pushed them down his trousers pockets.

"I believe that would do for now. When you are finished with the pain, get yourself out of my cabin."

Since that incident, the crew member kept coming for *protection fee,* as he came to refer to it. By the last day in the ship, she had parted with one thousand three hundred pounds as protection fees. Another one hundred and fifty pounds saw her through France from Marseilles to Boulogne where she boarded a ferry through the English Channel into London by way of the famous Thames River. She had to part with a further two hundred pounds to get herself the appropriate immigration documents with the name *McHenry* instead of Henry to avoid unnecessary alarm bells about her surname.

Down to under a hundred pounds only, she had to find herself a low budget accommodation. She landed a boarding house a few kilometres from the Thames.

The rent alone took a massive five pounds from the money she was left with. A further ten pounds went as she settled herself into the boarding house.

By the time she was resting in bed, very exhausted, she was down to twenty-three pounds in all. And as she looked at the sprawling city of London, she visualized herself in a canoe and London like a battleship which she had to conquer no matter what. London had something she wanted – livelihood. She would have to get it.

The place was mostly covert boarding and lodging that was frequented mainly by people on clandestine missions such as husbands and their mistresses or underage girls, wives and their secret men and boys, high school run away kids, adventurer groups, sailors, prostitutes, and all types of ostracized pairs, groups and singles.

The building itself was a mess. Heaps of agglomerated garbage all over, with rodents and stray cats very much at home around the heaps, broken windows on almost every window pane, broken tiles on the roof, pale patched ceilings on the insides as a result of ignored leakages that had gone unrepaired for much too long, cobwebs in every corner of the rooms, broken door locks, discoloured walls due to layers of dust left undusted, and rhythmically oscillating spring beds, especially when couples disappeared into their rooms to perform their amatory roles.

However, Wendy could not afford better lodgings with her limited amount of money and was hopeful that employment would be found and she would get herself out of the mess, but as days turned into weeks and weeks into months, it was always the same story.

"Good credentials. We'll get back to you." The interview was over.

"You know something; you are really a pretty girl. You don't have to go into all this trouble if you know how to use that body..." She would storm out of the office.

"Could you get some time off?"

"I am looking for a job sir, I have all the time in the world."

"Good, then you could see me later this evening and try to convince me why I should employ you. I presume you understand." Moreover, his hungry looks would betray his intentions. "I'll be at the Palace Pride restaurant at eight. If you really want this job you will be there."

At exactly eight o'clock, she would be fast asleep. Men, they always want to take advantage of every small opportunity in their relentless quest for sex. It was a stormy month of bus fares and meals, especially when the boarding house provided an indigestible breakfast that often left her with indigestion and constipation. The net effect of that kind of expenditure was that she was down to three pounds. She had to find something to do otherwise she was in trouble.

"You know something lady friend, I want you to join me tonight. I got myself two clashing dates and I'm alone. Tracy's got herself occupied tonight and is not available to cover for me," Sally Washington, the tall, slim, oval faced lady who occupied the opposite room to Wendy's in the boarding house said.

Nocturnal was what they referred to Sally, Tracy her roommate, and many other girls in the boarding house. The reference was in fact a befitting description of them, for they offered nightly sexual pleasures to clients, who in turn dug into their pockets for the services rendered. And that was what the ladies lived on.

"You don't know what you are getting yourself into; you'll probably get yourself thrown out of this place for lack of rent as I once did before I settled for my job. It is the only job where you could earn money, attention, experience about sex, and enjoy the benefits of self employment tax free, and probably woo a very rich husband if you can, all at the same time. Besides..." Sally kept telling her.

"Besides wooing a clap?" she would always interrupt to stop her from going on.

"I guess every money making venture has its drawbacks. Listen, they go for beauty and innocence, furthermore, inexperience appeals to a lot of them. You got it all wrapped around you, Wendy. You could move mountains when it comes to this trade. But you are throwing your chances away. Tracy has just left the door open for you. It's a good omen to begin in-house before going to the streets. Tonight is your chance, if you are smart, grab it."

"You call commercial sex and selling your body smart? Christ, where did you dump your manners and language."

"Don't call it that. Say something like offering love in return for gratitude and favours."

"I'd rather languish in poverty than give myself as a garbage bin for men who don't even care what happens to you or who you are."

"I also said that once, but now I know better. Knock off the preaching virgin and help me with my shoes. I hate cleaning muddy shoes just as much as I hate men who don't want to pay. Would three shillings do the honours?"

"You know very well I wouldn't mind little small ones for change." And that was the genesis of a shoe cleaning service that would keep her afloat.

TEN

The saying that time has a way of working things out was definitely right. Two days after she had cleaned Sally's shoes, the number of pairs had increased to three, then to six with one male pair, then to ten with four male pairs, then to fifteen and to the twenties. A month later she didn't end a day without having cleaned about twenty-five pairs. The fee had now increased to five shillings and she had now become the *shoe-girl*.

Sally and Tracy finally changed their ways after a heavy fight erupted between them over a client they all ended up sleeping with, and eventually both ended up catching the clap.

Sally had hooked a male nurse and ended up falling deeply in love with him. Finally, she was talking about future plans and Wendy was surprised. Tracy laughed at the thought. Nevertheless, three weeks later, Sally announced that they were getting married.

At a small in-house ceremony with a few friends from the boarding house, some relatives from the groom's side, and themselves as maids, Sally and John Trylon were joined in matrimony.

Tracy had taken to knitting of babies' clothing as a hobby to keep boredom at bay and ended up putting her work up for sale to make a few pounds.

Her fate had been sealed when a banker walked over to her and ordered a cardigan for a baby boy.

"Specifications," she asked. "Please sir, do yourself some good and be a little compassionate when talking about your baby. Remember, you did participate in bringing him forth, or did you not," she added when he seemed hesitant.

"I didn't, it is my brothers son. He went with the *wrong*

kind of girl and got himself a baby, my nephew."

"And who exactly are the *wrong* kind of girls?"

"Hookers, but you know something, it should not matter what somebody does or did. If you love that person, you should be able to work it out. What I don't like is the way he treats the boy and his mother."

"You are saying that he loves her but shuns her because she is a..."

"A hooker? Yes. He says he loves her but can't associate with her because of that."

"You must be a very considerate man. And anyway, you shouldn't be talking to me like this."

"Talking to you was a pleasure. I really don't have anyone to talk to about what is in my heart. It really made me feel better."

One week later, he appeared at her place again.

"Another cardigan, eh," she said when she saw it was him.

"No, I think you could do with a little time outside... how about dinner at a place of your picking?"

"You need to know something. I didn't expect this." She was genuinely flattered and surprised.

"I sure hope that's not a no. God help me if it is. Oh, I know. I forgot to ask if you are married. I should have known better. A beautiful girl like you could not be unattached."

"No, it's not that. I'm still single. I am not saying I don't want to go to dinner with you, but I don't think it is such a good idea."

"How's come?" He was genuinely puzzled.

"My past would not permit us to have a normal relationship. I... I was..."

"Take your time. You can tell me."

"A...a hooker..."

"I see. Can we talk about that through dinner tomorrow?"

"Can I say no to that?"

"No, you are not supposed to say no to that. I'll pick you up tomorrow at seven."

And that was the beginning of a healthy relationship that blossomed into a marriage three months later. Tracy became an Angston and moved in with her husband, Tommy Angston.

Being the only one of the three friends left in the boarding house, Wendy took over the room next door that belonged to Tracy and Sally to accommodate the extra number of pairs and employee she hired due to the pressures of work. The number of pairs she would clean in a day now averaged forty, and the charges per pair had now gone up to seven shillings. She managed to save at least twenty-five pounds a week, after she had paid the two and a half pounds on rent for each of the two rooms, five pounds on food, and ten pounds for the materials. Her clothes and hairdressing set her back by thirty pounds. She had also to part with twelve pounds for paying Tony Shingel, the helper she had hired.

Then Mr. William Loone, the owner of the sub-standard fifty-room boarding house, adjusted his rent to four pounds a week per room. With that, she lost five pairs of her daily average takings, and that threw her twenty-five pounds a week savings out the window. Mr. Loone was already talking of an adjustment to a round figure - that's five pounds per room per week.

If the rent went up again, she would not survive, especially not with everybody trying to save on every single penny that they could lay their hands on. Ideas like 'not liking to clean my muddy shoes' would soon have to be discarded.

Then the notice came. In one month's time, she would have to pay ten pounds for the two rooms. The people at the boarding house would have to adjust their lifestyles accordingly. She was thus to expect fewer pairs of shoes to clean. She had to find an alternative – fast. It was like driving on a highway and coming across a signpost saying *'hell, one metre ahead.'* Then looking at the speedometre and seeing that the pointer is at a hundred kilometres an hour and the brakes are not functioning. It was like a destiny that could only be changed by daredevil antics.

****

Peter Snell, the Liverpool tycoon had moved into London, not on holiday or business, but in pursuit of elusive love. His real hobby was the adventure of making money. His real passion was gambling his assets for others and succeeding in turning them into great businesses. His dream girl, Elizabeth Winston (or read correctly, Elizabeth Jerkin, since she was married to Hunk Jerkin Jr., the son of a local Liverpool MP, for the last two years) had moved to London for a holiday.

Snell had had feelings for Elizabeth since his high school days but had never managed to summon enough courage to tell her how he felt for her. He had always thought that she would mock him the moment he opened his mouth to express his feelings, especially since she was two years his senior at the same high school.

Elizabeth had the reputation of pulling pranks on boys, especially those who approached her. One afternoon, Snell was passing near some girls of the same class as Elizabeth and overheard them chatting about how she had pulled the prank of the year on a boy of the same class as her who had asked her for a date since his parents would be away for the weekend.

He lingered out of sight, just an earshot away, to catch the facts about the incident. Elizabeth had kept the boy, Jack, waiting for an hour and a half before appearing and letting things heat up for almost an hour. When Jack had crossed the point of no return, she had pricked the swollen organ with a pin. He screamed. Jack's cries had attracted the neighbours who had come to investigate, only to find the stark naked Jack trying some therapy on himself.

Such tales had made Snell as silent as a grave about his feelings for Elizabeth. One thing he realized was that he could never feel anything near what he felt for her for someone else. Since then, he had always kept a close distance and hoped for a miracle. Her wedding to Hunk Jerkin Jr. had devastated him. Then the rumours that Elizabeth had been pushed into the marriage came in. Peter intended to find out the whole truth. It took two years before his operatives came across a letter written by Elizabeth to a cousin in Switzerland, Maria, which practically presented a whole new angle, in black and white.

> *"I only married him to save my family from being thrown into prison for our dealings in illegal goods and my father being in debt to their family to the tune of three thousand pounds worth of merchandise that he could not deliver to Jerkin Senior. Otherwise every time we have sex, it is always a nightmare to me, though he seems to be enjoying himself. He threatened to expose us all if anybody said anything. I feel cornered like a caged animal."*

Those were the all-important lines that sounded like music of the greatest tune to Mr. Snell's ears. It was just the kind of a chance he had been waiting for all along.

The letter also revealed that they could be in London for a while as they were waiting for some merchandise, though it would take a month before the goods actually arrived. While they were in London, Elizabeth's husband often made regular visits to Liverpool and this time was no different.

Peter waited patiently until he saw Hunk board the Liverpool bound train. He then walked casually to the hairdresser's salon that his operative had told him Elizabeth frequented. He took his place in the lounge and waited patiently because of the thought of finally capturing his chase of a lifetime, and impatiently because of the adventure of not knowing what would come out of his chase.

Finally, Elizabeth walked into the lounge on her way into the salon. She was looking straight up and was almost walking past him. He stretched his leg to obstruct her path, pretending to be dead busy with the magazine he was holding high up. When she tripped and almost fell, they both looked at each other. The surprise on each face was apparent, though one was masked and the other was genuine.

"Peter Snell! God! What on earth would you be doing here?"

"Elizabeth! What a surprise."

"You brought some one special with you, eh," she said decidedly.

"No, I came here for another reason. He decided to go straight to the point. "Tell me, how come your husband is not here with you. I would surely love to meet that lucky chap." Sarcasm crept into his tone.

"He had a busy evening last night. He had to stay late in bed."

"I see. I thought I ran into someone taking the Liverpool train who I can swear was him."

"You know how it is, people can look alike." She could not succeed in camouflaging the tinge of guilt in her voice.

"I don't think so. The brown leather jacket, the red checked shirt, a pair of blue jeans – looks to me more like his style."

"What are you implying Peter?" Her voice was now an angry pitch. "Does it mean that wherever my husband is has suddenly become your business?"

The heads in the lounge began to emerge from behind

the books and magazines and started paying more attention to the former schoolmates.

"Hey, not here, Elizabeth I'm down at the Country Hill Hotel, room sixteen. Be there as soon as you are through with your appointment with the hair dresser." His voice had dropped to a whisper that only Elizabeth could hear.

She looked at him for a long time as he walked out of the salon, not really understanding what it meant. What was he planning? Black mail?

The little she could remember about Peter Snell was that he had always been of a pleasant but broody character. That didn't look at all like him. She may have had a major crush on him but her interest had quickly faded when he didn't seem to take any notice. Or didn't it? No. If she remembered correctly, she had pushed him out of her heart and closed that door - unwillingly. She could not wait for him forever, and even if she had waited that long she could still have ended getting married to Hunk. What exactly was Peter Snell up to? He had everything spinning around his fingers. He was a tycoon for goodness sake. She realized there was only one way to find out. She knew Hunk would kill her if he ever found out she went into another man's hotel room. Nevertheless, she had no choice. The suspense was too much to live with.

"I know all about you Elizabeth. I know Jerkin Jr. is not your kind of man and he deals in illegal business. I know about your father's indebtedness to him and the nightmare of you being his wife."

"You surely don't beat around the bush, Peter. So what am I to do to keep you quiet?" Typical lines of a blackmailer. Except for a misplaced passion she sensed in his tone. Maybe that was due to the fact that he was dealing with a former schoolmate. If she were to be asked what she would choose as payment to keep him quiet, she would choose going to bed with him. That was one thing she would enjoy giving to him. She had almost forgotten how it felt to be making love. Hunk had killed that side of her two years ago. With Peter, it would be lovemaking though she would have to pretend to hate it. However, she realized he would not ask for such favours. He could get any woman he wanted.

"Elizabeth, I want you to know something." He paused momentarily. "I...I fell in love with you while I was still in school. Ever since the first day I laid my eyes on you."

Elizabeth could not believe her ears. She held her breath as if breathing would drown his voice and she would not hear him clearly.

"I want to help you with your little problem. Elizabeth. But first you have to trust me." His firm voice had now given way to an emotional passionate appeal.

"Peter, do you know there was a time I could have killed to hear those words from you. But you never said them," she said after a long silence.

It was his turn to look at her, blankly stunned. He had not expected anything like what she had just said.

"I assumed my feelings were just one way. You should realize by now I am beyond help. Hunk has me exactly where he wants me. I'm even risking being in this hotel room with you. If he finds out.... Forget about me, Peter. You can get any woman you want. Take the chance and don't put yourself through this misery. Thanks anyway." She started picking her things to leave.

"Remember your reputation with pranks, Elizabeth. And don't forget you were two years my senior. You still are. I didn't want to risk being another of your victims."

"Sorry if that scared you off. None of those boys meant anything to me, Peter. Anyway, mine is sealed. Ours, you and me, was never meant to be. Hunk would have destroyed what we would have built anyway. That would have been worse. Let's just be contented with our separate fates. Thanks for your concern and for helping me figure out just why I missed out on the relationship I had most yearned for. At least now I know you cared."

"I still do care, Elizabeth. Give me this chance to help you out. I love you Elizabeth and I know I can never be happy without you in my life. Hunk murdered a man sometime back. You could put him away if you testified as to what kind of a man he is. I believe you and your family could get off if you pulled him down. I want to surrender the case to the Liverpool police. It would be airtight, if your testimony supported it. Help me so I can help you, Elizabeth." He walked over to her slowly, taking her in his arms.

Suddenly, she lost control. She had never felt anything like that for a long, long time. She could not resist the urge to let him go on. And when he realized what was happening, he asked her if she was sure that was what she wanted.

She looked into his eyes and all she could trace was passion. Inside her eyes he could only read the abandoned fires of passion. The two pairs of lips came together, and the banked amorous abandon took over, inhibitively at first, and to both, it was like a new found treasure, none willing to let go.

Two weeks later, the unfolding events led to the arrest of the son of the MP, Hunk Jerkin Jr. Two days after Hunk Jerkin Jr. was arrested, the MP himself, Ron Jerkin Sr., was arrested. The Liverpool police opened a file on the case and incorporated the report of Rawlins Peterson's, the detective Peter Snell had hired to nail the Jerkins. The one year old cold blooded murder case of Jonathan Lyce had found a suspect at last - Hunk Jerkin Jr.

When the police stormed the Jerkin's hotel room in London, Hunk was busy trying to pin Elizabeth into bed, and she was vigorously fighting him off.

The bottled emotions that Elizabeth and Peter had been keeping a secret for fear of Hunk's reaction must have stormed the bottle cork for they ran into each others' arms, as if without doing so they would have dropped dead.

"I no longer intend to be your wife, Hunk Jerkin. Our little arrangement is over," Elizabeth heard herself say. They were some of the sweetest words she had ever said in so many years.

"Do you realize you can not talk against your husband in a court of law, Elizabeth?" Hunk insisted as he was being led away.

I'll see to it that you don't have a wife by the time it comes to court, Hunk. I can't wait to be married to my fiancée here," she said leaning to Peter.

And when the doors finally closed and the noise subsided, the monsters of passion must have been let lose, as the two lovers celebrated their victory in amatory companionship.

And between themselves, an agreement was made that London was gong to be their home. But there was one thing Peter wanted to do. He needed to dispose off a Liverpool supermarket he had won through a bet about the movement of some shares that had been introduced into the market.

The supermarket had not made profits ever since, and Peter Snell had no intentions of being branded a loser in any business venture he ever undertook. He really did not know what to do with the supermarket. He placed an advert in the *Chronicle*. As soon as he confirmed that it would appear for five days, from Monday to Friday, especially in the Liverpool edition, they joined the weekend holiday rush in London.

****

She was in the dinning hall when a wildlife documentary, 'Footprints of Nature' was running on the television. The feature this episode was on eagles and what stuck with her was the eaglets leaving the nest. To her, the boarding house had for the last three years been a nest. It had supplied her with enough market to keep her afloat until very recently. Now the nest was not sufficient and there was need to find the market elsewhere. A new challenge was in the offing and even if she was uncomfortable with the change, she realized it had to happen.

She walked the streets and identified a spot she felt the shoe shine business would be ideal. It was a busy street in the East End, full of labourers, traders and jobseekers seeking to explore the post war opportunities coming from World War II, and right at the heart of British optimism, with the lowest overheads that the East End richly offered. A street shoe shiner would offer services of convenience of having the shoes cleaned affordably.

The process of setting up the road side business and identification of the cheaper but suitable residence was a tedious exercise which she nevertheless successfully concluded in a few days.

Within three months she had established a routine, as the business settled to equilibrium. She would pay her workers, pay the rent, put some decent food on the table and she would save the little that remained.

Finally, her dream of a college lower diploma in Business Management and Secretarial Operations was within achievable distance and she took full advantage and enrolled for the three year course. The course was both tasking but also satisfying and putting the knowledge in business helped her in slowly but steadily growing her savings. Three years later, graduation was celebrated by enrollment into the two year higher diploma course.

New city by-laws had endangered this balance and she had to look for even cheaper rental residence. Then plans to regulate roadside businesses were hatched and she was one among many businesses that were staring at extinction. Moments of uncertainty followed as their union painstakingly negotiated with the city fathers. She decided to purchase the Tuesday edition of the *Chronicle*, in the hope that she would look over and get a place where she could start anew.

In the end of it all, she wished she hadn't bought the paper and had saved the few shillings she had spent on it. The places she found in the classified section were either too small or too expensive, and the few that she felt were a fit had already been booked. She folded the paper once and tossed it aside. The lower half of the back page landed upwards. There was an eye-catching advert on that part of the paper, printed in bold.

Up for grabs! Medium sized supermarket in Liverpool for sale. Bids invited. Deadline: 15 days after the final advert appearing this Friday. Send your bids through the address given below. Decision on the winning bid is at the discretion of the management.

There was an address given at the end of the advert. She looked through it for a moment, and then she realized she could not even think of placing a bid. Her savings could only total three hundred pounds. If she sold the shoe shine business, maybe then she could only do one thousand two hundred pounds. She was simply out of the bracket. The bid would probably be worth three thousand to something like five thousand pounds. But a voice within her kept asking 'what harm would it do to try?' She kept telling herself, 'who knows, maybe a miracle could happen.' She imagined herself an owner of a supermarket! But reality slapped out of it. 'Get real shoe girl, three hundred pounds can never make you an owner of a supermarket - unless it belongs to a *good* father of yours,' another voice within her said.

Then on Thursday morning, one of those nocturnal ladies she had business-friended visited her premises while she was having a meeting with her workers, her muddy pair of high-heeled shoes under her arm.

"Guess who gives me a ride to the city last night?" she asked anxiously.

"Oh, damn. How many times do I have to tell you I don't want to hear about your nighttime activities? Would you please stop?"

"I know you don't give a shit, but this I have to tell some one. I am walking down towards the bus stop and at a corner a car bumps into me. I lose my balance and fall on my knees and hands. I raise my eyes to see who the bastard was and, *abracadabra!* A full length limo stops in front of me. And who steps out? Remember the Hunk Jerkin scandal?"

"What 'bout it." Wendy answered nonchalantly and without any real options but putting up with her tales.

"The Liverpool tycoon who effortlessly helped put Hunk in prison, and Hunk's wife. They grab me from the ground and 'are you hurt, are you alright?' they keep asking."

"And, I go 'thanks a lot, but I'll be fine. Don't trouble yourselves'."

"You owe me the favour of accepting my offer since I at least owe you to make up for running you over," the tycoon says, and before I know it, I'm being driven in the lengthy car. I tell you it feels like paradise."

"Those guys have cash. There was this one time she was asking him how much he expected to get from the sale of the Liverpool supermarket. He thinks it could net thirty thousand pounds. God if I could lay my hands on such kind of money."

That took her by surprise. Tycoon Peter Snell was the owner of the Liverpool supermarket she had read about in the *Chronicle* just two days back! Not that knowing this fact would change anything, but it was interesting to note the expected price range. The nocturnal lady talked non-stop, but this time around she was all ears.

"And can you imagine what I got myself off with when alighting at the town square? A ten pound tip for pocket money and a job offer to work as a maid for them, just to get me off the streets. Twenty pounds a week, can you believe that? They want me to meet them at the Sky Height restaurant the day after tomorrow. If I decide to take them on their offer and it takes me too long to reach the decision, I have the directions to their residence. Once the limousine disappears, I take the bus back here. That's why I don't look sleepy today."

ELEVEN

By 1968, Juve had bought the parcels of land around the cottage and had applied for the title deed from the government. He got himself some gardening tools, and on it he and Mark practiced subsistence farming, selling whatever was excess and settled to a quiet life.

It was he alone who knew what he was still waiting for. But he kept quiet about it since he knew his friends would make him their laughing stock.

To tell them that he had a feeling that the white lady who promised to return for him was saying the truth. Or that the white lady he briefly came into contact with, due to his own contrived actions, was missing him just as much as he was missing her, and somehow they were going to meet again and something good would come out of it.

Juve promised himself one thing though. Until he could get Wendy out of his system, he was not going to burden somebody else with feelings that were not genuine. He realized that it may take him a long time to get over her. But once he was ready to move on, he would find someone and get on with life. Not that there was much hope in waiting for her would be attracting a lifetime sentence of ridicule by them.

****

Winifred McAlester, the lady who Mr. Snell's chauffeur had bumped, was undecided on what she wanted to do. She wasn't quite sure she was ready to give up her freedom to go and work for somebody else, the salary not withstanding. Wendy had to do some real talking before convincing her that going for it was the right thing to do, and that by so doing she herself, might get the chance to meet the tycoon personally. Maybe then the unrealistic dream of owning a supermarket or maybe just bidding for one would somehow work out. Not that even Wendy herself believed it would happen or even seeing the owner of the supermarket would help anything. It was just her superstitious self that believed that could be the perfect action to take towards achieving her ambitions. Moreover, Winnie insisted that Wendy must accompany her to the visit for moral support.

Thus the unmatched pair composed of a reluctant Winnie and the superstitiously optimistic Wendy left for the restaurant. They found the couple thriving on each other's company in a secluded section.

It took two attempts by Winnie and a louder one by Wendy to finally capture their attention.

"Excuse us please," said Wendy, not liking to be the one responsible for spoiling the couple's nice moments. They both looked up.

"Look who's here darling, our new maid. I take it you have made the decision to work for us. You'll never regret it," Elizabeth said sweetly.

"Take seats and order please." They sat on the remaining two seats that filled up the table. "So Miss Winnie, I can see you brought a friend along," the tycoon noted.

"Yes, please meet a friend, Miss Wendy McHenry."

"She literally pushed me here as I wasn't sure whether I should take you up on your offer, and I asked her to accompany me here as a condition for my coming. Wendy, please meet Mr. Snell and his fiancée Elizabeth. Or should I just say Mr. and Mrs. Snell." Everyone broke into a hearty laughter.

The waiter brought two more cups of coffee. They had to have the coffee with doughnuts when Mr. Snell insisted.

"We can accommodate your friend too if she is willing to join you to work for us in the house," Elizabeth offered.

"I believe it is Wendy alone who can give us the answer

to that suggestion," Winnie said, looking directly at Wendy with anticipation for a positive answer.

"It's a pleasure to meet you Mr. Snell and Eliza... Mrs. Snell." They all could not hold back the laughter before letting her continue. "Thanks for the generosity. But I guess I'm not a perimetre woman. I mean I'd rather leave my options open."

"Would you rather venture into business?" Peter Snell asked jokingly.

"Actually, yes," Wendy had to admit.

"Wow, I am impressed. Not many ladies even think of going to the forefront, let alone hope for going into business," Peter Snell had to say.

"So what business did you have in mind?" Elizabeth wanted to know.

"I reckon anything where my decisions account for my successes and failures." She had to keep herself from adding, 'the supermarket business for instance, if Mr. Snell would let me to have it.'

"You know something. I might just be having something for you. Can you run a supermarket business in a busy town?" That question caught her unawares.

"I honestly believe she can." Winnie chipped in. "She opened a self-invented shoe cleaning service in the streets of London with 5 employees under her.

Now Peter Snell was truly awed. "How impressive. I get to know of a lady who's also a business wacko," Peter said approvingly. Wendy was still yet to recover from the surprise of how things were turning out.

They talked for sometime about some things such as the weather, current news, sports and the likes, before Winnie finally asked to be allowed to leave.

"Listen Miss Winnie, I'll send a truck to come and help you move tomorrow. And you, Miss Wendy, I'll expect you to apply through a bid as advertised in the *Chronicle*. Of course there are formalities you will have to abide with.

And please not a word about this to any one, it might spoil your party," Mr. Snell said.

He then pulled out a black piece of electronic equipment from an inside pocket of the three-piece suit and pressed a button.

"I want you ladies to take the limousine to wherever you want to go. My wife-to-be and I will wait for Mr. Williams to return." Before he was through with the sentence, the chauffeur was already standing next to their table.

"But Mr. Snell, we can find our way..." Wendy started to protest but Peter Snell wouldn't hear about it.

"That's my treat to you, ladies. They will tell you where to take them. We will be waiting here for you, Williams."

"Consider it done, Sir."

"One thing, Williams, don't ever call me Sir. The name is Peter."

"I will not, Sir...Peter."

They all laughed as the byes and thanks were exchanged. The chauffeur and the two ladies walked to the lengthy car.

Peter Snell watched as they walked away. He wasn't stupid. It was from such situations that he learned how to conquer the world of business. Watching as people struggled their way up the ladder of success, watching keenly as they were faced with difficulties and how they reacted to certain situations. It was an adventure that he loved to witness. It had helped him learn how to deal with people, how to pick the weaknesses in people, and how to use this to his advantage. It was one exercise that had never failed him before. He had learned how to smell a company in trouble through the management's thick skin of camouflage and all he had to do was to wait for the best opportunity in order to come in and pick the remains that he reorganized and rebuilt with great success. He had literally moved from rags to riches, as his companies put up huge profit margins. In the Liverpool business world, they called him the gambler eye.

He began his fairy journey to wealth on the streets of Liverpool, just fresh from college, when he paid a hundred pounds to a friend for a newspapers stall that was ailing from lack of profit. He had to convince his obstinate uncle that the hundred pounds he had finally agreed to lend him would not be lost in his unorthodox investments, as he had disapprovingly referred to Peter Snell's latest venture.

It miraculously took Peter Snell just three years to turn the stall into a low class bookshop in Liverpool's low rental streets, before transforming it into a high class bookshop cum publishing house in Liverpool's elitists quarters, rubbing shoulders with some of the wealthiest, most powerful, and most influential personalities in the city and all of England.

Perhaps, as his friends and critics alike agreed, his qualities of buoyancy could be traced back to the boating tragedy that left him an instant orphan when he was just ten years old, loosing both his parents and a young sister, and being taken in by his disobliging uncle.

Peter Snell had even, on numerous occasions, sold out his companies cheap, only to repurchase them months or years later, exorbitantly, though most had often slid the downward trend. Peter Snell had offered paying more than twice as much as he had sold out. It was only he who knew the true value of these irrational sells and repurchases. To him, it was a way of letting in a completely new and different personality, dedicated and industrious in its own way, into his own court, just for the sake of learning, while to them, he was a psychopath who should be watched carefully lest his psychosis began being manifested in a different form.

In this Wendy McHenry package, he intended to include an extra. He would set a limit and he knew Wendy would fall for it. She was too inexperienced to notice the bad deal and too inept to succeed in beating the deadline he would set for her to pay up in full. Once this deadline expired, the supermarket would revert to him again, this time incorporating all the novel ideas Wendy would have pumped in to try and beat the deadline. No matter how little the figure she would owe, at the expiry of the deadline he would repossess the supermarket. That would be one heck of a great time he would have, especially with Wendy being one in a million, a woman. It was going to be a great thrill, almost as great as getting married to Elizabeth. He could not wait. Life was turning into one big dream.

When Mr. Snell returned to his office to act on the bids, he found out that his ever-efficient secretary had already selected some ten bids she believed were valid by any standards and placed them on his table.

There was an A and A, for Allen and Alex, Mark Wright and Sons, DD for Dover Duncan, Lincoln Enterprises, Marson Supermarkets, Sam's Departmental Stores and Alvin Stores. They had all offered to pay for the supermarket on lump sum basis. The bids ranged from thirty-five thousand to fifty thousand pounds.

Those were all solid good bids. However, one ingredient they all did not have was the thrill of watching as the new owner sweats it out, trying to complete the payment. Giving the supermarket to an established bidder, who would pay for the establishment in a lump sum, would be like truancy – nay failing to attempt some examinations and hoping to get a pass mark. Can't happen. Peter Snell was not the type to skip lessons. It was those lessons that had sharpened his instincts to such excellence. Besides, an established entity could come across some secret about the previous owner of the establishment they just bought, if they are keen enough. He could not forget those several instances in which he had used this system where he would purchase the subsidiary of the organization that was eluding him, and from that, lay his offensive relying on the management's weaknesses he had picked up here and there in that subsidiary. He had managed to eventually lay his hands on his now second largest organization, Skyways Aviation, after a long running contest for ownership, through employing this tactic.

"Wasn't there a Wendy McHenry bid, Helen?" he asked his secretary after looking through those on his desk and not finding it.

"I don't really remember, sir. I disposed off the rest of the bids. None were good enough."

"I don't really remember delegating the powers of deciding what is good enough around this place. Would you please get the Wendy McHenry bid from wherever it is you disposed of it." he ordered.

She couldn't really understand all this. She had always been the first judge of what he was to see and what he was not to see. Maybe he had a fight with his lovebird, Elizabeth. She wondered if that could be the reason. Maybe this Wendy McHenry was blackmailing him. On the other hand, maybe he had met Wendy and suddenly realized that Elizabeth wasn't good enough. It was funny as to what length men would go for women. Finally, she remembered Wendy's bid, one whereby she was offering to pay for the supermarket for ten years from the earnings of the entity itself, with an initial deposit of five hundred pounds! That lady must be totally insane. Others were ready to pay even fifty thousand pounds spot cash!

Helen couldn't even wait to read the third line of that bid. That Wendy had to be a nut case. That proposal must be the most ridiculous she had ever come across all her lifetime. She had disposed it off without a second thought. Wendy was not even qualified to be a non-starter.

She had an easy time retrieving the Wendy McHenry bid from the waste paper basket. It was easy to tell from the rest, because it was of poor quality paper and without even a letterhead. She straightened it out and took it to her boss' office. She was expecting to make the return trip to the waste paper basket with the document, once Mr. Snell had finished perusing it and decided it was ridiculous.

"Please dispose off the rest of those bids," he ordered.

She could not believe what he had just said. Did he mean that she should get rid of those juicy bids, like A and A, DD, the three from those politicians, and the rest of those front runners?

She watched in shock as he pushed aside those juicy pieces of proposals, not even looking to see what they were proposing!

This Wendy McHenry must be some real bad news. She could not even wait to tell her friends this shocking tale.

One of the secret admirer's hirelings was one of those friends. She made the call.

****

Wendy did not have to wait for long for the reply from Mr. Snell. She received it through Winnie, who was now a maid at the Snell residence. It said her bid would be accepted, subject to some two conditions.

One, she had to deposit a sum of three thousand pounds at the bank account belonging to the supermarket. There was a bank name and number for her to do that, within a specified period of ten days. Already a day had strolled by. At the expiry of those days the management would assume she had withdrawn her bid and go on and award it to another person.

The second condition was that once she had placed the deposit, as required, she would have to agree to make the final payment within five years from the day of the deposit. In total she would have paid forty eight thousand pounds for the supermarket with three thousand upfront as deposit. Failure to make the final deposit would mean the supermarket reverts to its original owner, regardless of how small the balance would be. No refunds would be made, as those would cover the breach of the contract.

She looked at it for a long time. She realized she had just lost it. There was no way she was going to raise three thousand pounds, and certainly not in ten days. The dream was over even before she had a chance to start on it. Mr. Snell had given her the chance of a lifetime that she could not hold on to. She wondered how many other people had placed bids for the supermarket. She wondered how tempting they must have been to Mr. Snell. He had overlooked those and given her the chance.

On the second day to the deadline she had five hundred and fifty pounds if she included the three hundred pounds selling price for the shoe shine business (worth over one thousand five hundred but grossly undervalued due to the uncertainty of a new set of city by-laws). She would have to find a cheaper place to live and try to get a job if she could. Maybe she would pay rent, rent, rent, and finally become broke. Maybe then she would go to the Snell's residence and beg to be allowed to join Winnie, who seemed to be doing well. Or maybe Mr. Snell would give her a job in one of his many organizations. If that did not work out, then maybe Sally's prediction would hold true, for there would be no where else to turn.

Then it crossed her mind that maybe Sally or Tracy could help. She found Tracy's number and called. The telephone just kept on ringing. Tracy and Tommy had the tendency of going for prolonged holidays. They must be on one of those. Sally's number could not go through either. The line had a breakdown. She was alone in this. Nobody was going to bail her out. It was the end of the road for her. Time had come to find an alternative. Mr. Snell must be choosing some body else at that very moment.

Wendy's landlord delivered the only mail in her letter box a day later. She was in no mood for opening letters.

She was certain the letter was not from Mr. Snell. One thing she had learned about the tycoon, during that short period she had been acquainted to him, was that he was a man of his word. He had categorically stated in the letter he had sent to her that there would be no communication what so ever upon her failure to act on the proposal. It can hardly be from a friend, as they did not write much. She soothed herself to sleep as tears of failure rolled down her cheeks. She felt the need for a final deep sleep before she would settle to tackle the unknown that next day and the following ones. She would call the person she had promised to sell the shoe shine business to had her proposal been agreed to by the tycoon, and tell him the deal was off.

The following morning, she woke up distressed as never before and literally pushed herself to the café where the union members frequented. She unwillingly started to bite through the fried egg and scones sandwich, as she sipped on black coffee. She realized she had to eat, for few months into the future she might not even manage to put food in front of her through her own means. Suddenly, everybody's eyes were looking at her like she was from another planet. She stopped eating wondering what it was everybody was seeing in her. Her willpower to fight her failing appetite had just been destroyed. Suddenly she could not bite anymore.

Everybody must have gotten a brief on the story of the *shoe-girl's* foolish and unrealistic attempts to own a supermarket! She wondered how that information had leaked. Did Mr. Snell let out the secret? Or was it Winnie who told it? She raised her eyes to look back at them, blatantly. In a way, the stare conveyed the intended message - 'mind your own businesses.'

Somebody walked over to her and leaned on the table. It was one of her shoe polishing business customers. "I did not know you had such huge ambitions, Wendy. Wow, owning a supermarket..."

She had had enough. She was not going to let them put her through that. She was going to act on him as a lesson to the rest of them. Her hand slowly inched for the half-filled cup, as he kept talking.

"...Congratulations are in order I believe. But how on earth did you manage to raise three thousand pounds, obviously not from your shoe-girlie business."

Her hand had already gripped the cup and she was on the verge of projecting its contents on Bob Staily's face. But his statement hit the mark just in the nick of time.

"Bob, what are you implying, some stupid practical joke or what?" she had to say, finally fighting hard to keep her sudden anxiety camouflaged.

Somebody else opened the business section of the *Chronicle,* folded the paper appropriately and tossed it on the table, under her face. She found herself staring at the small gallery insert at the base of the page.

TYCOON SNELL SUPERMARKET BID AWARDED

Liverpool tycoon Peter Snell has awarded the supermarket to a virtually unknown bidder, Wendy McHenry.

The tycoon insists that the decision was purely on business terms and has refuted claims that he had in anyway been forced into his choice of the winning bid.

There were reports that some bidders cried foul and questioned the capability of the *Shoe-girl* to raise the three thousand pound deposit tycoon Snell had asked for.

Shoe-girl, whose shoe polishing trade is said to have been her livelihood at the boarding house where she had been a resident before venturing to the streets, (thus her nick name), is said to have beaten a seasoned field of bidders such as Allen and Alex, Dover Duncan, Mark Wright, and some three senior politicians, among others, who it is believed had offered to pay for the supermarket on a lump sum basis.

But top business analysts insist there was nothing out of the ordinary with the awarding of the bid to the *shoe-girl,* judging from the tycoon's history of unorthodox business decisions.

McHenry has five years to pay the total price of forty-five thousand pounds, having deposited three thousand to get the supermarket at forty eight thousand pounds.

She looked up and threw a moment's apologetic look at everyone. She then excused herself and took off to her place, as Bob and everyone else began to protest. She had to see exactly what was in the envelope. Once in her room, she grabbed the envelope she previously ignored. She did not know what to think. Maybe the letter would give a direction or at least shed some light to this dream she was going through. How could it be possible that she had *paid* the deposit that she could not afford?

She ripped the envelope open. A small piece of paper fell to the floor. She picked it up and perused it.

Verill Bank

Depositor's Original Receipt
Depositor's name: - Anonymous
Sum total: - Three Thousand Pounds
£3,000
Account no. AV. 50062
Account name: - Snell Supermarket
Date: - 28th February 1968

There was another piece of paper addressed to her. She unfolded it anxiously and perused it.

Please receive and keep your receipt for payment of the deposit as required. I paid on your behalf. Burn this note after use.

Secret Admirer

Please fulfill your dreams.

There was no forwarding address. There was nothing else in the note or envelope that could give her a clue as to the identity of the sender. She wondered why anyone would bail her out and wish to remain anonymous. Some one probably had a crush on her and could not bring himself to tell her. She looked at the possibilities. Maybe it was Bob Stainly or Steve Raleigh, the other man who had tossed the paper in front of her. Why would they want to help out and how did they know about the deal?

Could it be the tycoon himself? She found herself playing with the idea of confronting him. But that would be taking the joke too far. Snell was currently overwhelmed by his lovebird. Or maybe it was Elizabeth. She realized there was no way to find out.

****

After four years in the streets of London operating her shoe shine business she moved to Liverpool and found herself a small cottage near the supermarket, upon requesting the tycoon to guarantee her so she would secure it on credit. Of course she was not aware that Mr. Snell loved to extend her liability to him as a business strategy. Once she and Mr. Snell were through the formalities of signing, she changed the name of the supermarket to Wendy's supermarket.

It was a gallant performance on the first year. But it would fall short if she had to complete the forty-five thousand pounds payment. She was in fact running behind schedule. It was just a matter of time, and she would be on her way out.

In the second year, she had worked extremely hard. Everything was beginning to look up within the year. She expected to recover a substantial amount on the payments and maybe start making prepayments for the third year. However, her chances were blurred midway through the year, as a shipping accident wreaked havoc on her hopes. The insurance company refused to budge claiming that she had changed freights by using a different freight from the one they had arranged for her, and did not surrender her changes to them on time. At the end of year two, she was more behind in payments than ever.

Year three: - she did well and more customers walked into the supermarket. She made some positive changes on product outlook and arrangements that started to pay off. She then introduced lottery competitions for her customers and donated to charity. She brought in imports that were an instant hit. Finally by the end of the year, she had recovered almost three-quarters of her overall overdraft on payments to Mr. Snell. She also managed to clear the credit on the cottage.

Year four: - things went on to improve all through the year, and for the first time she was at par with the payments. By the end of that year, she had made some prepayments and was looking optimistically at the final year. The dream of being the owner of the supermarket was well within reach and realistic.

Year five: - this turned out to be a disastrous year. At first, everything looked well and on track, until mid-year when the store was robbed several times. Gangster terror had caught up in Liverpool, setting her back yet again. Then, just a few weeks after the bold and rude robberies, a South American importation was certified as stale. She ended up losing over a thousand pounds on that deal. And as if that was not enough, the supermarkets warehouse was consumed by a mysterious fire. The fire brigade took several minutes to bring the raging inferno under control, but that did not help as the fire did almost total damage on the goods in storage. The insurance firm agreed to compensate for the damages, but that would not help her desperate situation. She needed to recover in her payments as the deadline drew closer. It would take months if not years for the insurance money to be released. The reality of the situation was that she had lost yet again. This time there was no way out. Five long years of building a dream had been consumed by the inferno. It was one bitter pill to swallow. Even if she were to dispose of her assets, it would not be enough to cover the five thousand-pound final payment. It was over.

A call came through and she let it ring persistently before summoning the energy to move across the room to pick it up.

"You've got six thousand pounds in your account. Take it to Mr. Snell." It was a feminine voice at the other end of the line.

"What? Who is this? What do you want with me?"

Secret Admirer."

"A lady? Why are you doing this? Don't you think you are being too generous to a stranger...?"

"The supermarket is yours, Wendy."

"How much do I owe you, please tell me how I can repay..." Suddenly Wendy wanted to say a million things to her.

"You owe nothing. One day you will understand. Good luck, Wendy."

"Hey, don't hang up. I need to know..." But the line went dead, leaving the baffled Wendy staring at the box for a long time, a million and one questions suddenly crossing her mind all at once.

Her years of hard work had some romance in it through some two men.

First, Jack Dicholson came into her life. Every inch of that relationship was healthy, except when he tried to kiss her, something she found very repulsive. This went on for a few months, before it finally eroded Jack's interest.

"How can you profess to love some one and not find making love to them exciting?" he kept telling her now and then. Her pleas that she needed some time to get ready met an overly disappointed Jack, who broke off the relationship officially and advised her to seek some professional help.

Then, there was Roy Burns, who waited only two weeks before trying to force her into bed. She had asked Roy to take it slowly, as she had to get used to the idea. But Roy must have been too impatient to wait for the rewards of his involvement with such a seraphic lady.

When she first came to England, she always dreamed of Juve and the promise she had made to him. But as her hopes of ever succeeding to earn a meaningful life in England quickly dwindled, she had to admit that the chances of ever returning to Kenya and finding him still waiting for her were growing slim by the day and the night. She had unwillingly given up on that dream and had thrown herself into building a life for herself in Britain. However, the only man she had felt love for continued to visit her in her dreams. Then that also died off with time. What she had not realized was that gone with those dreams was her appetite for sex. She consulted her doctor over the problem and the doctor confirmed her fears when she casually observed that may be she was yet to find the man she truly loved.

Suddenly, Juve had returned to her dreams. No wonder Jack and Roy could not find real feelings with her. Juve had always been there, blocking their paths. Suddenly she felt light hearted, anxious and wishful, all at the same time. Jane Banks, the doctor, immediately prescribed a remedy when she told her about Juve.

"Take some time off and board a plane, go find this Juve guy and find out what he is doing with his life. It's only if you start from there that you can get back your lost appetite. Now, get your things packed," she told her smiling.

And she took her advice and left everything in the hands of her able assistant, Bryan Ronald. She wondered if by now he had found someone and settled down to marriage. She wondered if he had children. Probably yes. Or maybe he could even be...dead. She pushed that particular thought out of her mind. Where would she start looking? She remembered the big hug and the passionate kiss they had exchanged at the coast. The feelings of warmth, lust, love, unwillingness to let go and extreme happiness replayed themselves to her, just as she had felt them on that occasion. She smiled at the prospect of meeting him again. 'Here I come, Juve.' And she could not help but slide into the utopian amatory world of the two of them, as the plane ascended deep into the clouds on its way to Kenya.

****

The secret admirer hired a private charter plane to Kenya. She did not know how long she was going to stay in Kenya, but she knew this was going to be one of the greatest moments of her life. She was not going to miss this for anything. She had made sure everything was in good hands of her assistants back in England. She relaxed and waited impatiently for the moment of a lifetime to arrive. She had kept her informers strategically stationed to give her a clear picture on what went on in Wendy's life. She was in the know when Wendy was kidnapped, when the Wendy - Juve romance began and when she landed in Europe. Her people were reliable and out of the way. She paid them well.

TWELVE

The plane touched down at Nairobi's Wilson Airport at sunset. She didn't know where he could be at the particular time. She decided she would start looking in the morning.

"Where exactly, madam," asked the taxi driver when she said "city centre."

"Hill Crest Inn." It was the only place she could remember.

The second plane touched down at the same airport fifteen minutes later. The passenger it was carrying had paid a fortune for the private charter. The secret admirer knew exactly where to check - the Hill Crest Inn.

A Wendy McHenry had just checked into the inn. She booked herself at an adjacent lodging, overlooking the Hill Crest, where she had an appropriate view of the Hill Crest's entrance. It was time to wait for tomorrow.

The following day Wendy got up at nine, had a quick shower, then breakfast, dressed up and beckoned a taxi to Thika. She would start looking for him there. What if he had gone to work? Or simply did not remember her at all? Questions kept coming. But she realized she owed it to herself at least to carry out this fact-finding mission in order to lead a normal life. On two occasions, she had almost stopped the taxi and asked the driver to turn back and take her back to the airport. Maybe she was making a fool of herself. By now, Juve could be a happily married man. She then realized she wanted more than ever to make sure.

The second taxi tailed the one in which Wendy was carried in. "Don't lose them and don't let them know we are tailing them. I want to keep this a surprise." The secret admirer spoke passionately and the driver understood.

****

Juve was watering the nursery bed. It was here that he would seek refuge when thoughts of her came invading. It was twelve years now. His life had stopped moving. Maybe everybody was right. What would a *white* woman want to do with a *black* man anyway? She had obviously found her kind in England or wherever it is she went. Suddenly, it occurred to him that he did not even know where she could be. It really was time to move on. He had to find himself a good partner for a wife, get married and start a family before it was too late. He was not getting any younger, as Mark was fond of telling him. Reality was what it was. 12 wasted years.

Theirs was over even before it had started. It only took him that long. Precisely twelve years, to realize this fact. White for white and black for black, Mark kept saying. Maybe that was what it was. She had just used him to get out of the country she could not stand.

****

"Stop!" she told the driver at the junction into the driveway leading to the cottage. She wanted to walk the rest of the way. She paid him his due and started the journey. She needed to prepare herself for whatever surprise would happen.

Her pursuer saw what she had done and opted to give her some space in between them. She waited for some twenty minutes before instructing the driver to proceed, slowly.

When Wendy reached her destination, she stopped due to the unfamiliar outlook. A wooden gate stood majestically in front of her, blocking her way into the compound of the cottage. Maybe even Juve had sold the cottage and moved some place else.

The compound had totally changed. There were flowers and grass, tended to a perfect harmony. The cottage now displayed characteristics of good care, so unlike Juve, or even Mark for that matter.

She climbed the two step stair, leading to the door. She listened in briefly, half expecting to hear the sound of children playing. But there was silence.

Through two undecided, rapid knocks she tried to seek attention but it went unanswered. She tried again a bit harder, but no answer came. The door moved back a little, under the tiny pressure. She had decided that should a woman answer, she would claim to be a foreigner who had lost her way and was trying to retrace her way back to the road, and then she would be out of there as fast as lightening. She pushed the door slightly and knocked again. The response still did not come.

The furniture in the room was clean, sophisticated, Victorian type and well arranged. The floor was covered with a matching carpet, and a wall unit of a matching type stood majestically at one end of the living room. This was no longer the cottage in which she had been held captive. It had been transformed into a self-contained bungalow. A tic-tacking sound came from the copperware-hung clock. This was a totally different place from the one she knew.

"Any body home!" she called out. No response came. She did not know what to do next. She came back outside, pulling the door behind her to return it to the position in which she had found it, and allowed her eyes to roam the Eden-like gardens.

Her eyes came across a vaguely familiar figure on one side of the compound. The figure was facing the other direction, and under its right hand was a watering can that was letting out a shower of water through its spout onto a nursery bed covered with a green carpet of seedlings. The person was seemingly lost in either thought or concentration.

She walked slowly towards him and stopped a few yards away, not sure whether to run for him or just to wait and see how he reacts to seeing her again after so long. He had not noticed there was someone there. That left her with only one option, call him by name. She hesitated for a long time, studying him as if to see some indication of what to expect the moment she drew his attention, wondering whether all this was a mistake in itself.

"Juve," she called out in a low, uncertain voice.

That familiar, gentle voice hit him with a bout of surprise. He jolted upright as if stung by an arrow. And the instance of expectation and uncertainty seemed to last much longer than it really did. He turned with a start to see what he could only explain as a figment of his imagination. This could not be true. She was standing there looking inquisitively at him. Finally, her pretty angelic face broke into a smile.

His once long rusty and shaggy dreadlocks had given way to a clean, well kept horde of hair on the face and head. He looked much more in control, more composed, calm and undisturbed, yet his eyes bore the characteristics of loneliness and wishfullness.

In her eyes, he could see the uncertainty and toughness only printable by being through the roughest of times. Evidently, under the well matured all round beauty camouflage was the abandoned passion.

And on that momentous occasion, time seized to be, worries disappeared, reality vanished, and dreamland took over as the sea-parted finally found each other, again. Celebrated by a tight squeezing hug and long sensuous kiss, the insouciance of amorous abandon was shuttled back to reality via a rude and unexpected flash and flick.

Behind the Desmonds camera, was a middle-aged blond haired, exultant woman.

"Nellie! What in the world would you be doing here?"

"It's a long, long story. Right now I will give you half the answer. You are looking at the secret admirer," she said, as her face disappeared behind the camera and a series of flicks and flashes.

"What! You are the secret admirer? You must be kidding."

"No time to explain yet. Everybody, get in the car. You two have got a *marriage* priest to catch. You should let lose those beasts of love and romance only when you've got past that man."

The ceremony took place at a nearby church, where Nellie had already finalized the arrangements for a simple wedding that previous evening, catching both Juve and his friends unawares, and leaving Wendy at a loss for words with the joy of being wedded to the one only true love of her life.

For the newly weds, being united together in matrimony, however simple the ceremony had been, constituted the happiest of moments in their lives. And when the priest finally declared them man and wife there was no hiding the joy.

And finally when the festivities disintegrated into physical oneness behind closed doors, they made passionate love and talked late into the night and early into the morning, each telling a tale of 12 years of loneliness, successes and failures and hopes and expectations. Both had to agree on one fact - the night and the day they had just been through was the single happiest of days of their lives. Pledges and vows of remaining united through thick and thin were exchanged amorously though they both realized that was an understatement. Their special relationship was largely ineffable, unselfish and befitting. It was one that they both realized they would cherish for a lifetime.

Late the next morning when the lovebirds finally came out for breakfast, Nellie told Wendy about her one hundred and fifty thousand pound inheritance, of her mother's secret account, and an expense of thirty thousand pounds over the years as she went about looking for and after Wendy and helping her out when she got stuck.

Nellie refused the gratitude of half the inheritance offered by Wendy, insisting that she had already taken a loan to start a hotel in England.

"I got a confession to make Wendy," she said abruptly. Wendy was just about to ask about her father.

"I...I killed him, I'm sorry Wendy. I didn't...it happened so fast," Nellie explained how it happened.

Her face dropped and she took a long moment before whispering back "don't be, Nellie, you have been there for me for so long. I could not ask you to kill yourself for me."

"I heard the story," Juve regretted.

"Nellie, I'll always be in debt to you. We will always be in debt to you," Wendy added.

"I'll leave you two to your celebrations of love and devotion," she said mockingly, and walked out of the room, pulling the door shut quietly behind her.

And like two unlike poles of a magnet, the two could not resist the temptation.

THIRTEEN

It was only after three weeks that the newly weds managed to defy every rave of their nerves to stay away from the rest of the world and reluctantly flew to Liverpool City. Their two-week honeymoon had taken them through the Caribbean, the Americas, the coastal town of Mombasa, and the Maasai Mara.

The first thing that Wendy wanted to do was to rename the supermarket. The new name tag now read: *WENJUVE SHOPPING POINT,* derived from the names of Wendy and Juve.

It did not seem to bother the shopping populace. In fact, the African sounding name seemed to have pulled in a few extra shoppers as the accounts testified, and that gave Juve an idea.

"Did you notice that the African sounding name pulled a pound or two here and there?" Juve commented one afternoon as they were having a terrace lunch at the famous Liverpool Grand Eaters restaurant.

"Yes, I did notice something of that sort. I only don't know what it means," Wendy answered, looking puzzled.

"I think I know the significance. Ask yourself, why explorers visited Africa in their large numbers."

"I'm all ears."

"They wanted to see what they hadn't seen, a new culture, new traditions, new scenarios, new resources and all that which was different."

"Are you saying they responded to the Africanization?" Wendy was beginning to understand.

"I'm saying, how about giving the supermarket a totally different design from the ordinary. Make everything African, and if possible, sell some African wares. I'm sure Liverpool and England will love it."

Despite its new name and increased appeal to the populace, the Wenjuve Shopping Point was still rated as one of the most unfrequented supermarkets in Liverpool. In fact, the picture was clearer on the balance sheet, where the shopping point was yet to start counting profits and breaking even.

The *Supermarkets Independent*, an authoritative periodical that looked into the statistics and performance of supermarkets, had described Wenjuve as a fast dwindling supermarket. The periodical in its just released ratings put Wenjuve at grade E and depicted it as 'standing on quick sand.' "You know something, Juve, you are the most brilliant man I have ever met." Wendy beamed gleefully, enthusiastic at the prospects of the undertaking her husband had suggested. "First things first, we are going to close down and open anew after repairs and necessary adjustments to complete an all round African look. Imagine the person who would love very much to visit Kenya or Africa and can't afford to travel. They can do it right here in England, every time they go shopping," she said, raring to go.

They placed the official announcement in the media.

The following morning the *Supermarkets Independent* reported the Wenjuve shopping point close down must be more out of necessity, than 'to carry out pressing repairs and to do some upgrading' as had been claimed by the management. The report went on to say that Wendy and her husband Juve were cash strapped after their globe trotting honeymoon. The *Supermarkets Independent* wondered if there ever was going to be a Wenjuve in Liverpool's list of supermarkets again. It continued to say that the minimal populace that was dependent on the Wenjuve Shopping point would easily find replacements in other supermarkets for their shopping needs. It even criticized the move to close as it would be hard for the Wenjuve shopping point to win back its minimal command of the market when it re-opened, if that would ever happen.

But Wendy and Juve were not cowed by the report. A week later the supermarket was closed down. Wendy paid a six months full advanced salary to the fifteen staff members and asked them to report to work in exactly five months so that one month will be for preparation.

Not much of Liverpool activity was affected by the closedown, just as the *Supermarkets Independent* had predicted. The minimal populace that did depend on the supermarket easily found new places to go and shop from. The plot that the supermarket stood on was fenced off as construction work went underway.

Six months later, as the supermarket prepared to reopen its doors to the public, the list of invited guests and those who confirmed attendance was a study of imbalance. Very few invited guests actually declared their intention of being at the ceremony.

There were a handful of supermarket owners, under half a dozen journalists, and a few concerned professionals who appeared for the ceremony.

The small group was ferried to the site in two vans. The building was covered under a huge, dark cloth, attached to a small hot air balloon that was anchored by a long tough silk chord, carefully fastened to a crossbar lock that was only short of turning. The crossbar lock was to prevent the balloon from ascending away and dragging with it into the skies, and onto a football field nearby, the dark-cloth, thereby revealing the secrets behind the curtain before hand, the new Wenjuve Supermarket.

In the absence of most of the distinguished guests and honourables who had snubbed the occasion as inauspicious, the *Supermarkets Independent* 2nd vice-editor, Mr. Chris Wande, in attendance on behalf of the editor-in-chief, Challie Perry, was given the honours of twisting the bar in order to release the balloon into flight.

Once all the formalities had been performed, the

'revelation' ceremony as it came to be referred to, went underway. The third-in-command of editors of the *Supermarkets Independent,* Chris Wande, twisted the bar and released the balloon, which smoothly lifted off, carrying with it the huge dark cloth that had kept the building hidden.

Sporting the sculptural African façade, the new look Wenjuve Shopping Point that was dreamily uncovered as the cloth rose with the airborne balloon was in every sense a magnificent masterpiece.

Instead of the common-place British architecture they all expected to see, there stood a majestically appealing, peculiar, alluring and mesmerizing piece of architecture that seemed pleasantly out of place with its environs, in a regal aura of uniqueness.

Faces that were seemingly sleepy and lost in thoughts elsewhere suddenly brightened as the new wonder of Liverpool was revealed. The cameramen who had earlier looked full of regret for their abject decision to be there were suddenly gripped with a new burst of energy as the cameras went on a wild flash and flick spree. Suddenly, everybody wanted to grab a greedy look at the latest wonder of the city of Liverpool. Juve and Wendy leaned on each other, smiling satisfactorily.

The façade was composed of a brief door width veranda, which was about two metres in length of the *terrazzo* floor, suitably designed, with the typical African zigzag patterns on it. On both sides of the veranda was a raised platform of jaggedly curved stone with a flat face facing away from the building itself. The writings on the platform announced: WENJUVE SHOPPING POINT. The ground around the jaggedly curved raised platform was a well-balanced bed of flowers and grass.

At the outer edges of the veranda stood perhaps the greatest lookers ever, a welcoming sight of a pair of giant innovative elephant tusks, curved to perfection and rooted on either sides of the veranda on a thatched concrete square block platform, before coming to a tiny crossover at their semi-tips, then letting to a brief overlap at the top.

On the opposite end of the veranda stood thick heavy wood two-way sliding doors. The veranda roofing was bamboo ceiling on the inside and roof tiles on the outside hidden under the grass-thatched roof, shaped according to the giant tusks. The cash register point was designed from thick dark-coloured, receipting tables with custom made covers for the cash register machines.

On one end, inside the supermarket, stood a tinted glass partitioned cube that served as the manager's office. The rows of shelves were characterized by sculptures of faces of famous legendary African warriors, and consisted of metal fixtures that were concealed in bamboo grass.

A thick well-decorated table separated the luggage point from the rest of the areas. The luggage point was characterized by pot-like shelves from the table level, way up. From the pot shelves, hung leather and bead luggage tags that could easily be confused for earrings, except for the numbers innovatively printed on them, which had the same values as the numbers on the pot shelves. Below the tables were matching cubic cabinet, of different sizes.

The trolleys consisted of large rectangular baskets about a metre by half, made of strong bamboo fiber and mounted on well matched metal frames that also consisted of four small adjusting wheels, and a push handle. The trolleys were designed using the swallow and crumble technique, to ensure space utility. There were hand held baskets made of similar bamboo fiber of various sizes, ideal for small and medium sized shopping.

The lights, hanging under the wooden, well-patterned ceilings, were projected from multi-arm, metal chandeliers, wrapped all round in bamboo grass.

The concrete plastered walls were concealed behind well-decorated matching paper and ceramic tiles to complete the all-round African outlook.

African artifacts hung from well selected points all over the walls and ceiling. The outer roofing was composed of tiles that were hidden under roofing grass, giving the building its overall look of alluring quaintness in a line of routine architecture.

The new-look Wenjuve Shopping Point was an instant hit, and the *Supermarkets Independent* periodical had to swallow its previous words.

'If I were to grade the grade 'A' five star supermarkets, I would give this particular establishment an A1 grade. This is an entity of its own class, far ahead in innovation than any others.' Those were the exact words Charlie Perry, the tough, frugal-worded editor-in-chief of the *Supermarkets Independent,* had to settle for at the end of his editorial column.

The supermarket quickly established itself as the most frequented supermarket in Liverpool. Its image quickly gripped England and Europe. The supermarket was suddenly continental as tourists and wealthy personalities visited the landmark of Liverpool, as it came to be referred to. The management had to resort to the membership card procedure for admission of the shopping populace in order to control the numbers.

Riding high, Wendy and Juve had to agree on one thing - there were far too many people who wanted to shop in this kind of supermarket. They decided to invest in the idea, and it culminated in the opening of similar Wenjuve franchises in London and Nairobi within the year. All branches reported high profits in the next year.

The couple established Nairobi as their business headquarters and soon plans were laid to put up more branches worldwide. Wenjuve Shopping Point now became Wenjuve Group of Supermarkets.

In the next 3 years, branches sprung up in every corner of the world. Customer membership was filled to capacity.

The group quickly attained VIP status and was now visited by presidents, ministers, kings, celebrities and some of the most wealthy and powerful personalities all over the world. The two lovers had in a period of just a few years worked their way up the ladders of wealth. A report in the authoritative edition of the *'Achievers'* estimated them as being worth 50 million dollars. Most analysts dismissed this report as being too conservative. Tour agents saw the opportunity and rushed to book the few business cubicles at the Wenjuve Shopping Point. Many Safari deals were struck from there, creating a mad rush and helping to place Kenya high among the club of the most preferred holiday destinations.

FOURTEEN

One morning Juve woke up to a pleasant shock from his wife. She had moved a chair next to the bed and was just waiting for him to wake up. She watched as he rolled from side to side, then she smiled when he stretched out his hand to stroke her gently as he always did every morning. On missing his target, he opened his eyes lazily, and the angelic sight of his wife was looking down at him.

She was in white, tied her hair in a pony tail with a white ribbon, and wore ivory earrings. The outfit was completed with white high-heeled stylish shoes and matching neck chain.

"What's the occasion?" Juve asked inquisitively on seeing that she was dressed just the same she was on the day they met – the day of the kidnapping.

"I'd ruin the surprise if I told you. Now get up and get dressed, prince."

When he was about to dress in one of his ordinary favourite outfits, she stopped him and pointed to a stool on one side of the room. He was amazed at her spark of taste.

On the stool was a V-shaped T-shirt made of unique African material and glowing with tiny particles of gold and diamond stones on the central chest area just below the neck line, as well as a leather coat that overlapped all the way to the knees, leaving the glittering chest area for admiring eyes. The leather coat was fastened at the hip by a leather belt dotted in gold and diamond across the strip.

Once dressed, she led him outside. Parked in the driveway, was a grey Mercedes, exactly the same model as the one the judge owned.

"What is all this. Are we commemorating something?"

"Quiet, you'll make me ruin the surprise. Now get in the car, prince. I'm driving." She stressed the word prince and the driving.

"Just like you were on the day I kidnapped you, eh."

"No. On the day you came to my rescue."

She engaged the gears and released the pedals. The car rolled to a smooth start. Soon, they were on their way to the city centre, before branching off to Ngong road.

At exactly the same spot they had changed cars on that day was a similar red Ford Cortina. Juve almost thought time had moved backwards. They changed cars and were back on the Thika road, before making the same turns just the way they had done on that day. Soon they were parked outside the battered cottage.

"When I passed here about a year ago, I found this place had been ravaged by a mysterious fire," he said, wondering how far she had gone.

"I had it reconstructed."

"Do you realize its over 18 years since that day, six of which we have spent married? I'm wondering why you chose now this moment to remember." he said hoping she would tell him the motive behind her move.

"Don't try being too clever sweetheart. You will find out soon enough, but don't hope to con me into telling you yet." She smiled sweetly.

Juve smiled at being so well analyzed. "You win, angel," he had to admit.

They walked hand in hand into the cottage. She had prepared the most enormous and elegant breakfast he could remember. Through the gigantic meal, they talked and revived memories of good times together.

And once through the meal, she took from under one of the trays a paper and handed it to him. As he unfolded it to read, she grabbed it from him before he had a chance to read a word.

"Three guesses please."

"You don't intend to make this easy for me, eh?"

"You'll only add to the maze if you grouse."

"A reservation to some...great place."

"Miss one."

"A title deed to some wonderland."

"Miss two."

"A second honeymoon trip," Juve answered confidently. This time he must have got it. The suspense was killing him.

"Wow, I'd love that. Won't you?"

"Did I just guess right?" he asked excitedly.

"Miss three."

"Okay, I give up. Give me the paper, darling I am dying of curiosity."

"Want try again? I got the feeling this is going hit you like a bomb."

"Don't do this, gosh I am curious," he said, getting up and trying to grab the paper from Wendy, but missing.

"You know something, prince, you just dug your own grave. Now you have to wrestle it from me." She pushed the paper deep inside her bra, as she ducked a Juve grab. She managed to survive several other grabs, before falling for a cheap trick when he deliberately kicked the leg of the bed, then tossed himself on it pretending to be in great pain. At first, she hesitated, but when he continued to writhe about on the bed, she quickly ran over to offer help.

"Got you." He beamed satisfactorily when she had moved close enough. She tried to struggle free, but he gently turned her over and pinned her to the bed.

"Pinning me down does not mean you got it yet." She smiled glowingly.

"Want a bet?" he challenged.

He slowly lowered his face to meet hers. She raised hers to meet his. His lips found hers, and hers found his. His tongue probed and she probed back, finding each other's. At that moment, time stopped as they ascended into their own private world. And while he worked his way down the bridal white dress, she worked up his T-shirt. Their eyes met and locked in a passionate embrace. When she moved downwards for the garment underneath his trousers, he undid her bra, then down to her briefs. The paper went down lazily and nobody seemed to notice.

And when the two bodies were completely rid of all the earthly imposed coverings, they submitted to the golden rule of sensuality. The bonds of tenderness, affection, desire, and love were consummated in ardor.

And when finally and reluctantly they returned from their world, Juve picked the paper everybody had forgotten about. He found just three words:

Daddy! Daddy! Daddy!

He looked at her blankly. She looked back at him, smiled sweetly, before looking at her tummy. Then he understood.

"I...I missed my periods," she told him anyway, the last part of the sentence ascending to jubilation.

His joy bolted skywards. It was the best news anybody had ever told him. And the couple went into a moment of uncontrollable insanity of happiness and jubilation. They were going to be parents, finally. It was the beginning of great things to follow.

"Come on, get dressed, daddy prince. I want you to see something."

"Isn't being told you are going to be a daddy enough for a day?" he complained sweetly.

"Maybe, but you need to see this."

She talked him into getting in the car and after driving for some minutes, she stopped the car at the outskirts of the city on a seemingly endless land of grass and fencing.

"What is this place Wendy? It looks lonely to me."

"What can you see on this land?"

"Grass, shrubs, a few trees, a barbed wire fence and more grass." This time round he was careful not to miss the right answer.

"What do you think that signboard reads?" She was referring to a signboard facing opposite them which was still not legible from the distance they were.

"At this rate, I won't be surprised if it says, 'we are going to have a baby'."

"Wow, you almost got it right this time."

"You must be nuts darling, do you realize?"

"Probably because I happen to be the wife of a man I love so much," she said giving him a huge passionate hug. "Okay, here we are, prince." She ran the few steps to the signboard. He joined her shortly, running the last two steps due to curiosity.

The writings on the signboard read:

'The Proposed Site of the Wenjuve Hyper-plaza and Amusement Park'

"Imagine, these one hundred acres of land will be ready in the next eight months and will be opened on the day our baby will be born. Present for our baby, Juve."

Words could not express his gratitude to her for being in his life. And at that moment, words would not explain enough how he felt. He just took her into his arms and kissed her as if he had just learned that the world would soon be ending. She had managed to keep this away from him just to surprise him. He had not seen the picnic bag at the base of a huge tree nearby, or the portions of land where grass had been ploughed and flattened for their picnic.

She spread the picnic blanket and other necessary materials and they settled to a hearty picnic of burgers, sausages and fruit salad, and finally lovemaking in the open fields for dessert.

Wendy had just made him the happiest father-to-be with those wonderful surprises. He listened gaily as she told him about how hard it was to keep it away from him.

A multi-storied shopping paradise, complete with everything from safety pins to automobiles all under one roof was the idea. A five star hotel, some low cost lodgings somewhere in there, and the rest of the land covered with an amusement park. A casino, a studio, a theatre, an aquatic park, a circus arena, roller coaster drops, swings, a horse racing track, an indoor stadium, a car race track and all that could be described as amusement, would all be a feature of the park.

And that would mark a new chapter of growth for the couple and their investment. Diversity was what Wendy preferred to call it.

A new lifestyle was established from the old one. A new set of rules replaced the old ones. The mother of the prince to come, as Juve would put it, and princess to come according to Wendy, had to eat well, keep off heavy work, do only the lightest of jobs, exercise, and cut back on working hours.

But as it turned out, Wendy would not be banished from the new project, as work on the hyper-plaza and the amusement park went underway. Juve and Mark on the other hand, had to run around to ensure that every single piece of tool and implement required by the contractors was always available. Every morning she would proudly show off her bulging tummy and he would kiss her passionately and make a promise of his intention to be the best daddy in the whole world, and she would say the same about her motherhood to come.

They had made a deal that she would be the one to choose the name of the baby if it turned out to be a girl and he would do the honours if it turned out to be a boy. It was the reward for the bet they had made about the gender of the baby. She had chosen Catherine, after

Juve's mother, who she wished she had met had fate been different. He had settled for Stephen, after the grandfather of Wendy, who she loved very much and could not stop talking highly about. The couple would have easily won the nomination for the 'most-happy parents to be.'

Everything was going well and the doctors were predicting an easy birth, to a bouncing baby. The financiers of the 100 million dollar project deposited the lump sum amount with the contractors. Juve and Mark had finally secured the word of the American chief project supervisor that the project would be ready for opening on that material day, as it would be completed weeks before. The second phase of the project would take off soon after the official opening, and would take some two years to complete. Juve himself would perform the unofficial opening at the birth of the baby, before the inauguration and official opening two weeks later, with mother and child present.

That was on the sixth month of the pregnancy. On the seventh, just some two months to the D-day, everything came crushing down.

FIFTEEN

Two men walked into the hospital ward in deep thought and sorrow. For a week now, they wore the same expression on their faces.

They took the same corners they had taken through the hospital for the last week, and came to the door marked, 'Out Of Bounds for Non-Staff'. They were not part of the hospital staff, but theirs was a special case. All the doctors and nurses knew that the 'out of bounds' limitation did not apply to them. They walked into the room and, as always, held their breath and said a little prayer, anticipating for the worst, yet hoping for the better and ultimately the best.

This room was characterized by heavy life supporting machines that allowed the doctor to know of any change in the patient's condition, for any such change for the worse, would mean disaster - death, precisely.

Lying lifelessly in one of the six beds in the room was Wendy Teluve, wife of the elder of these two men, Juve Teluve. She had become mother to Mark Lubevu, by virtue of her marriage to Juve, who considered Mark as his real son.

The solid friendship of Juve and Mark came into being when Juve decided to pursue the government colonial police, who had butchered his family and arrested a huge number of members of their ethnic community. Mark was one of the loyal followers during those trying periods.

As usual, they routinely left the ICU and went to the maternity section of the hospital. In the incubator was Juve's premature daughter, Catherine, which was quickly shortened to Kate.

They watched for a while, as they always did, silently praying that everything worked out as they wished. It was a trying time for them. Though the doctors had said Kate was in stable condition, they could not guarantee that the stable condition meant that she would graduate from the incubator into infancy.

****

Tom Mbuke had made it a habit. Every afternoon, he would come to their ranch residence, change into some suitable gear, take his bike and ride into the countryside.

It all started one afternoon when school ended unusually early and Tom went straight home. He knocked on the door for a while but nobody answered. So he decided to use the back door, surprised about where everyone had gone to.

The door was shut but unlocked, so he let himself in. His attention was attracted by murmurs and groans from Mr. Davidson Randall's room.

The thick door was ajar, letting him into the well-kept room. On the huge bed were two nude figures of a striking contrast in skin colours, entwined and moving rhythmically on the bed. He watched for a while, transfixed, as his mother and Mr. Randall went on with their lovemaking, each expressing pleasure at every thrust, unaware of the young boy watching them.

Unable to control his shock and disgust, he ran outside, grabbed the bicycle that his late father had given him for his seventh birthday, and rode off into the countryside, not knowing where he was headed. That was just two weeks after his tenth birthday. Since that incident, he just rode away every other afternoon, unable to deal with the betrayal.

Every time he rode on the bike, he remembered his father. How his father had made everyday a day in paradise by treating him just the way a son should be treated. The time he used to have for his son, the presents he used to bring to him and the compliments he used to shower on him.

Then one evening, the bullet from a drunken Mr.

Randall's barrel abruptly curtailed this blissful father-son relationship.

Mr. Randall returned unusually early from his afternoon hunting sessions and accidentally ran into two stark naked bodies curled together in the banana plantation, adhering to the sensual dictates of intercourse. There was no mistaking it. The white female figure belonged to his wife and the black male counterpart was that of his servant's - Dovan Mbuke, Tom Mbuke's father. The two did not even see him and the amorous liaison continued, as Randall made his way past them.

Mr. Randall, overwhelmed by the treacherous act by the two closest people to him, went berserk, cursing and furiously throwing unprintable words at anyone on sight, to his penultimate destination – a bar where he went on a drinking spree, before the fatal confrontation that followed.

One thing led to another. Soon he had the two unsuspecting lovers cornered, holding his hunting rifle on the offensive against them. It ended with two deaths, leaving Mr. Randall a widower and Mrs. Mbuke a widow.

The eight-year-old Tom Mbuke had no real experience of dealing with this tragic episode. His mother on the other hand accepted the situation as tragic but unavoidable and was thankful the two of them were still alive, even with the death of the head of the family. The two bodies were buried at one end of the ranch and their deaths reported as accidental to the local authorities, who asked very little, especially after some palm greasing.

****

One afternoon, Tom overstayed and sunset caught up with him. As he started back to the ranch, the light of day slowly and gradually disappeared into the horizon, and the big bright ball in the sky gave way to the thick blanket of darkness. Tom had no idea what time it was until it started getting dark. He lost track of time watching as water birds caught fish in a pond. It was when he realized that time had flown by that he started feeling hungry. He knew he would find food at the ranch but that would be after at least an hour of riding. He got to his bike and started back for the ranch.

After he had been riding for about half an hour he came to a blockage, the result of a serious accident on the main road involving a trailer and a bus. The road was completely sealed off and he had to take a detour through the farmlands nearby.

After he had done the detour for a while, his attention was drawn to a mango tree with ready ripe fruits a few feet away. He stopped his bike and jumped over the half height fence into the compound. No sooner had he climbed the tree (after failing to pick a single fruit using an iron bar he had found inside the compound), did a dog start barking. He realized he had stirred trouble. As the dog barked persistently, the security lights of the house went on. The dog was a huge overgrown Alsatian. He had to find a way to escape the dog's wrath before his chances expired. Climbing further up the tree was only the way to safety he was left with.

****

The hidden figure kept waiting. It had been waiting for several days now, just for the chance to press the button on the remote control infrared wave sender. The timing was crucial.

A bike had stopped near its targeted backyard. The kid jumped the half height fence and started trying to pick ripened fruits from the mango tree in the compound.

"Wow! This had to be it. The mother of all chances!" The figure took position and waited.

It did not take long before the watchdog went on the

alert. It had sensed where the disturbance came from and ran to the tree, barking wildly.

Tom was caught off guard. Thank God, he had the option to climb further up the tree. The overgrown Alsatian was threatening to pull him down. He moved further up. His chances had just expired. If he dared moving down, the dog would tear him up. Some one from the house had to come and tame it, first.

It took some time before the back door of the house opened. A white lady stepped outside. The dog was now barking wildly and viciously as if emboldened by its master's appearance.

The hidden figure watched as the security lights went on. The figure aimed the ray and pushed the button. The signal was sent.

Suddenly, three figures appeared as if from nowhere and jumped over the fence with the precise perfection of high jump athletes and went on to carry out the operation. Two of the three attacked Wendy. One was carrying a syringe and the other some textile of some sort. The third figure attacked the dog with a club without mercy. The huge dog collapsed to the ground, lifeless. A handkerchief was quickly shoved into Wendy's nose. Tom did not see the strange contents of the syringe being emptied into Wendy's left arm. She too collapsed, lifelessly. The whole operation took lest than three minutes and the figures jumped the fence and vanished just like they had appeared.

The figure in hiding smiled satisfactorily. It tossed the remote control infrared sender into the bush and walked away. Mission accomplished. The call was made to report.

Tom watched in shock as the attack unfolded. None of the attackers paid any attention to him. It was well a planned operation no doubt. Once they were out of the compound he climbed down the tree to see what he could do to help.

He had to put to practice the little first aid he knew and

some common sense. She came around in a few minutes though dazed. He could see she was nearing the final stages of pregnancy. And that complicated an already delicate situation a million times over. There was no telling how the pregnancy would react to such a violation.

He supported her into the house, as he tried to figure out what the next move had to be. He saw a set of keys on the table. They had to be car keys. There was no time to be wasted.

"Know any neighbours around who can help get you to the hospital?" he asked slowly and soothingly.

"We are a bit far apart," she answered laboriously, in between breaths.

"Okay, let's get you to the car." He decided he would drive her to the hospital. There was no time to think.

"Now, you are not so good, so we can't afford to waste any time. You are going to be my driving instructor and I'm the learner and we are headed for the hospital. Thank God I'm not completly driving illiterate." He used to drive the tractor his father used to work with when some rare opportunities came by, with the full support of his father of course.

She nodded sickly. It was the only way she could get to hospital as fast as was necessary.

And that was how Mrs. Teluve was driven to the hospital, by the ten year old Tom Mbuke.

Soon Wendy was in the able hands of doctors. He furnished the doctors with the necessary information, including about the handkerchief he had carried to the hospital for tests. Once he felt he had done his part he disappeared from the scene. He felt responsible for the lady's unimaginable suffering.

Juve was regretful for the boy's disappearance from the hospital, as he wanted to thank him personally for assisting his wife to the hospital and against the attack. He wished he had found the boy. He would have then made a feast in his honour.

"I'm Doctor Renna and I suppose you are the lady's husband."

"I'm Juve. I just got the news that my wife was attacked. How's she."

"Stable, but I don't want to assure you that she is out of danger, sir."

"What do you mean doc? I've got to know."

"I'm trying to say that such attacks are not often fatal but if a victim is a pregnant woman, well that's a situation that can get complicated and we won't rule out any possibilities."

"Are you telling me that she is in danger?"

"I'm not saying that to an extent and I'm saying so to an extent."

"You doctors sure know how to scare people to hell. Can I see my wife?"

"Give it time, sir. And something else, do we have your authority to perform surgery incase there are complications with the pregnancy?"

"Listen doctor. I want to go back home with both my son and my wife. So do all that you have to do to make sure my family stays intact."

It wasn't long before the doctors had to perform surgery to save the baby from dying in the mother's womb. This resulted from a sudden re-channeling of the nutrients to fight for the mother's life automatically being put in motion by the body's defence mechanisms. The doctors were now convinced that the condition that Wendy Teluve had slid into was one that they could refer to as 'two lives in one' as it could easily mean needless death of both the mother and the child in the womb.

Juve was thankful a million times to the young boy who had been there to save the situation. He regretted the boy's decision to keep offs. Probably, he blamed himself for provoking the situation. He was impressed by the boy's intelligence. A ten year old kid driving to the hospital and having his wife admitted! He wished he could find him and thank him personally. That boy was his hero, no matter what the outcome would be.

****

Tom Mbuke went to the hospital every single day, but could not trust showing his face to the family of the lady in admittance. He reasoned that had he not jumped over the fence stupidly just to get a Mango fruit, all would not have happened. He wanted to make up for the pain he had caused. He prayed hard for the lady and her premature baby to recover. He feared for the worst.

SIXTEEN

The longest two weeks of Juve's entire life had slowly dragged along. The doctors worked around the clock to ensure Wendy received the best medical attention.

The initial tests revealed that chloroform had been used in the handkerchief. The doctors realized they were faced with a potentially fatal situation when two days after admission, Wendy slid into a coma despite the doctors frantic efforts to keep her medical situation from further deterioration.

Three days after Wendy had gone into coma, the doctors suspected they had won the race to unravel the suspected poisoning. They quickly put her on treatment for arsenic poisoning. They hoped they would win but when the symptoms such as skin complications, heart disruption and brain damage continued to manifest themselves, the doctors realized they were fighting a losing battle.

Two weeks later, Wendy's condition deteriorated and as doctors tried to wrestle life back into her, she quietly slid into the big mysterious unknown, permanent sleep - death.

Juve sensed it the moment he had walked into the hospital. A certain seemingly dark feeling greeted him on entering the hospital, but it was nothing compared to the looks on the doctors' faces. Yet all that was just an iota compared to the verbal confirmation from the doctors, who seemed contrite at being responsible to break the news to Juve.

When the doctor started "We did all we could Mr. Juve..." he couldn't even wait to listen to the rest of the statement.

A dark cloud suddenly caught up with him. It was like a dark curtain had suddenly enveloped the whole world. For a moment he wanted to die and join her in the other world.

It was a familiar feeling he could only remember on the day the colonial police butchered his family. Suddenly, it was like a very heavy load that he could not support, had fallen upon him. His head started to spin, his legs went spongy, his eyes were blinded, his heart beat raced and his mind went insane, for the moment.

In Africa, it is customary for a man not to cry in front of people, especially women, even if the pain is unbearable. He could not contain himself. Not only did tears roll down his cheeks, he wailed at the pain of the loss. Nurses automatically looked elsewhere. He had to be assisted to find his way to the gents, locked himself up and let the tears roll down freely.

He had come this far. She had brought him this far. He could not understand why nature would mount a fatal blow on such a perfect relationship, as theirs was. He wished the ground would open up and swallow him away from here, or an angel would come and take him to her.

It was when they were together that they had come this far. And now she was gone. Gone never to be touched or spoken to again. Death was so final. A part of him now had been brutally cut off. A part he knew he could never replace.

There was a knock on the door. "Listen father, if something somewhere is telling you for even a moment that you are alone in this, then you are terribly wrong. She was "mummy" remember? Open up and let's travel through this together." It was Mark. Maybe that was what he needed at this moment of sorrow, somebody to help him through. He composed himself and unlocked the door. Tears were rolling down Mark's cheeks too.

"Let's put up a strong show for Kate. Remember she is there in the incubator and needs us to pull through. I'm sure Wendy would have wanted us to be strong. Not break down like this," Mark said.

And he knew Mark was right. They had to fight on.

That was what his wife would have told him had she been present and alive. Ironic, but that was it. Life had to go on.

****

Tom sneaked into the hospital unnoticed, as he had always done. He wished very much that things would work out, somehow for the better. He had had dreams about the day she would walk out of the hospital, a healthy recovered woman.

But he also had nightmares. They were nightmares about a bad day. A day he prayed with all his might and willed that it should never come to pass.

That evening he did his usual routine. But he felt uneasy and sweaty. He had an ominous gut feeling, but he could not place a finger on what it all meant.

When he peeked into the ward, she was being attended to by an unusually large number of doctors and nurses. The expressions in their faces wore the unmistaken attire of panic and confusion. These attires were reluctantly replaced by symbols of defeat and surrender and it was then that it hit him. It was over. The battle for survival by Wendy, helped closely by doctors, nurses, her family and friends, had been lost to the fateful mystery called death.

A small Mango fruit prank had developed into trespass, assault, serious injury and now death. He had now become a killer. He realized he wanted to get out of there fast. He laboriously struggled with his trance but managed to trudge his way out of the hospital buildings to his bike. He rode off not knowing where he was headed. Anywhere his legs and bike could take him.

He found himself at the detour he had made on that eventful night, and outside the fence he had jumped. It beats logic how death was so easy to come across.

Tom vowed to bring to book the people who had attacked Wendy and caused the death. It was the least he could do to make up for his wrong doing. The police had not succeeded in bringing anyone to book with the incident. He decided he would report to the police the following day so he can share all he knew.

He was brought back from his thoughts when he stepped on something hard under his foot. It was a wooden device, as large as four matchboxes. At one end, it had a small dark screen just in front of a tube globe circuited to the rest of the box. There was a button. The device looked home made, but out of curiosity he decided to take it with him, anyway.

He got to his bicycle and rode slowly to the ranch. He took one of his school lesson folders and removed the papers from it. He then took a horde of plain papers and began writing about the chronology of events from the day of the attack to the dark day that was the death-day of Wendy Teluve.

He recorded every single detail about the two weeks Wendy had been in hospital. He recorded doctors' statements, nurses' statements, the husband's statement, and friends' statements. He recorded all events including the picking up of the homemade device. Every single bit of information that he knew concerning the final days of Wendy Teluve appeared in his files. He then took a black marker pen and wrote on the folder in bold: **Wendy Teluve** - just as he had learned through reading the criminology book and records of Mr. Davidson Randall, all by himself.

The inquest into the death of Mrs. Wendy Teluve had just been opened. He was the detective to get to the bottom of the case. It did not matter how long it would take, he was eventually going to get to the bottom of the case.

****

Operations at the Wenjuve supermarkets worldwide nose-dived. The world had great respect for the Teluve couple and their businesses. Wendy was like the heart of the organization. Everybody who worked or shopped at the Wenjuves was affected.

The Wenjuve hyper-plaza and amusement park projects had slowed with the attack on Mrs. Teluve. And when she had lost the battle of survival after two weeks, everybody knew it was the end of an era at Wenjuve. The big question was: - could they pull through the loss of the queen of the organization, Wendy Teluve?

****

Diana, the nurse, placed the all-important baby girl in her special crib. Another nurse walked into the room.

"Where is the baby girl called Kate Teluve?. She is due for her medical check-up. I have been asked to take her to the examination room."

"You are new I presume, never seen you around." There was something out of place about this particular nurse. But Diana could not place a finger on it. She looked strange in her long, shinny, bushy hair, her medium coloured complexion, and her strange voice. She was tall and plump.

"Sorry for not introducing myself. I'm Lorna. I'm just joining the nursing profession and they want me to get a little training. So here I am, your student for the next few weeks. Months I suppose."

"I'm Diana, I've worked here for the last five years and I must say welcome. I'm surprised they didn't tell us we were getting some students."

"Maybe they did not remember to tell the nurses."

"That would be odd. They always said something. Anyway, who is the doctor you are representing?"

"Doctor Andrews."

"He must be planning to leave for someplace. It's a bit too early for the baby's turn."

"In deed he is. He has a meeting with the medical board."

"I thought that was going to be tomorrow's business."

"I don't know. Probably they decided to have a pre-med board meeting or something."

"Yes, they did that once, sometime last year. Anyway, there is the Wenjuve heiress. Handle her with care."

"Pleasure knowing you, teacher," Lorna said as she reached for the baby.

"Pleased knowing you, Lorna. And don't ever call me that again. It's one profession I can't stand."

"I'll try not to. By the way, can you make some space for tea at ten, my treat?"

"Okay. I will make some space. I think I'm going to enjoy this training," Diana predicted.

"See you then," Lorna said as she held the baby carefully and walked out of the room.

"See you then, Lorna."

Diana wanted to make sure everything was all right as soon as she had the chance. It was only after some twenty minutes that she got some time.

Lorna, the student nurse, and Kate, Juve's daughter, were no where to be seen. She checked all the other places she thought Lorna could have taken the Wenjuve heiress, but there was no trace of either the nurse or baby Kate.

She ran into doctor Andrews in the corridors. She asked about the examination he was supposed to be performing on the baby. The doctor insisted he did not have any knowledge about an early examination that he was supposed to be undertaking on the baby. He did not know of any Lorna. And neither was the description familiar.

The hospital staff went panicky. They called in the police, who responded promptly and launched investigations immediately.

The *nurse* had been seen in a blue Datsun with a baby and a male driver.

The blue Datsun was later found abandoned a few kilometres away from the hospital. The Wenjuve heiress had been kidnapped.

****

On her kidnap, Kate was just one week old from her development into an infant in the incubator.

It had been a long two months of waiting for Juve, Mark, and the hospital staff. With every passing day, the baby improved and finally came out of the incubator.

Doctors had insisted she had to stay in the hospital for sometime in order for them to perform some examinations on her to ensure nothing was wrong with her and to determine if there was anything that could indicate some complications in the future.

Kate had shown normalcy in development and growth and the doctor's examinations were full of positive indicators.

One week after the incubator birth, Kate was almost being ruled out of danger. Juve and Mark were already preparing to welcome home the newborn when Lorna the nurse struck.

****

Tom took yet another of his school files and marked it **Catherine-Kate Teluve.** It was yet another case he could not overlook. Something weird was going on with the Teluves. He had to know what it was, even if it would take his lifetime. He owed it to the dead lady to know what was going on.

SEVENTEEN

The demise of Wendy Teluve was too much a bitter pill to swallow. But Juve knew he had to face reality. And that meant life had to go on. When he looked at a picture of Wendy, her lips seemed to move and they seemed to be telling him to move on with life as they had planned together.

If everything had been smooth, the hyper-plaza would have been opened with Kate's arrival to symbolize the end of phase one of the project, with the second phase taking off immediately. They had promised each other to move ahead, no matter what stood in their way.

Juve looked back at how vividly happy she was when they raised their glasses and toasted to their new found motivation. He realized that not working towards that goal would be betraying their commitment. He just had to fight on, alone. Mark would help him. Kate would one day rise and take over. He had to prepare the way for her.

When he told Mark about those moments, Mark supported him in the need to keep the commitment alive. That was the destination. For it was what Wendy would have wanted.

They called a press conference and announced their intentions to continue with the project they had begun, the Wenjuve hyper-plaza and Amusement Park, and in-fact add on to it. They were planning another five star hotel and a burial ground for Wendy Teluve. They had already acquired a few acres of land from the neighbouring landowners for this purpose.

For the new additions, the mausoleum that was to be a burial ground and a five star commemorative hotel, the group was inviting all interested contractors to attend a bidding conference in the next three days or hand in their proposals.

The meeting, three days later, was a success and over three thousand contractors were represented from all over the world. It marked the beginning of the bid acceptance period that was to lapse in three weeks.

Once the period lapsed, Juve and Mark engaged a contract award independent committee to look into the bids on their behalf since they were more conversant with the contractors. Out of the fifteen thousand worldwide applications, the contract award independent committee narrowed them to just three thousand.

The three thousand were asked to submit a detailed plan for the mausoleum.

An Italian firm, Lucianado Constructions, won the bid. It was while Lucianado Constructions was winning this bid, that Lorna the *nurse* was kidnapping Kate, the heiress of the Wenjuve fortune and daughter of Juve Teluve. Rumour went around that it was the end of the road for the Wenjuve group. It was feared that their motivation was now spent.

They did not know how the group's top brass was going to deal with the new development, so close on the heels of the demise of the 'heart' of the group, Wendy Teluve.

The police investigations about the kidnapping case were hitting a brick wall. The wait for a call for ransom money was proving a futile exercise. Their trailing of the vehicle used by the kidnapper had hit a snag when a second car was found in a bush abandoned, with virtually no trace of the kidnappers. The police realized they were in a maze without any clues of how to get out.

Juve could not drink nor eat. He stayed three long days sitting beside the telephone awaiting the ransom call. He could not believe his bad fortunes. What was life going to be, first without his lovely wife, and now the only thing that linked them together, their daughter? He recruited a bodyguard to watch over Mark around the clock. He could not stand losing him too.

The police kept assuring them that maybe the kidnappers were those 'lets try something adventurous and gain some finances' types, but Juve knew better. Changing three vehicles, to shake off the police trail was the work of professionals. He was worried that if these guys struck again, the police may not manage to stop them. What was the essence of success if every criminal targets you? The kidnappers could not have chosen a worse time, while he was still mourning the loss of his wife.

Everyday, Mark sent in a maid with food and water but Juve rejected it. He could hardly eat while he didn't know what was happening to his daughter. On the third day Mark had to go in himself.

"You know something, father. I was at the police station this morning. We looked through this carefully and realized maybe the kidnappers may have had other motives."

"What are you saying, son?"

"Look at the timing, the cars, and the knowledge about the hospital. All this seem to point to one thing – a rich person with enough resources and information to do the kidnapping successfully."

"Having known that, how will it help to bring my daughter back?"

"We concluded that maybe the kidnappers are not here for monetary gain. This has to be something more complex. It may have been planned by a rival who has learned about our diversity program and is trying to throw us off the boat."

"How on earth could somebody hope that by kidnapping my Kate, they would succeed in stopping me from proceeding with business as before?"

"We looked back into some police files and came

across a case in South America where a rival group kidnapped the other group leader's son. Their plan was to keep the boy for as long as they could as a guarantee of their victim's poor performance in business issues. They managed to hold on to the boy for some two years. The victim's business faltered and the kidnappers were succeeding until a new board was put in place at the victim's company. The victim went back into business with zeal and reported instant success. The aggressors on seeing this realized the kid was not that important after all and released him. Maybe that is the situation we have got ourselves into. According to the inspector, these kinds of people don't like to end up as murderers."

"Are you implying we could be faced with a similar case?"

"I'm merely suggesting that if it's that, then what we are doing right now is letting the kidnappers win and thereby guaranteeing themselves that as long as they hold on to Kate, they can rule over our business capabilities."

"Are you people sure that can be it?"

"We can never be sure, father. God only knows how far the kidnapper's intentions could go. Nevertheless, there would be no harm done putting up a fight. Let's not make Kate the guarantee of our poor performance in business. We should however not rule out ransom. But you realize that everyday that passes by without the call, means there is more to it than just financial gain."

"If that's the case then they must have found a way to counter our intentions incase we decided to put up the fight. They must have obviously learned their lessons from the South American case, just like we are doing. And remember my daughter is just a week old. She can't just be let lose to bring herself back here. They would be running the risk of having to bring her back. If you asked me it looks off the mark to me."

"Yeah. We talked about that at length and we had

to conclude that going for it was more beneficial than harmful. Besides, they don't have to bring the baby back. They could easily place it somewhere and give us a call as to where the baby is."

Juve had to agree with Mark that there was not much to lose in trying to fight for Kate, just in case they were faced with such a situation. They could not just sit back and do nothing. They had to fight for Kate's safety, whichever way possible. Juve started the grand battle for the return of his daughter by putting some much-needed energy into his body by eating and drinking well.

And as the two men were just finishing their meal and were leaving the room, a call came through. The baby was fine and would continue to remain so, as long as the Wenjuve groups did not think of diversity, was the message relayed from the other end of the line. The caller hurriedly hung up. When Mark called the police to see if there could be a trace on the call, the answer was negative. Kate was indeed being held hostage as the guarantee to the derailment of that diversity program the Wenjuve groups had been planning to undertake. The police and Mark were right.

Juve and Mark braced themselves for a battle of life and death. A truly grand battle it was going to be and they expected it to be long and grueling. At stake was Kate's life. They did not know if the kidnapper would resolve to kill Kate altogether. However, they realized they had to fight on. They would start by calling the Italian firm, Lucianado Constructions, and the American firm that was building the hyper-plaza and the amusement park to echo their intentions to proceed with both projects.

Juve was looking at the plan for the mausoleum, for the very first time. The plan was of a grave site complete with a pyramid-like structure about twenty-five metres high on all four sides supported by four pillars standing to the height of about three metres. The wall-like structures linking the four pyramid-like structures were to be made of marble, cement and irregular stones. An outer perimetre fence was designed of monoliths about one metre high and cylindrical stone made of concrete and patterned in irregular shaped fire-stone were to link the monoliths to form a circular fence around the site. The floor was to be of blocks of concrete and irregular firestone.

The twelve-storey majestic five star hotel was to be of marble, firestone, and bleached concrete.

Juve had to agree. Lucianado Constructions had submitted a great plan.

Even as the high-keyed funeral, graced by all kinds of dignitaries and ordinary folks alike took place, Juve could not restrain his tears. She had been his livelihood. And now he had to proceed without her. It really was ironic, but that was how things had turned out.

The funeral took place some three months after the kidnaper's call. Kate was still being held captive. Mark had to support Juve as they walked from the mausoleum to prepare for the grand opening of the hyper-plaza a few days later. Juve wanted to name the whole project after Kate. Mark advised him against such a move. They had to portray the image that they had gotten over Kate. The Wenjuve hyper-plaza was an instant hit, and nine months later when the twin hotel package opened to mark the end of stage two, the site was a beehive of activities, especially with tourists. The courtesy vehicles that provided transport to the site were always filled to capacity. Taxis were doing roaring business on the route, as families and groups arranged outings to the Wenjuve paradise, the reference that quickly came to denote to the place.

Exactly one year later, Juve flew to Europe and the Americas to assess new sites for the Wenjuve paradises on those continents. This led to the opening of the London and the New York Wenjuve paradises a few months later, an investment program which was described as an instant success by the media and the business fraternity alike.

Juve then flew to Paris and opened the Paris Wenjuve paradise, which threw France into a shopping frenzy as everybody tried to have a taste of the shopping in a paradise of a supermarket. Next, Juve was in Argentina's Buenos Aires to lay the foundation for the Wenjuve paradise there.

It was when Juve was about to fly into the Middle East to lay the first stone for the Wenjuve paradise there that, from the blue, a newspaper report uncovered a scandalous story about the millionaire.

This episode suddenly turned the life of the millionaire and his associates into a living hell. Each day brought with it new evidence and more sensational scandals than the previous one. Rumours in Nairobi were abuzz like a huge wind that could carry with it roofs for miles and had anyone blown something into this windstorm, it would be carried away for miles and miles. And once the newspapers had started on Juve's story, every mouth wanted to add something to it.

The opening of the Buenos Aires Wenjuve paradise and the laying of the foundation stone of the Riyadh Wenjuve paradise had to be cancelled indefinitely, though the exercises took place the following month.

The battle of words raged for several months and it was marked by attacks and counter attacks, accusations and counter accusations, with the Wenjuve group in vehement defence of their president Mr. Teluve and the newspapers and government officials asking the Wenjuve president to clear his name beyond any reasonable doubt and prove that he was not in-fact 'a wolf in a lamb's skin'.

Mark insisted that the accusers had no solid evidence and their outbursts were driven purely by selfish and egocentric engines. He accused those behind the allegations as people filled with bad blood and jealousy, who were only out to ruin the reputation of the Wenjuve Group. Once he referred to Juve as being among the

144,000 men described in Revelations in the Holy Bible, and that threw the clergy into the fray as they expressed their disgust at Mark's statements and warned him of dire consequences should he continue dragging the name of God into worldly issues.

Those allegations caught Juve flat-footed and he remained mum all through the period, though he occasionally came out to deny the charges leveled against him.

Events quickly overtook the line of defence forwarded by the Wenjuve group, as evidence emerged linking Juve to ownership of a brothel which also stored smuggled goods and acted as a headquarters for drugs trafficking in the city.

He denied this charge vehemently, but the police, armed with overwhelming evidence of ownership of the brothel, acted quickly. The company's top brass were arraigned in court to answer charges of drug trafficking and graft among others.

Two days before he was to appear in court to face the judge for hearing, Juve took his car, drove off and vanished into thin air. He did not tell anyone about his destination or when he would return.

The court found him guilty in absentia for contempt of court for not appearing before it as was expected, and he was to face three years imprisonment. A warrant was thus issued for his arrest.

Three days after his disappearance, the wreckage of his sedan was recovered, halfway burned beyond recognition.

The police only managed to identify the millionaire's vehicle because the registration numbers were confirmed to be his.

Some significant items had been recovered near the wreckage. When the investigators recovered the charred remains from the wreckage, they found a golden wedding ring that bore the initials JT on the site. They identified it as what should have been the victim's left hand. Mark identified it as Juve's wedding ring. Unofficially, it was confirmed. Juve had lost his life through a road accident, as his sedan descended three hundred feet into a deep valley.

Then the new angle started forming.

First, an officer recovered a loaded .38 millimetre caliber pistol which Mark and other friends and associates of Juve identified positively as Juve's. The pistol had been carefully placed under the driver's seat of the wreckage. Mark insisted he had personally unloaded the gun fifteen days earlier when they had been asked to surrender their guns to the police during their arrest. Juve must have reloaded the gun.

Then another officer found a brown envelope a few metres away from the wreckage. It contained twenty-four tablets of *Camoquine,* a medicine meant for fighting malaria.

The company's staff dispensaries worldwide stocked drugs in bulk, but their issuance to the staff was purely after a doctor's check-up. Juve could have easily taken the drugs unnoticed. Being the head of the organization, he was well above regulations. After an inspection of the *Camoquine drug* records, it was discovered that the stock did not balance. Twelve pairs of the drugs were unaccounted for. The company dispensary clerk had not issued the drug for the past one month. The company doctor had not authorized an issuing of that particular drug either. None of the organization members could confirm that Juve had ever complained of any form of failing health even one month to the incident.

Two days after the half-burned wreckage was recovered and taken to the police station for further investigation, a witness presented himself and swore to have seen Juve leaning on the rails of the bridge where the accident occurred, as if admiring the breathtaking scenery. The yellow sedan was harmlessly and sanely parked at the roadside. Asked how sure he was that he had seen the millionaire, his description fitted that of Juve.

Another person came up and supported the first witness's story. He said he had in fact found the millionaire reversing the yellow sedan.

Both of them had no prior knowledge of the millionaire's disappearance and had only learned of it from the press.

They both signed statements to the effect of their observation.

The Wenjuve Company hired two accident investigators from a U.K. firm, Accidentquire, to investigate the cause of the accident. Two weeks later, they submitted their report which passed a clean sheet on the sedan's mechanical condition, described as mint and new.

The police force adopted this report as the two accident investigators had more specialized knowledge on the subject in question and had advanced equipment to perform the task. With the vehicle having been certified as free of any mechanical problems that could lead to loss of control, the absence of brake tracks to symbolize the abrupt use of brakes and Mark's confirmation that the car had just returned from its monthly mechanical check-up were revealing.

Only one theory could adequately explain the strange chronology. The millionaire had simply left his residence knowing he was not going to return – alive. On his way towards Nakuru, he was only contemplating the best way to end his life. He had finally settled for the accident when he saw the valley, three hundred feet down, just a few minutes from Nakuru. He calmly chose the site, reversed, and drove through the rails to his death. The fire must have been caused by an electrical mishap during the plunge, as the Accidentquire report found.

The millionaire had committed suicide. He could not face the volumes of evidence against him.

Mark insisted that was not the Juve he knew, especially not when fake charges were being leveled against him.

But everybody knew Mark was alone in believing that. There was no changing the reality. The man who had been a hero to many due to his clean ways was in fact a pretender and a coward who could not face and admit guilt and preferred to take his life instead. His action had shown that he was guilty of all the crimes leveled against him. The media had it all in black and white. The story was guaranteed headline material for several days to come. The world could not wait to rid itself of such imps.

Juve was laid to rest next to his late wife, Wendy. The funeral turned out to be as dull as the man's life had turned out to be.

The politicians who had been accusing each other of having something to do with the disappearance of the man were merely out to gain political advantage over their opponents. Nobody was going to gain such kind of political mileage as it turned out to be. The man had killed himself.

It was the end of an era and the beginning of another at the Wenjuve Group of Companies. They hoped the new president of the Wenjuve Group of Companies, a company that touched on millions of lives worldwide, was going to be genuinely clean as opposed to his predecessor.

****

Doctor Fexwell Makaza had ended up in a native village after admiring the simplicity of life there. A trained and renowned chemical physician holding several international awards, the doctor fell in love with the vast untapped vegetation and questioned the civilized world's overlooking of botanical input of such untapped vegetation and technical knowledge of the local herbalists in medicine. He decided he would shut himself out of the world and proceed to turn the vegetation into medicine. And so began his self imposed exile from the 'modern' world

Guided by a local renowned medicine man, in whose beautiful daughter Doctor Makaza had found a soulmate and an interesting companion for a wife, through the thick forests, the doctor was enjoying his trade of discovering new and more effective medical formulae with these untapped local inputs.

To the local community, he was a magician whose concoctions had saved many lives that according to them had already been lost. The doctor's discoveries proved very effective against some persistent diseases that had waged decades of war against medical science and technology.

It was no wonder when the villagers brought to him a half-dead victim, probably from a road accident, on returning from a hunting expedition.

He asked them to keep mum about it. His new patient was somewhere around his fifties and terribly in a bad shape. Once the doctor was done with the necessary crucial steps, he realized this was not going to be an easy task. He put his new patient on the life support machines.

Finally, he was left with just waiting helplessly for the best or worst to happen. The good side would be if the patient came out of the coma. The bad side would be if the patient never came back and slipped into death.

He realized he was faced with another problem, the patient's identity. That would have to wait until the patient came out of the coma. He understood the need to keep this person away from ever being found until he had fully recovered and was healthy enough to face whatever it was he had left behind. He knew the exact spot where they had found him from the interrogation he had held with the villagers, and when he went there and found the wreckage, he figured out just how he would go about concealing the patient's whereabouts. He wanted to prevent any one from finding a clue that would lead them to his hospital.

The doctor then started the long uncertain wait.

BOOK TWO-THE PROGENY

EIGHTEEN

Tom Mbuke roamed around his low budget semi-executive office. He listened as the main door of the office letting into an inadequately furnished reception and office of his secretary slid to a close.

He knew the next sequence in the chain of events. She walked into his office, slowly closing the door behind her, before walking over to him in a sensual manner as she usually did.

"You seem preoccupied," she commented as she unbuttoned his shirt slowly.

"Indeed I am. I don't seem to be getting anywhere on those cases."

"Believe me, things will work themselves out. Right now let me rock your world."

"Who am I to say no?"

The couple hit the couch as they had been doing for some three weeks now.

It was when he was just ten years of age and in his third class that he came across the Wenjuves. He had cleared his primary education in class seven, and was one of the few lucky pupils to be declared eligible for admission to prestigious Alliance Boy's high school. But that was not without a set back, as Davidson Randall refused to honour his pledge of paying for his fees. What Randall did not say, which was an open secret, was that he believed a black boy's education was limited to the lower classes. A church organization had come to the rescue on seeing the superb grades Tom had achieved. All that time, his mother had been trying to talk some sense into her lover's head, but his decision was as rigid as a rock. Not even his friends or his lover would make him change his mind.

And so, after the hitch, Tom finally took his place at the prestigious Alliance School where his grades effortlessly continued to give him an edge over the rest of the students.

He had to wait until after a year to again take his place at the highly regarded Makerere University in Uganda, where he went to study a three-year law degree course after completing six years of secondary education. The church organization had to step in again to see him through the university.

As soon as he had sailed through three strenuous years of study and had finally secured his aims, Tom participated in a competition in Nairobi and won a full scholarship to study at the university of his choice, in the United States.

But his plans to travel to the prestigious Harvard University for a criminology degree hit the snag when his mother developed a serious strain of malaria, which eventually claimed her life.

Once his mother had been laid to rest, Tom found himself in trouble. Mr. Randall had not minced his words.

"Well, bloody black stuff, your mama's gone now. I expect you to be all vanished by nightfall. And don't try my patience. I shoot at anything I don't like. I believe you know me well enough."

Not that Mr. Randall was that much of an actor to succeed in keeping his racial fanaticism and laboured tolerance of Tom's presence a secret during Tom's mother's lifetime, but to spill it word for word and at the very first opportunity available hit Tom completely unawares.

Tom had to spend two nights in the cold before he came across a former college mate who offered to take him in temporarily as he looked for an alternative set up of his own.

He visited the local office of the firm that had organized the scholarship competition in order to try and explain the predicament which made him not to report to Harvard on time, as had been earlier arranged. The officer in charge was not willing to listen, leaving a dejected Tom to walk himself out of the building, wondering what his next course of action would be.

A secretary at the firm, on seeing what happened, followed Tom outside and gave him a piece of paper on which the address of their overseas mother firm was printed. She advised Tom to write to them and asked him to forgive her boss, who was never blessed with the gifts of being logical and reasonable.

"What's your name, good Samaritan?" he asked once she had explained herself.

"My name is not important, do as I say and you might get yourself some golden chance."

"I am going through hell right now and I don't have an address. Can I get to use yours?"

"Okay I understand. Give me a minute," she said after thinking for a moment. She disappeared into the offices before reappearing. She handed him another small piece of paper. "That's my address. Just make sure you write your name above that and the initials 'care of' in front of my name."

"I'm Tom Mbuke. I hope you do not think it's some trick I used to get to know your name."

"Nice meeting you. I would have told you who I am anyway. Well I got to run before my boss starts missing me."

"Thanks for your concern and help. Believe me, you've just made an investment. Someday you will harvest the fruits."

"Welcome," she said as she hurried off.

It was at that time that he got the chance to look at her well. She was swarthy, of middle height, with almost every curve of her body well developed. He looked at the name - Sally Winde. Nice name for a nice person.

He visited the office once every week, soon after he had

posted the letter. It took six weeks before he got the reply.

His case had been ruled as exceptional and they wanted him to travel and take his place at Harvard, the university he had chosen as per the scholarship. All he had to do was to present himself at the US embassy and they would make travelling arrangements as instructed.

It took him just two days to sort himself out and bid bye to his temporary host and Sally, thanking them for the support they had given him when he needed it and promising to keep in touch, before presenting himself at the US embassy. Soon he was on his way to Harvard.

Four strenuous years later, he was through Harvard University and with the degree he so desired at hand. During his stay at Harvard, Tom went through any odd jobs that came his way. Today he was a truck driver, tomorrow a baby sitter, the next day a pizza-man, a deliveryman, a gardener, a florist. That had earned him the nickname 'Oddy.' He had the reputation of a miser and saved almost everything he earned from those jobs.

On several occasions, he was caught up in a dilemma when his work schedule overlapped with his studies. He had on many such occasions opted to earn some money, knowing very well he had studied well ahead in the topic involved. However he had always opted for class where the topic was giving him problems or where he was expecting a practical class.

Tom went through some three romantic escapades through his four years at Harvard. Those died out as naturally as they had appeared.

First there was a lecturer's daughter who he met at a campus party, Suzie Whitelake. He could swear she had the best tits he had ever seen. Suzie's father landed a new job in Mexico as an envoy and the family had to move with him. The lovers did not keep in touch.

Then there was the pretty sociology lecturer who had summoned Tom to a disciplinary session when Tom could not explain why he had not attended her lectures three times in a row. They ended up being amorously all over each other. These sessions lasted for another one and a half months before coming to an end when Tom felt the student-teacher relationship was too much for him to take.

There was Jennie, the dining hall waitress who somehow found her way into Tom's room and asked his roommate for some privacy with Tom. This continued every other night for three months before she got married to a rich insurance agent and went on to be a house wife.

With graduation drawing nearer, Tom approached his sponsors and explained to them that it would be to a great benefit if he could enroll for a year-long sandwich program with an actual police department and if he could obtain an international detective's license.

Their answer was affirmative and led to an extra year's attachment with the Los Angeles Police Department where the chance was secured. Here, Tom learned to deal with crime first hand. He quickly won the respect from his colleagues in the police department for some heroics that brought ends to some persistent criminals' domination in the streets.

When he was through with his one-year sandwich and was to leave for Kenya, his colleagues from the LAPD and Harvard organized one big farewell party for him and composed songs to try and talk him into staying a bit longer. They offered to bring together some of their savings to offset his travelling and resettlement expenses.

Tom eventually received his international license and was soon on a flight back to Kenya. He had gained more than enough education on how to fight crime. He had saved enough money and that together with the money he had received at the farewell party, made him believe that he was ready to open his own firm and settle. He was facing a new page of his life.

The bulk of his capital went into buying and furnishing a house in Nairobi's Kimathi estate. He rented and affordably furnished an office space and cleared the rent for the year.

He realized he could not work alone. He needed someone to mind the office, answer the telephone, collate the files, and fix appointments. He needed a secretary. He decided to take his time about it, since after all he did not have much to do in the office as yet.

One afternoon as he was taking a stroll through the city's streets, he ran into a seemingly disturbed beautiful Sally, who still managed to look somehow younger than her age. She was some three years older than him.

"Sally! What happened, why did you just stop writing?" She had stopped replying to his letters during his last quarter as a freshman. Juma, his temporary host when Mr. Randall had thrown him out of the ranch, never even replied to any of his letters.

Tom had walked the places he thought he would locate Juma and Sally upon his return, but had found that Juma had shifted and changed jobs before eventually flying to Scandinavia. He found that the organization that Sally worked for had closed down and he could not locate her current address. Five years down the line and things could really change.

"I lost my job," Sally started once they had received their orders, tea and scones, at a café across the street from where they met.

"As in - fired or resignation?" he inquired.

"As in – 'You are fired.'" The tears slowly filled her eyes.

"I thought you were very competent. What happened? Or was it too much competence?"

"No, that wasn't it."

"So what was it?"

"My boss used to tell me I was one of a kind in the field and I worked my level best. Then came lunch treats. At first I thought it was just a normal reaction of a boss to a staff member who works hard. When those persisted, I got suspicious. I thought I was imagining things. So I decided to ignore it all together."

"Then my salary started getting abnormal increments. Then he started, conveniently forgetting his files at his home. But I must have been too naïve that I didn't suspect his intentions, especially since his wife was always there. My guard must have dropped."

"But one afternoon I went and found the door locked. His car appeared and he stepped out and apologized for not remembering she was going to be away. He would have given me the keys if he had remembered. He invited me for a while, as we would go back to the office in his car. I saw no need to decline as it would look silly."

She stopped not sure whether to continue.

"Hey, you can trust me," Tom encouraged.

"He took a seat next to the one I was sitting on. I got nervous and found an excuse to move to another seat. He followed me there. He started telling me how beautiful I was and how we could use up the time we had real well. I reminded him he was married and I was sorry if I gave him that impression. I wasn't interested in sex or a relationship with him for that matter. I just wanted to do my job. He threatened that I would lose my job if I did not agree to his advances. He started being forceful. I kept my resistance. The telephone rang and in that moment of confusion I slipped from his grip and took off."

"But I knew I was a jobless case from that moment on. And sure enough when I got to the office, he had already made it there before me and personally handed me the hand written 'You are fired' letter. Since then, I have been in between jobs and I'm not making ends meet. Nobody seems to be keen on hiring me."

"Sorry." Tom could not find words enough to console her. "But cheer up, just your lucky day. I'm glad I have not hired some one else, yet. You got yourself a job."

And that marked the foundations of a flirtatious relationship between employer and employee. At first, everything dangled on a professional relationship basis, then suddenly, things moved quickly and the two found themselves in each others arms, both more than willing and both realizing that none had any intentions of commitment.

One afternoon while they were reclining on the couch, the phone rang beggingly as she struggled to fit into her tight skirt. She gave up due to the sense of urgency and fitted herself into Tom's trousers although they appeared clumsy on her.

Tom laughed his heart out through most of that before his wild imagination captured something interesting. He quickly got up and reached for the file of Kate Teluve's kidnapping. He scrutinized the drawings of the kidnapper nurse. He asked Sally to call the artist who had done those drawings.

"Can you produce similar drawings without the hair?" was the all itchy question.

Within days he had those drawings in his files and they went on to confirm his suspicions.

The nurse who kidnapped Kate Teluve could have been a man in disguise.

Sally was right. Things would work out somehow. Thanks to her and his trousers. It would be really hard to trace a person when you were led to believe they were of the opposite sex. The kidnappers had used that basic rule of survival to their advantage, and managed to hoodwink the law enforcement team. The police had all this time been on a wild goose chase. He was personally not giving up on the Wenjuve cases. That was a lifetime commitment.

****

Some fifteen years before that, in a primitive private hospital, Doctor Fexwell Makaza took a long relieving breath. It was after three long months that his patient had come out of his coma. The doctor soon realized he had another battle to fight. His patient was suffering from total amnesia. He gave his patient a name - Mann.

The doctor realized he could place an advert in the media and that might solve the identity problem. But he knew that would be risking something. Who knows what such an action would result in? There was no telling. He would only release his patient when the patient himself was ready. That would have to be a carefully well-planned process. Or was the doctor just looking for a personal solace for what he was about to do? Maybe, but Doctor Makaza knew this was a chance in itself. A human guinea pig. No rules, no restrictions, no questions. He intended to emerge victorious with an effective drug formula to combat amnesia. It would be the greatest victory of his life's works. He went into his lab to begin the battle.

Fifteen long years of hard work and perseverance later, Doctor Fexwell finally stumbled upon a formula that started the new chapter of recovery for Mann.

After two doses of his wonder drug, Mann murmured something in his sleep. The doctor did not hear clearly, but concluded it was something like – Wen... When... A few days later after more doses that the words came out audibly - Wendy.

That was when Doctor Fexwell realized that Mann was in transition from total amnesia to partial and maybe full recovery. That had to be a memory. The doctor jumped into a relentless search for the connection between his patient and this Wendy.

It was eight years later that Doctor Fexwell came across

something interesting. Could it be? Was it possible? The resemblance, the Wendy name, the age... everything, but one thing - the alleged death. He had to find out.

Doctor Fexwell knew one thing that would work. He had to move into Nairobi with Mann for this purpose.

Soon Mann and his doctor became frequent visitors to all Kenyan dailies' libraries. Any item on the man whose looks and coincidences came close to Mann's was worth being looked at.

The exercise took off in a futile manner and Mann could not even relate to anything from the old newspaper clips. The doctor had almost given up when Mann suddenly started seeing familiar faces and scenes. The doctor was excited. He now realized who Mann was. It was going to be the biggest shock to ever hit the world recently. He had to be a hundred percent sure.

Doctor Fexwell took Mann in for a forensic check up. The prints, the DNA, the dental identification check, all matched perfectly. It was unbelievable. But there was the evidence.

He didn't have to wait before Mann confirmed it himself. It suddenly came to him bit by bit at first, then all of it. Everything he did everywhere he went. Everybody he knew. Everything came back to him, finally.

Time had come for Mann to prepare for his grand return. He was back in flesh and blood! Who would believe when he declares who he was? The world was full of surprises.

NINETEEN

Tom was beginning to get tired and worked up by visiting the police stations in Nairobi and not getting any tangible information he could use in tracking down the person in the drawing. Honestly, he was beginning to feel that his hunch that the kidnapper nurse was a man was just an illusion.

He realized what failing in the police stations in the city would mean. He would have to start walking the whole country. Then widen his manhunt to government registration offices, then churches, mosques, entertainment spots, bus stops, shops, any place somebody would have to pass through as they go about their daily routines.

He walked into the Jogoo Road Police Station on the sixth day of his search hoping for a miracle. He had made photocopies of the drawing and had them pinned on the notice boards of the police stations, hoping somebody would call him through the numbers he had given below the sketch. He had shifted from sleeping in his house and was now 'sleeping on the job' in the office using the couch as his bed, hoping somebody would call even during the night. What made his life a living hell was the fact that he had no names to go with the drawing, no places to associate with the face in the drawing. He had absolutely nothing to accompany the drawing.

Some officers suggested he put a public advertisement in the mass media, but he realized that would be absurd without a name. Also, a public announcement would blow open the silence he needed to catch the kidnapper off guard. He had to be discrete to avoid warning off the suspect.

"Who is he, some lover of your wife or something?" an officer asked when Tom caught his attention.

"No, no, I believe he could help me find the daughter of a client I'm working for who went missing a long time back.

"My, my, my, what have we here, some psycho who thinks he has more capability than the whole police force, or maybe the case wasn't reported to the police?"

"Indeed it was. I got a lead I want to follow up on. I'll probably give up sooner or later."

"Interesting, so have you got us some lubricant for that kind of information. You realize engines don't run without fuel."

Tom knew. He also knew that almost every policeman in the Kenya Police Force would not help someone without some form of handout, also referred to as *TKK (Toa kitu kidogo)*. He had been losing an average of three hundred shillings a day and getting nothing tangible in exchange. He passed a fifty-shilling note. The police force had surely become a rotten bunch.

Once lubricated, the officer disappeared into an inner door and came back accompanied with a uniformed officer.

"Do you know this man?" Tom handed him the drawing and the fifty. It was his first test for that particular officer, to see what kind of a person he was dealing with.

The officer took the drawing but declined the fifty.

"Who's asking?" he questioned after looking at the drawing for a while.

This man had unknowingly done well in the test, so he could gamble with telling him the whole truth. So far he had not been letting out the fact that the man he was looking for could in fact be the person who kidnapped Kate Teluve. He decided on the whole truth.

"I'm chasing a lead on the Wenjuve kidnap case," Tom started, showing the officer the identification that proved he was a private investigator.

"Impressive. You must have some real will to be chasing that case now. Well, I think I know of someone who fits this description. He was a neighbour briefly before shifting to some place I don't know."

"When was this and how long? Was it brief?"

"Back in seventy-nine. We were neighbours for just three weeks. His name was Johnny Mulano. People called him Johnny.

"Have I got a name for this portrait, finally?"

"I'm sorry that's all I can help you with. You must understand that I didn't get the time to get to know him well. I was still in high school, which took up most of my time. But I'll give you the house number he used to live in, maybe you could try other neighbours. Some one might have some vital information that you could use."

"Do you realize something? You are one in a million. If the police force had a million men like you, crime would cease to be." He was indeed glad to learn that there were some clean officers in the reputed rotten police force.

Inspector Steve Ponde and the private investigator Tom Mbuke wished each other good luck, shook hands and went their separate ways, promising to keep in touch.

Tom was soon visiting the houses neighbouring the number Inspector Ponde had given him. Nobody seemed to know about Johny's three weeks residence at the place. He sure was a discrete man.

"Maybe you should see the girl he used to spend some time with. They had some chemistry between them."

Tom was relieved to finally find someone who knew about John. "You mean his girlfriend?"

"She said so herself. They had met way back, before he took off to God only knows where. The lady used to live with her parents on that block. But they have since moved to Kaloleni Estates.

"Do you have any particulars on exactly where they shifted to?"

"She gave me the directions if I ever wanted to visit."

"You seem to have been good friends," Tom commented.

"You could say we were good neighbours. Her name is Judith Palo Angi."

"Did you ever visit?"

"We kind of drifted apart since then."

After thanking his informant for the crucial information and taking the directions keenly, he was on his way to Kaloleni, a rejuvenated, optimistic man. At last, now he was headed somewhere with the Johnny lead. He must have crossed paths with lady luck, somewhere along the line.

At Kaloleni, Judith's parents still lived there, but Judith was now married and lived with her husband and family in Buruburu phase four. He thanked the aging couple for the information they had reluctantly surrendered, only after he had exhaustively explained the circumstances surrounding a fictitious case and assured them that it meant no trouble for their daughter. He could not bring himself to ask them if Johnny was Judith's husband. Next stop – Buruburu Estate.

His trip to Buruburu was more prodigious than he even thought it would be. When a petite, short-haired lady opened the door, Tom could see that she was familiar, for he had seen her in a wall picture at Kaloleni, though she looked a bit older in person. He introduced himself and she invited him in.

"So, what is this all about?" she inquired curiously, once she had handed him some fruit juice.

Tom had gotten just enough time to look around the wall pictures and managed to get the answer that he needed before starting his interrogation. Her current husband may not be Johnny. There was not a picture of him among those hung on the wall. Neither was the man affectionately sharing most of the pictures with the petite short haired lady anywhere near the image of the face in his files.

"Nothing to worry about." Tom avoided going straight to the point. He wanted first to be sure bringing up the name Johnny would not get a hostile reception from her. Chances were that as long as she was never married to Johnny, then their relationship must have died a natural death. "You and your husband?" he asked referring to one of those wall pictures.

"Right."

"You make a nice couple."

"Thanks."

"Ever been married again?"

"No."

So he could go directly to the point. Chances were that she would not be hostile to the mention of Johnny's name.

She admitted to having been Johnny's girlfriend. Johnny died just months after he had moved to Pangani, when burglars broke into his home and hacked him to death, before taking off with everything of value.

"We met at a dance hall two and a half years prior to his death and became lovers within three weeks of our meeting. Then he used to live at Bahati Estates, paid for by his boss, whom he worked for as a driver."

"Did you know his boss's name or anything about Johnny's job?"

"No. I didn't make it my business. Anyway, after we had been going on for three months, he disappeared without telling me where he was going. He wrote and told me not to worry as he was doing well in Arusha, living with a friend. He claimed he had to leave in that manner because he was running an emergency errand for his boss and could not leave a forwarding address as the nature of the errand would risk being compromised. He promised to explain when he returned to Nairobi. He could not say for how long he was going to stay in Arusha or Tanzania for that matter."

"He came back to Nairobi after about two and a half years and rented a house in Jericho Estates, a few blocks away from my place. He wanted me to go and live with him. I was not ready to do that though he had always written regularly when he was in Arusha to tell me how much he loved me and missed me and wished to return and be with me. He kept reassuring me that he was doing that for us. I was not sure he was the same Johnny. I needed time to think about us."

"Did you get to know what he was doing in Arusha, Tanzania?"

"Never. I did not bother to find out. He gave up the Jericho house so suddenly and bought one in Pangani. He told me he had quit his job and was looking for another. He wanted me to elope with him and not to tell anyone about his new residence. I needed time to think about the eloping issue. Of course I could not betray him by telling anyone about his Pangani house."

"When I asked him why he thought we should elope, as it would make everybody angry, including my parents who were not against the relationship, he only gave me the address to the house and asked me to go and visit him whenever I felt like it. I loved him very much so I ended up going to his place. I decided I would remain with my parents but I would visit him every time I got a chance."

"His personality had changed and he seemed jumpy, vigilant and nervous, as if determined to keep away from someone. He had changed a lot. Even in between the sheets, so naturally I got suspicious. I asked him if he had someone else. He denied."

"I waited until he was away before I ransacked the place, hoping to find something that would clear those suspicions."

"I came across a photograph of him and some light-skinned bitch, fondling some bastard she was holding, with his other hand around her waist. You can imagine how that felt like."

"Yeah, I can imagine how it felt." Tom waited before asking the next question. "Do you still have the photograph?"

"I believe it was taken together with other valuables at the Pangani robbery."

"Would you describe the woman who was in the photograph if you were asked to?"

"I believe I could. I looked at her well."

"I'll need you to describe to an artist how the woman looked. Will you agree to that?"

"Gladly, when do you want me to do that?"

"I'll arrange the session. But, beware: I'll make it soonest possible."

"That's okay with me."

"So tell me, what did you do once you found out he had another family else-where?"

"I confronted him and he insisted the woman meant nothing to him. I asked him about the baby and he said it wasn't flesh and blood. It was only his daughter by adoption. I did not understand what he meant. I however did not intend to let him continue poisoning my mind with lies. I walked out on him, a confused, broken-hearted woman, once in love. Finally, I composed myself and was ready to face him. I walked to the house and found a vacuum and his lifeless body in one of the rooms, hacked to death."

"Sorry about that. I'm sorry to have taken you through that experience again," Tom said in a consolatory tone.

"It's a long time back. One more thing, I got her address from one of his private belongings. I wrote to her twice to inform her about his death and hoped she would contact me but she didn't. I noted the address down in one of my old diaries."

"Let me not take much of your time. The information you have given me is exactly what I needed for the big break in this case. I will always be in debt to you for that. Thank for accepting to talk to me."

"Let me know what you find in Arusha," she said once she had given Tom the addresses of the Tanzanian woman. "I guess I was too naïve to think straight. Had I notified the authorities about his change of behaviour, maybe he would be alive and well today. Every time I look back at the circumstances surrounding Johnny's last days, I believe more and more that that robbery was too convenient, especially judging from his nervous, vigilant behaviour prior to his death."

"We can only speculate as of now. But believe me, I won't rest until I get to the bottom of this."

She gave Tom her contacts and saw him off, but only after he had promised to notify her of the progress they were making on the case from time to time.

It had been two long eventful days since Tom walked into the Jogoo Road Police Station, and he was looking forward to a relaxing evening at his Kimathi home before taking on his next destination – Arusha.

Soon, Judith and Fred Mongo, the artist, were through with the artistic production, and a distinct eyed, angular faced lady with a slender figure was composed. The trio agreed that it was the closest to the replica of the person Judith had described from the photograph she had seen so many years back. Fred did minor alterations on the drawing to cover for aging, and Tom was to carry with him three copies of drawings of the stranger he expected to come across soon enough, if he was lucky.

He took a pen and scribbled the name Monica Wambi below the drawing. At least this time around he had a name to associate with the drawings.

Once every formality was in place, he was off to the unknown. He wished Sally would accompany him, but they both knew it was best if she stayed behind and manned the offices. He was going to go it alone towards these new horizons of the case.

****

Arusha was like a drop of water in the sea, compared to the size of the country, Tanzania. The businesses here were small and it appeared like a street in down town Nairobi. The buildings consisted of mostly single floored structures and a few multi-storied droplets here and there. The streets were small compared to the multi-lane motorways he had to cross in Nairobi. Arusha was yet to attain city status. Tom was glad he was looking for someone in this place. It would be a million times easier to locate someone here than locating someone in Nairobi or Dar-es- Salaam. Here, it was even possible to run into your subject, by coincidence.

He booked himself into the *Modern Hotel*, a middle class hotel that he came across on the outskirts of the town.

The next morning, after a rejuvenating night's sleep, he was back out there deep inside the town looking from building to building for the names of the premises indicated in the address. He had to seek help from two strangers who helped him locate the old rusty single storied building with a half faded signboard that read ...NKE PRES.... He believed he could fill in the missing letters. It would then read, AROKONKE PRESS, the firm indicated in Monica's address.

He took bold steps up the stairs, hoping his hunch was right. Five minutes later, he found he was right. But the employees could neither recognize the woman in the drawings, nor the name Monica Wambi.

It had been fifteen long years and none of the employees seemed to have been there for that long. But one of the employees, who claimed to be the longest serving employee in that branch, told him that the employers had moved their headquarters to Dar-es-Salaam, and that most of the employees who worked in Arusha had moved there. He could however not remember an employee known as Monica Wambi, though he admitted the name sounded familiar.

Tom had to make the unwanted trip to the country's capital, eventually. After getting himself a sketch map to guide him to the Dar-es-Salaam branch, he said his thanks and went back to his hotel room to make preparations.

The journey to Dar-es-Salaam proved to be a grueling eight-hour affair and by the time he was checking in at the *Beach Land Hotel*, he was a feeble man drowning in exhaustion. He got into his room, after cornering a waiter with a massive tip for someone else's room service regardless of what the order was, and immediately ran the shower. Once through the infringed supper, he hit the pillow like a baby.

He was disappointed that next morning to learn that Monica did not even move to Dar-es-Salaam but had opted out of employment and gone on to embark on self-employment in Arusha. Nobody could tell what exactly she had taken up. An elderly lady however provided consolatory information when she told him that the last time Monica was in Arusha she lived in the Diluti area and that in fact, her daughter was a pupil at the Diluti primary school.

That meant another ten hours of an arduous journey back to Arusha. Diluti was a small area in the outskirts of Arusha town where Tom hoped he was finally going to end his pursuit by catching up with Monica.

Once there, he was yet again to find out that he was trailing events. A former neighbour of Monica informed him she had moved to an unknown destination.

At the primary school he landed on thin luck when he found a former class teacher of Monica's daughter, Judy Wambi. Judy had been transferred to another school when she reached class five.

"Do you know where she moved to?"

"No, I didn't get to learn that."

"Do you know of anybody who could help me trail them, friends, cousins, anything?"

"Maria Luni. She was her best friend way back and maybe she learned something.

"Where can I find her?"

"That's the problem. She sailed through high school just last year and after that nobody knows what a person's next move can be."

"Do you know the high school she was in?"

"A school called Hope Mission High School, in Mwanza."

Hope Mission High School was in countryside Mwanza and Tom had no problem locating it. When he inquired about Maria, he learned that Maria was in fact married to a wealthy business man named Juma Tembo and lived in Dodoma with her husband.

In Dodoma, the urbanite sprawling set up was not to cause a problem as the renowned Juma Tembo's reputation helped him locate the residence.

Maria seemed surprised at her guest's inquiry about her best friend way back when she was still in classes three, four and five. It was quite a long time back and her memory about those days was greatly marred by time. But she could remember the earring she was given by Judy Wambi one afternoon after school and the words very well.

"I might be leaving you for good. Mum says we will move to Mombasa and I will be going to finish school there at the Aga Khan Primary School. Keep this half of my favourite earring and I'll keep the other half, so as to remember each other."

The pursuit of the elusive Monica Wambi had taken him from Nairobi, right across Tanzania, and back to Kenya through the coastal town of Mombasa. He needed some answers and he believed Monica could provide them. He just had to hang on and catch up with her. He just wished he could accomplish this feat soon. And as he walked into the Aga Khan Primary School, he said a silent prayer. They knew which school she had gone to for her high school education - the Old Mombasa Secondary School.

At the Old Mombasa Secondary School, Judy had already gone through her O-level exams the previous year. He refused to admit he had reached the end of his unyielding pursuit. Someone in the school must be aware of Judy's whereabouts.

Luckily, information was available when he needed it. A certain teacher knew of a student who resided in the same estate as Judy when she was still in the school, though the teacher was not sure if Judy still lived in that estate. Tom found a former student at the school who knew about a cafeteria Judy's mother owned in Mombasa Island where he believed Judy and her mother spent most of their time. He could not tell exactly where they lived, but he said the cafeteria was called Stardine.

Stardine was a mid-class, well-maintained, low budget cafeteria in the heart of Mombasa Island. Tom walked in and went to the self-service counter to pick and pay for his order.

The lady at the counter captured his interests. She was of an exotic, delicate beauty, with dark free flowing hair and a mild complexion. Her delightful looks were further embellished by the beatific figure. He could guess who she was, for she was an exact image of Judy as she had been described to him.

He opted to keep his luck stalled around the cafeteria, as he waited for Judy to lead him to her mother, Monica Wambi, and hopefully to a big break in his case.

Six hours of waiting brought his wishes to fruition when a 'closed' sign took over the place of the previous 'open' sign.

Fifteen minutes later, two figures emerged from the main entrance of the cafeteria. One of them held a bunch of keys under her right arm, which she used to lock the entrance. The two figures went their separate ways into the eight o'clock moonlit night. One of the figures was that of Judy - or at least the lady he believed was Judy.

The lady boarded a K.B.S. bus after walking a reasonable distance to the bus stop. He had to run some few steps to the bus that was already taxiing off, to keep his trail intact.

She alighted about half an hour later. He took his tailing position a few metres behind her. She walked into a compound after a few corners, and knocked at the door. A few seconds later she disappeared into the house.

He waited for some minutes to lapse before knocking on the same door, hoping Judy was not going to open, or if she did, she would not recognize him as a customer she had earlier in the day served at the cafeteria.

He was in luck. A tallish, slender, and angular faced lady with some striking features opened it. He could swear it was a living replica of the drawing he had been carrying with him all along his peregrination - Monica Wambi! Bulls-eye!

TWENTY

At sixteen years, Linda Imako had seen it all and had had enough. Life was surely a drag for some unfortunate people. She had woken up one morning her left eye swollen from a beating she had received the previous night from her uncle who was all enraged with her for not being able to bear a child, the basis of an end to her one year marriage to one of the most eligible bachelors in the village. This was after her husband had rejected her.

Her uncle had now realized the mountain it was going to be for him to receive any bride-price payments from any suitors, seeing that the girl Linda could not bear children.

In the Rulinga community, children were a must for a marriage to be complete, and without them, the wife was at the mercy of the husband who had definite grounds for the renunciation of the marriage and eventual rejection of the wife. Once the lady had been proved unable to bear children, she became ostracized and was from then on considered a bad omen. She was thus kept away from the rest of the community until a suitor from another community agreed to marry her and take her away from them.

It was thus no surprise the kind of treatment Linda received from her relatives.

The door to her room was always locked from the outside and the wooden window had been hammered fixed the day she was condemned to ostracism. Her freedom had been completely curtailed.

But she had put up a silent resistance. She had for the last few weeks been pushing the fixed wooden window to and fro, weakening it with each day that passed. And one morning her wishes had been granted when the wooden structure had come tumbling down from the wall, letting in the blinding strange rays of sunrise, which had once been her favourite sight. She replaced the window loosely and waited for the next dawn. It would be time to implement the plan she had been pre-meditating the previous months.

Then the all-important morning came and she dressed for the occasion. She put on a maternity dress over the soft clothing expertly folded over the flat tummy to deceive prospective onlookers that she was in advanced stages of pregnancy. Then she pulled out the premixed charcoal paste from under the bed and carefully rubbed a thin even layer over her hands, neck, face and legs to completely conceal her light skinned complexion. The final image in the mirror was exactly what she meant it to appear. The disguise was a perfect incognito, especially in the inadequate light of dawn.

She removed the wooden window and placed it on the bed where she could reach it from outside. Once she was on the outside, she replaced it carefully and casually walked into freedom.

She easily found her way into Tanzania from Rulinga land on the east of Lake Magadi, where the community occupied its small ancestral land.

Once in Arusha, she became a different person, with a completely different identity – Monica Wambi.

She landed her first job working as a baby sitter, when the mother of her subject came down with an acute fever. Upon her recovery she was jobless again. The job had lasted just two weeks. She received her meager wages and was back on the road.

Her next job was an almost immediate blessing, since a neighbour of her first employer spotted her and offered to take her in as a maid in her house. Two months later she took off when the husband of her employer started making advances at her and on one occasion would have forced himself on her had it not been for the wife's early return from the plantations.

With nothing else to do with herself, she walked slowly into a church, explained her plight, and ended up landing herself an accommodation and a temporary job as a cleaner on the church grounds.

Then one afternoon while running an errand for the church in town, she ran into an unexpected crowd of ladies outside the offices of a printing firm.

The ladies, whose head count she estimated at two dozen, were all squaring it out for one post of a receptionist which had been advertised a few days earlier, as she was told upon inquiring. Most were carrying leaves of academic papers, as proof of their qualifications and suitability for the job and were dressed for the occasion. She was miles, behind in comparison.

She realized she would have nothing to lose if she stayed and watched how the interview would go. She would gain some valuable experience about interviews. She needed to move closer to the reception desk in the room, where she expected the interview to be conducted if she was to gain any form of experience from this exercise.

She gently pushed her way into the room, against the all-scornful rudeness and non-cooperation that the other girls threw at her. They all agreed to let her through when somebody shouted, "Let her through. She probably will be dismissed at the first sight and done away with." The rest of the group burst into contemptuous laughter.

The room was a mess and a mockery of an office meant to welcome clients to the organization. The papers on the desk were an untidy heap and someone could only tell there was a telephone on the desk because of the wires that were covered with a thin layer of dust, suggesting things in that office had been on a stand still for sometime.

Engrossed by her perception about cleanliness, she took out her handkerchief to beating off the dust, set the papers and magazines and finally organized the desk amidst scornful and despiteful remarks, laughs and jokes thrown at her by the contentious girls. While she was still at it, the interviewer walked into the room. He was obviously captivated by her concern and repulsed by the derision of the rest of the girls. "Well, ladies, the interview has been called off for the vacancy has been filled up. Congratulations on your appointment as the receptionist of Arokonke Press," he said, offering his hand for a congratulatory handshake with Monica.

That night she focused back on her life. It consisted of a background she wished would disappear. A background she was not at all proud of.

At two, she lost her mother to a mysterious fever that was sweeping across the coastal strip of Kenya. At four, her father followed her mother to the mysterious unknown called death, his death coming via tribal wars against the neighbouring Lamashi community.

Her uncle, who was more than pleased to wait and receive a huge bride price for her when she was to be married off, then took her in. If being an angel was all about beauty alone, then she was one of them. He knew she was going to fetch a very huge sum and make him rich. It was just a matter of patience. Where money was the issue, he was a patient man. He sent her to school when she was eight years old, for it would add to the value of the price to be named. She was entitled to nothing and her life was a prison. She earned a heavy beating at the slightest mistake. There was not a time they appreciated her for doing the right thing. Not even her topping the school in academics and managing to stay there earned a reward. Nor did her promotion to more senior levels at school for good grades attract any encouragement from them. When she was thirteen, he forced himself on her. Despite her spirited protests, he took her virginity and innocence by force, beating her half to death in the process for the resistance.

Soon her cousins and some friends of her uncle caught on the sex spree with her on the receiving end. Every single minute she wished she had not lost her parents. Her predicament went on until she was to be married off. The only thing she cared about was school. It provided some time away from her misery. When she attempted to run away, they caught up with her and that worsened her misery.

It was no wonder that marriage, when it finally came, was the best thing that ever happened to her. Though in Rulinga culture it was the parents who made the choice for their daughters, her uncle's choice, the most eligible bachelor in the village, was exactly the man she had in mind. He was the son of a senior politician and one of the few men in the community who had contacts with the outside world.

The ceremony itself was one of the greatest the community had ever seen and was not easily to be forgotten. It was that night that she lost her true virginity.

Eight months later, she had not seen any sign of pregnancy and was beginning to get worried. She knew what happened to women if their husbands rejected them for not getting pregnant. It was one very stinking custom in the Rulinga culture.

She prayed and hoped, but her nightmare was soon to be confirmed. Her husband had had enough. She was now a certified *manuna*, or a bad omen of infertility.

And that was when she decided escape was the only next option. And so when the opportunity to escape reared its tempting face she could not hesitate.

She soon pushed the memories away from her head. Now that she had a job, the sky was her limit. She threw herself into her job with zeal and willingness to face any challenge. It was her only chance in life.

With her salary coming in steadily, she rented herself a small single bedroom in a self contained house a few kilometres away from the Arusha town centre, where she lived by herself.

She no longer trusted anyone. She did not intend to invite any close friendships. She intended to remain an individualist at all costs. For her, men were especially a thing of the past.

TWENTY ONE

In the neighbourhood, burglary was a growing concern. Every night before retiring to bed she made sure all the doors were locked, windows shut, pulled down the curtains and anything of value kept away where it should be. She did not intend risking loss of what she had sweat for to a single burglary.

One fateful Friday evening was no different. She did her routine before retiring to much-deserved sleep and rest. It had been a busy day through work and she was looking forward to a peaceful, rejuvenating night's rest.

But that was not to be. At about one o'clock in the night, she came to a startling awakening to the blinding beam of a torch held a few inches away from her face. Behind it was a silhouette of a tall muscular figure, looking down at her and seemingly ready to pounce at her at any moment.

An abrupt duck from the beam and a concurrent defensive kick on the figure's groin, she charged to escape.

But the tall ghostly figure in the dark room responded to that pain for just a moment, before blocking her desperate make for the door.

The bout that ensued was one where each person tried to outdo the other whichever way possible. While she grabbed at every object her hands could come across in the darkness, he calculated his every move. There was not a doubt he was experienced. He managed to duck every object she threw at him and waited patiently for the right moment, before grabbing her. He tossed her back on the bed and pinned her to it, rendering her helpless.

She employed all the energy she was left with, struggling and kicking as ferociously as she could and screaming uncontrollably and madly. She gave up when someone else switched on the lights and was holding a gun on them - her.

The second man came closer and held the gun against her face. She froze with fear at the smell of deadly gunpowder. The scream choked back into her.

"Okay Bumo, let's see you have some fun," he said, the gun harshly on the offensive.

"Wow, Saso, she's a queen. I'm really gonna enjoy this," the man pinning her down said, pulling a penknife from one of his pockets. He expertly started cutting down the nightdress. Even the ice-cold blade against her skin was not as terrifying as the faces of these people or what they intended to do with her. Bumo seemed to enjoy every tot of her fright and looked like a zombie.

"Hey Bumo, don't think you are the only one whose in need of service around here."

"You'll get your chance Saso, just be patient. We have all night, remember." Bumo continued to prepare himself. Once he was rid of every garment she had on, he knelt over her and started unzipping his trousers, his bulge very apparent under his garments.

Suddenly, there was a lashing sound and the gunman was caught off guard. He lost balance and stumbled, before falling, agony printed all over his face. The gun slipped beyond his reach.

Bumo, whose pants were already down and his swell just short of forcing its way into the unwilling shocked victim, tried in vain to duck the already flicking lash. The whip registered its angry mean contact on his bare back with a sharp splitting pain, forcing him to let out an agonizing cry and diving for desperate cover in an effort to duck another stroke. He effortlessly slipped into some of his clothing and took off behind Saso, who had already gained the quickest of exits from the scene. The would-be rapists left the gun behind.

Her rescuer was a tall, medium complexioned and plump-bodied figure. His voice could easily pass for both sexes. Except for a short haired balding scalp and the obvious male-hood wrapped inside the tight fit sports gear, he was seemingly effeminate.

The violent sobbing of Monica, who was coiled and nude in her bed, abruptly succeeded the commotion. Not sure how to go about comforting her, he walked slowly and cautiously towards her, studying every step he made and hoping to read her feelings towards his being there. He picked up the sheets from the floor and tossed them carefully over her. He then briefly arranged the room which was in a topsy-turvy state, before taking a stool from the sitting room, pushing the main door to a close and then placing the stool at a far end of the room. He stayed there to watch over her.

Later, when she had composed herself, they both agreed that it was not wise to involve the police in the incident since the would-be-rapists had not fulfilled their intentions. The weapon was discretely discarded.

Three weeks later, with the incident pushed to the background, John Mulano, the rescuer from the neighbourhood, and Monica had their first bedly adventures.

To her, it was only the second time all her life that she had willingly given herself to a man. This time round, she was not going to make a mistake. Two weeks later, she decided it was not wise to keep the mystery of her womb and her background to herself.

She was surprised that instead of being disappointed in her, he had carried her tenderly into the room and made passionate love to her.

Once they returned to reality, marked with pleasant amatory exhaust, he spoke those golden words that declared that their relationship was to climb the ladder.

His firm, robust and confident voice was a pleasant rumpus in the stillness of the night, as the words "Will you marry me Monica Wambi?" came through his lips like a melody into her ears, forcing a soulful harmony to pervade through every inch of her like an ink drop squeezed into a jar of water.

The statutory wedding was solemnized seven weeks later and a few of her work mates attended as witnesses. A new chapter had been propitiously opened in their lives. And they were ready to face the challenges ahead.

Life must have been kind to them to let them find each other. And for the first few months they could not get enough of each other. Then that all reduced with time, and gradually boredom started to trickle in. Johnny's friends started to question his wisdom in the marriage. He started to leave books and newspapers half read, every time he came across the word child, children, son or daughter.

That aroused her to the plain facts. Offspring fever was catching up with him, them and their relationship. She went to the nearby church to seek help from the local priest. And he did not fail her. He awakened her to the idea of adoption.

When she popped up the subject with him, he was hesitant at first and then the idea caught up with him. Suddenly, he was crazy with the idea. And it quickly became an obsession.

Their relationship had in no time graduated to a second marriage. Their mutual love and respect for each other grew and so did their bedly prowess, which had earlier on slumped to a record low. He threw himself into the business of finding a good baby for them.

One evening, about a month later, he got home and refused to let her get their supper. Instead, he took her to a candle lit seven course dinner before making passionate love to her and finally announcing the purpose of the celebration. He had found the ideal baby for them. Suddenly, it was her turn to rock him, joyously.

Its teenage white mother and a black servant at a ranch in Kenya were giving up the baby. He would have to travel to Kenya to bring it home.

Everything had fallen into place. As the adoption agent

had put it, they were just waiting for the deliver. They would be notified as soon the mother went into labour.

The call finally came. She wanted to accompany him to Kenya to bring home the baby. But he was adamant of letting her join him on such a perilous trip. He managed to shake off her insistence, but only after he had promised to keep in constant contact through the telephone. He only made his trip after he had employed security men to keep watch over her through out his absence lest anything happened to her while he was away. A week later, he returned accompanied as promised, with the cute adorable half-cast.

"Call it love at the first sight," she commented when she first carried the baby.

"I did, too. You two will make a great team. Obviously, I'm the luckiest papa and husband."

"I'm obviously the luckiest mama and wife in the whole world."

Of the two names chosen earlier for the baby depending on the sex, Andrew was discarded and Judy remained, for it was feminine.

And life for the Mulanos was at its fullest until after two years of marriage, Monica woke up to a rude awakening one morning, when she found herself alone in bed. Judy was sleeping undisturbed in her crib. Her husband was no where to be seen. He had left a hand written note where he had scribbled to her not to wait for him as he was not returning, and which advised her to continue with her life and to forget about him. He wished her and Judy a happy full life, ironically. Two months of waiting and she realized he was really gone never to return.

After two years of marriage he had had enough and had simply walked out of their lives, though it took years for her to admit that he was gone and was not returning. She wondered what it was that she had done wrong to warrant such an action. She then changed their surnames from Mulano to Wambi. She promised herself never to trust a man again. Men were those weird creatures of the human species that happened to have a dangling piece of flesh somewhere in their mid section that they thought gave them so much advantage over the female species. No wonder none had any sense of what livelihood was really about. In her thirteenth year as an employee with the printing firm, she had simply gotten bored of employment and wanted to venture into something more adventurous, more exciting, more challenging, and more unpredictable.

Having saved most of her money through out her years of employment, she tendered in her resignation. Her bosses decided to treat her resignation as a retirement and approved all the benefits she was entitled to receive. They paid her a retirement lump sum once she explained herself to them.

She stopped Judy from going into her sixth class at Diluti primary and the two simply moved into Kenya's coastal town of Mombasa. Once there she enrolled Judy back on track in sixth class at the Aga Khan primary school.

Once Judy was back in school, she threw herself into finding a business premises to operate. She was able to convince the proprietor of a half-dead kiosk outside the railway station to sell. Once she acquired the premises for an inflated value, she embarked on capturing much needed customers.

Within several months, her kiosk had become one roaring entity among the many similar businesses outside the railway station.

Many months later, she had managed to save enough to afford the rental for a commercial plot. She put up a cafeteria, in the island's old town, just a few blocks away from the Mombasa Cinema Theatre.

And those were the humble beginnings of the successful *Stardine Cafeteria*. It became the pillar of livelihood for the Wambis, for it was the earnings of the cafeteria that Monica and her daughter Judy lived on.

TWENTY TWO

Tom was overwhelmed momentarily. There she was, standing in front of him, the Monica he had been looking for across two countries.

"Can I help you?" she asked.

"Detective Tom Mbuke here. I presume you are Monica Wambi?"

"Yes I am. What has my being Monica got to do with you?" She was getting agitated.

"A lot, Miss Monica."

"Are you here to accuse me of some murder or something, Mr. Detective?"

"No madam. Please keep your voice down. You don't need your daughter to hear about this yet. I'll have a table reserved for us under Mr. Detective at two o'clock tomorrow at the Oceanic Hotel. Please be punctual. He started walking away. He knew he had her in the bag. She was curious, especially after he mentioned her daughter. That was enough to get her to the Oceanic.

"Hey, you think your presumptuous approach would work on me? And don't dare drag my...." She trailed off and could not finish the "...daughter into this." part, when she sensed Judy's presence behind her.

The scene at the Wambis' front door was one of a mixed blend comprised of a satisfied detective who believed he had just made a big stride in his big case, a mother who was drowning in curiosity on the inside and struggling to wear a calm composed guise on the outside, ducking every question her daughter put across to her, and a daughter who was inquisitive and wanted to know exactly what was going on.

When she appeared at the Oceanic Hotel some minutes

past two that afternoon, Monica was still wondering whether this detective had something on her or her daughter. She minced no words in warning Tom that if he was just another of those men who thought they were any different from the rest of them, he was in for a rude awakening. The only person who mattered in her life was her daughter, whom she was going to protect by all means.

But her curiosity at the previous day's mention of her daughter was apparent to him, as she took the seat opposite to him. When he offered her some juice, which he had already ordered, she pushed the glass aside.

He pushed to her a small picture. Johnny was smiling back at her. She pushed it away on impulse.

"I want us to talk about him – and your daughter," he said the moment she looked down at the picture.

"I should have sensed this. You are working for him. He wants to take away my daughter. This meeting is over. Tell Johnny to keep away from Judy and me. He walked out on us seventeen years back when we needed him most. Now he wants to take away the only person that matters to me! I can't believe men. And you have the guts to show up here thinking I can even allow you to go near her!"

He waited until she had said all that she had to say. She got up and started picking up her things to leave. "And don't dare show your filthy Johnny errand self at my door again."

"I'm not working for Johnny. He is dead. He died some three years after he left you."

That threw her off, momentarily. She dropped back into the chair. "I see," were the hardly audible words that came through her lips, involuntarily. She clearly did not expect that.

Then she spoke up abruptly.

"You may not be working for Johnny. Then what brings

you here? Are you here to blackmail me or something?"

"That's not it, either."

"Let's get over with it whatever it is. I'm getting tired of this."

"You are the one who's not letting me speak, madam."

"Okay, speak your mind. Johnny is dead, so what?"

And he went on to tell her about the stranger nurse and the disappearance of the half-cast girl from the hospital and his involvement, the discovery that the nurse was actually a disguised Johnny, leaving out the part of Sally and the clues that led him to Judy and finally to her. He told her he was yet to establish who Johnny was working for and why.

She listened without interrupting, sipping slowly on the juice she had earlier rejected. And when he finally said, "...that's what got me looking for you," - she asked if he was sure Judy was this Kate he was looking for.

"A beauty spot below the lower lip and a crescent of a burn mark just above her left breast, where a nurse had accidentally dropped a hot tool and about which her father had made a big furious fuss regarding the hospital's safety standards. It would be no coincidence if Judy has these marks, and of course with her age and the obvious resemblance to her mother, there is reason to believe Judy is Kate. Everything falls into place," Tom said conclusively. He had seen the beauty spot.

"What you are saying is Johnny had me set up, right?"

"Affirmative."

"So the rape attempt was a lie. He paid those men to attack me so he could come to the rescue?"

"He needed something to get close enough and make you need his presence."

"What you are effectively implying is that because you want to solve some stupid case, you are ready to break me and my daughter up?"

"Listen ma'am, you've been a mother to Judy for the

last 21 years. Obviously you have been a good mother. But your attitude is what may just bring an end to this. I bet she thinks that her father was some warrior who died when she was very young and knows nothing about the adoption."

"Who do you think you are to start lecturing me about how I should take care of my daughter?"

"If you are afraid that her parents are going to take her away from you, then let me console you. They are all dead."

The expression on her face changed to surprise.

Tom took advantage of her surprise to get his massage across. "Now, you have three days to decide if you will be the one to tell your daughter about the adoption, whereby you stand a chance of a whole lifetime with her, or if I will be the one she learns it from, whereby you stand the risk of losing her trust. There is no way of telling what her reaction might be if she learns about such an important secret about herself from someone else. I hope you are not crazy enough to try running off to some place else hoping this issue will just evaporate. I will look around and I will definitely find you and you can guess where such a scenario would put you regarding your relationship with to your daughter." He took a small pocket size note book from his wallet, tore a page and wrote his name, room number, direct telephone contact number and pushed it under her palm. He paid the bill and walked away, leaving a pensive and confused Monica at the table.

****

Monica played around with not telling Judy that she was her adopted daughter. This made her nights sleepless. She could not stand it if Judy were to walk out on her. It was for Judy that Monica was still sane. It was due to Judy that life was worth living. Now some good for nothing detective had caught up with her and was threatening to break up her relationship with her daughter.

When Judy was twelve, Monica had considered letting her know. But she feared that Judy might want to go back to her biological parents. Then what? Monica had toyed with the idea again when Judy was fifteen and when she became eighteen but somehow the words could not come out. She was too afraid of the consequences.

Now Judy was 21. It was probably too late to tell her. She would question her not being told when she had attained a reasonable age. Monica would try to explain her dilemma, but Judy could walk out on her anyway. Even if she did not, things would never be the same again between them. It was too disturbing to even think about.

On the third day, she realized she had to do something. It was better if Judy learned the facts from her than from someone else, perhaps a stranger. She called Tom and told him that she would hold him responsible for whatever happens to her and her daughter. She vowed to file a lawsuit against him.

Tom, on his part, was relieved at the phone call. "Do what you have to do, Ma'am, but please make sure she learns about it from you and nobody else. And something that will help you - tell her I know about her parents and leave the 'death' part to me. And please don't go doing anything foolish. She may make very drastic decisions immediately, but with time that will come to pass, I promise you."

"What, are you pretending that you care?"

"Good luck, Ma'am."

"Any one else can tell me that but not you for God's sake..." She realized she was talking to her self. Tom had already hung up. She banged the phone in rage. Then she settled to make a decision.

It had to be during lunch. She could not risk telling Judy something like that over supper. She may walk out into the night, not even knowing where she was going. God only knows what would happen, should such a scenario occur. Judy had left early as usual and had kissed her goodbye on her way out.

She nervously called the cafeteria. "Can you make it here for lunch?" she asked Judy when she came to the phone.

"Of course I can, mum. What's the occasion? You did not talk about it yesterday or even in the morning, at least."

"Just something I want to do. Please be here, and please pick up the money from the counter and come with it." She wanted to be sure that Judy had some money in her pocket just in case.

"I will mum. See you then."

"Judy, I love you." It was more passionate than she could imagine.

"I know that, mum"

"Bye."

"Bye."

Then she embarked on a shopping spree. By lunch time, Judy's favourite half ripened boiled bananas and chicken stew was ready to serve. She also prepared some rice, chapatis, ugali, bean stew, and some fruit salad to Judy's preference. Once all was set, she put the mouth-watering dishes on the table and waited for Judy to arrive.

Judy walked into a surprising and unexpected sumptuous lunch her mother had prepared. It was not that this was the first of such meals, but such kinds of meals were reserved for special occasions, and they rarely happened during lunch. Monica insisted that they eat first. When Judy tried to pass her the collection from the restaurant she tactfully insisted that could be done later.

Therefore mother and daughter gaily went through the hearty dishes. After it was over, Monica knew she had to do it – now. At least she had made a point with the meal.

All through the meal she had kept telling Judy how much she meant to her.

"Mum, are you in some kind of medical problem or something?" Judy was curious.

"No. Certainly not, Judy."

"Oh, I know. You found someone and you think I will not approve of him. Is it that man who was here last Saturday?"

'*NOW*' – Monica heard the voice from inside, urging her on.

"That man who was here last Saturday, he knows something you should know about," Monica started once she could summon enough courage. She felt nervous and sweaty all over.

"Mum, what line is that? Is that what this is all about?" she said, smiling gaily. "If you need my approval mum, you don't have to go through such trouble. I think he is quite handsome and exactly the kind of a man you need. Younger than you to help you recover on lost days. And to tell you the truth, mum, I was beginning to get worried about you. Grab him mum, 'cause if you don't, I will," she said comically. Monica could not stop her. She was thinking of the next line. She had thought about it for the last three days.

"It's not what you think. He knows about a man and his wife who had a beautiful adorable baby girl - who they named Kate."

"Mum, what is it with two people and their adorable daughter?"

The smile was still there. Monica hated to think that she would be the one to kill that smile. She would relish avoiding this moment, but she realized she had to face it, no matter how unwelcome it would be. She had to drop the bomb.

"I could... not...I could not make a ...a...a baby when I got married," she finally managed to say.

"What?" Judy was caught off guard. Her expression changed to puzzlement.

"You are that Kate. I adopted you, Judy." Monica rushed the next line before Judy had the chance to focus. Monica wished she was dreaming. But this was real.

The statement finally registered. The ceramic cup Judy was drinking from slipped her grip and spilled coffee all over her white poplin dress before hitting the tiled floor and collapsing into hundreds of pieces. She looked for a trace of a joke on Monica's face but none came up. Monica was dead serious.

"Did I hear you right...mu..." She could not bring out the word 'mum.' Her voice was now tearfully suffocated.

"Yes, yes, you did, Judy. I always wanted to tell you but I was afraid of losing you." Her voice was hardly audible. She could not look at Judy. Her tearful eyes wandered and finally settled, face downwards.

Judy could not say anymore. She got up from the table as if she had just seen a snake, her movement claiming a number of plates as they dropped from the table into hundreds of pieces.

Monica's pleas for understanding and her appeals for a second chance were shut behind the thundering front door that Judy slammed as she stormed out of the house.

"Keep your sanity and wait for her sweet return," was all Tom could say when she called, swearing to kill him for breaking up her relationship with her daughter.

It was after such four sleepless nights and tiresome days that there was a light knock on the door. Her tears had never stopped coming. She wiped them off and reluctantly got up to go and open the door.

'Who else could it be except the son of a bitch detective?' she thought as she walked unsteadily towards the door. She picked up a kitchen knife on her way. She was going to put some scars across his face for this. She flanked open the door with a start, her cruel weapon hidden behind her back, ready to strike.

Suddenly, tears vanished from her eyes. The knife dropped from her hand, impulsively. She thought she was dreaming. Standing there, staring back at her, tearfully, was Judy.

For that instance, an odd pride and overwhelming speechlessness saturated the air. Then the pangs of separation cut in and mother and daughter could not resist the urge for a passionate embrace of reunion.

"You'll always be my mother, mum." Judy was first to speak up.

"I prayed each and every second, for these last few days for this moment to come. You'll never know how sorry I am for not letting you know earlier."

"I know this wasn't easy for you. I probably would have done the same if I were in your position. I love you, mama."

"I love you, daughter."

TWENTY THREE

Tom was reclining on the sofa in the cozy living room of his rental apartment watching his favourite program on television, *Derrick*. Murder had been committed and Derrick and his assistant Harry had just been notified. Suddenly, his concentration was disturbed by the beggingly ringing telephone. He cursed under his breath as he made a quick step to pick up the phone.

Monica was calling to make the triumphant announcement. Her daughter, Judy, had returned home and was ready to hear the story about her real parents. Monica too wanted to know why the detective was involved.

"Sorry Derrick, some very important business to be attended to." He drove to the Wambis home immediately.

"You know something Judy – Kate, you are a very rich woman but you don't know it yet. Your parents were the couple behind the prestigious Wenjuve group."

"You said 'were'," Judy was quick to point out.

"I also said you are a very rich woman." He took a moment's pause before confirming the already spilled news. "They have been dead for a long time now, Judy. Sorry."

"Yeah, I've heard some history about the company. Some beneficiary named Mark is the current president," Judy said.

"Before you show up anywhere on this planet we must make sure nothing threatens your safety. We don't know who these guys are yet and what they are capable of. Obviously your showing up may upset something. So naturally, a good detective will tell you nobody is to be trusted."

"What you are essentially trying to say is you are trying

to find out who exactly is responsible for my kidnapping," Judy inquired.

"Yes, Judy. I can see you are catching up fast," Tom answered.

"I read a lot of detective novels."

"And no, you are not coming with me if that's the next question on your mind. It's too risky to start showing you around. These people may catch up with my investigations and you can imagine what they would do to us. Talk about putting a world champion wrestler and a three year old kid in the ring," Tom answered, reading Judy's mind.

"I have to start catching up on what my life as a Wenjuve would have been. I can't wait ten years when you will finally come to identify the person responsible."

Tom realized she wasn't going to change her mind. Maybe it would be useful for him to take her along so that he can keep an eye on her.

Monica told them about Johnny's friends, the main one being Sam, the adoption agent. She could remember one evening when Johnny and Sam were arguing about something in low tones as if she was not supposed to hear and she overheard Johnny call him George.

Tom set up an arrangement with the artist to work with Monica to produce a drawing of Sam's face. Fred Mongo, the artist, agreed to make the trip from Nairobi the following morning.

Tom made arrangements with the Arusha telephone exchange to obtain the transcripts of calls entering Kenya.

While Monica and Fred worked on the drawing, Tom made the trip to Arusha.

Two days later, he was back with a long list of numbers called from Arusha to Kenya and those that entered into Arusha from Kenya. He found out that the artist Fred and Monica had performed their task, and Fred had even made four different drawings to allow for aging.

Monica, Tom and Judy got started on the painstaking

task of finding those numbers that proved consistent with times and dates that could allow for communication between Johnny and his cronies. Monica could remember five occasions on which Johnny might have made and received the calls.

And at the end of the exercise, the long list of numbers was reduced to just twenty-six. Tom added 'George' to the names for the drawings Fred had produced. It was time to move into Nairobi.

TWENTY FOUR

The seven hour uneventful trip into Nairobi, the Kenyan capital, from the coastal town of Mombasa was an exhaustive exercise, and so immediately the *Coastside* bus stopped at its designated terminus, the quadruple travel mates alighted and walked several streets to the *Wimpy* for a late lunch.

Tom hired a taxi to ferry them to his Kimathi residence but Fred opted to use other means to get to his South C residence. Tom drafted him a cheque to offset his debt for his handy services including travel allowances. Tom felt lucky because he could survive on the few cases he had to work on for some insurance companies and private clients. The Kate Teluve case was quickly becoming a financial and time consuming matter. Monica had asked him once to let her inject some capital into the case because it was all about Judy, her daughter. He had declined, insisting that the case was a personal commitment for him.

Sally was a bit jumpy but pleased to see Tom back. She was a great hostess to their guests, Monica and Judy. She ran the showers, prepared their rooms, and offered them some delicacies she took time to carefully prepare. T h e y both declined the food, on the account of having had a late lunch and instead settled for a cup of coffee before dropping dead asleep on their beds in the guestroom.

During the entire evening Tom thought that Sally was acting rather strangely. He associated this strange behaviour with the presence of guests around. But the bombshell struck Tom like a thunderbolt when he inquired about the seemingly strange behaviour. Sally confessed that she had found a 'true love, a soul mate,' as she put it across.

Tom knew what losing Sally meant. She had been of great value to his firm. Together they made a great team. When he asked her what her plans were she answered with a question. Could they keep their relationship purely on professional terms? He answered affirmatively, but only after a long pause.

"Are you sure, Tom? I don't want to strain my affair and that needs your solemn promise."

"I need you, Sally, if not in my bed, then at least in my office. I'm positive."

As a secretary, she was the best and the only one who could understand his kind of job and therefore he would respect her decision. He wished her good luck.

She told him he would understand fully when he himself met someone one day.

The following morning, Tom was as busy as a bee; he chose the Kenya Post and Telecommunications Corporation as his first choice of places to hunt for answers about the twenty-six numbers he had to check on.

Monica was the other early riser, at his side. They had to settle for the huge directories when the man at the counter proved to be a very uncooperative and unfriendly character. Tom had to 'buy' some two old copies that were lying around at the counter. They went back to the house and the pains-taking task of checking the numbers against the names registered beside them began.

Two hours later, and with Judy's input, they finally managed to put names against twenty-two out of the twenty-six numbers they originally had. The other four probably did not appear in the directory, Tom concluded. They were soon to discover they had another problem. The directories did not offer enough residential addresses. They had to get that information from somewhere. Probably the Post Telecommunications Corporation would be helpful.

Tom walked into the building and demanded to be taken to the supervisor. A short, half-bald man came and introduced himself as the supervisor. Tom introduced himself as a private detective, showing his licence and identity card. He then gave him the list of names he had, disclosed that those were crime suspects and requested information on their residential addresses. He eventually walked out of the building with twenty-two residential addresses for the twenty-two names he had.

With the help of the ladies, he went down the list carefully.

First there was a George Matatana. Anything with George besides it was worth looking at twice. The second name did not look anything Kenyan and Judy could swear that they had a Matatana in class when she was in primary school in Arusha. They noted it. Further down the list came a second George, this time a George Maloni. Maloni was a Kenyan name. They noted it down.

Then there was an interesting finding. There were numbers that looked very familiar to Tom, but he was yet to place a finger on why until the name Wenjuve Companies was written next to them. Those two numbers happened to be the official numbers of the Wenjuve Companies' offices in Nairobi some years back. The numbers had since been changed to new ones. Tom knew the new number off head. The other one had been the direct line to the vice-presidents office.

Tom was elated and surprised by this latest finding. Could Johnny have been in direct contact with the Wenjuve Groups' management? Could he have been threatening someone? Maybe the Wenjuve Group had been paying a ransom secretly. He had to know. He did not understand how this information had remained unknown to the authorities. Now he realized they were headed somewhere. He noted the prized information.

The last section of the list went on to push more adrenaline up within them. A number at Muthaiga Estate was listed under a M. L. Taboni. Tom filled the initials.

Mark Lubevu Taboni. Could this be a coincidence? Mark resided at Muthaiga too, back then. It would be a rare coincidence. He noted down the observation.

And as if to confirm these fears, another familiar name came up beside the last bunch of numbers in the list. Jama Toki was a personal assistant to Mark.

"What does all this imply?" Judy asked.

"Did I tell you we can't trust anyone? Well this goes a long way to prove so. And it tells us we should carefully look at the Wenjuve Group of Companies' top brass. They are obviously concealing some vital information."

"Could Mark himself be involved?" Monica wanted to know.

"Anybody could be involved. But I don't want to commit statements yet. Let's wait and see what turns out," Tom answered.

The next day would be a very crucial day and the trio could not wait for it to come.

TWENTY FIVE

That next day, Tom and the two ladies, Judy and Monica, roamed the various destinations related to the residential addresses. Tom had established that George Matatana was a Tanzanian-born Kenyan with no relevance to his case.

George Mulano, whose description they had established was an exact match to the artistic impression done by Sam, was long dead. Gangsters in a burglary had killed him in his house. Word had it that he had been disposed off by a powerful person.

When Tom displayed the photograph of Mark, the informant nodded. They knew him well. He was that stinking rich person George used to associate himself with. Rumour had it that George had done some dirty work for the man, after which George had come across an old friend of his who had gone through a restless spiritual search and finally settled with Jesus as his personal saviour. George had listened to his old friend and had decided he would do with that Christ his friend was professing for his spiritual guidance. With such a decision, there was the chance that George could talk.

M.L. Taboni turned out to be Mark Lubevu Taboni. The rest of the personalities in question did not seem to bear any relevance to the case.

Now there was Mark Lubevu in the thick of things, suddenly. Mark's telephone numbers proved consistent with the calls Johnny Mulano made. Johnny's death was similar to George's, and both men had been acquaintances of Mark according to the primary investigations. Mark had all the opportunity, space and cover in the world to carry out the crimes and get away with them.

There was also the suspicious coincidence. In a space of

only a few weeks after the death of Wendy, her daughter Kate was kidnapped, and Juve committed suicide. Tom could not help wondering whether the kidnapping was orchestrated to seize the opportunity arising from Wendy's death. Everything appeared much too convenient for Mark. Mark became the prime suspect.

Suddenly, adrenaline was pumping within Tom. When Juve's accident occurred, it was Mark's idea that specialists inspect the vehicle for any mechanical failure. He had to start by eliminating the wild possibilities. It was Mark who had hired the two British accident investigators who carried out a thorough inspection of the vehicle and later made a report on it. The police had adopted that report as conclusive and exhaustive. It was this chronology of events that led to the conclusion that Juve had committed suicide. The case was then closed. And now, some twenty years later, Tom was asking questions. Anything on which Mark's name appeared was worth looking at carefully.

Tom dug deep into his files. He knew he had a copy of the report somewhere. He found the copy, finally. He realized he had to do something else - open a new file on Juve's death.

The report clarified that the two Britons, John Reilly and Kent Mulley, were employees of a Britain based accident insurance investigators firm called Accidentquire.

The British High Commission was cooperative in volunteering information about the present state of Accidentquire. But it was only three days later that he would receive the brief from the office in Nairobi. And when it came, the brief shed new light on the case.

The firm was in brief existence between 1978 and 1989. It was a partnership that started off soundly before falling victim to poor management that reduced it to a moribund firm within three years. By 1984 when Juve's accident occurred, the company was not in active business, therefore had no employees.

Accidentquire must have been floated just as a blind-folding device. Somebody had run into a cover-up kink and had seized the opportunity to the fullest. Mark was the first name that came into mind. What would somebody be covering up? *What would Mark be covering up?* Suddenly, a wild thought struck him. That was the only possible reason Tom could come up with for Mark's involvement. He would have to verify. He had learnt a long time ago that anything was possible. And the explanation in his mind constituted a very logical explanation due to his recent findings. Every piece of the jigsaw was suddenly falling into place. The Kate Teluve kidnapping, Johnny, the telephone calls, George, the present Wenjuve status quo, even Wendy's death. He had to check carefully before jumping to conclusions.

Wayne Stelle, a long time friend from the Harvard days, had called him and said he was to visit the country some time soon. Stelle had promised to call as soon as he arrived in the country. Tom called up Sally and alerted her to expect a Wayne Stelle's call which was very important to him, just in case it came when he was out. Wayne had worked for two years in the motor crime department while Tom was still in the Los Angles Police Department on his sandwich course.

Three days later, Stelle called as he had promised he would. He was at the Nyali Beach Hotel. He had already spent two days in the country. His choice of Kenya as a destination for his vacation was one very wise decision, Wayne said boastfully. His family was having the greatest time ever.

Tom picked up a few personal effects and was soon headed for Mombasa. Wayne's coming was a blessing to the case. The only problem was whether Wayne was going to accept doing the job over his vacation. He had this rigid principle they remembered him for, and it was that when its work its work and no play and when it's play its play and no work. Tom wondered how he would get around that principle to get Stelle to helping him out.

It took every trick in the book to convince Wayne to help him out. His wife Shelly was helpful in convincing Wayne to help a friend. Wayne finally agreed to help, but insisted it was only because Tom was a great friend. They bade Tom goodbye once Wayne had promised to travel to Nairobi as soon as it was convenient for him.

Tom didn't have to wait long for the call. Wayne called within a few days to announce his arrival in the capital city – Nairobi. They arranged their meeting place for the morning next.

The two friends met as planned and did some catching up over a hearty breakfast. Tom took the time to brief Wayne on the case. Wayne was pleased to meet Judy and Monica. Once through breakfast, it was time for work. Both Judy and Monica wanted to accompany the two detectives to where the wreckage that killed the millionaire had been grounded. But the two detectives were against the idea, as they could not tell who could be watching. That could mean putting to unnecessary risk the lives of the two ladies, especially Judy. Tom waved down a taxi and Wayne objected, insisting that they commute to the site on a Matatu with music. He was obviously captivated by the music and the colourful allure the vehicles were wearing. He kept taking photographs of the vehicles as they passed by him. "Kenya is one country I'll never forget, the famous wildebeest migration on the Maasai Mara, the scenic countryside, the scenic landscape such as the Great Rift Valley, the beaches, the hospitable people and those public transport you call matatus. Its fun being here and every time I get a chance I'll have to holiday here."

"Thanks for the vote of confidence. Tourism gives our country huge earnings. I'm just sorry I interfered with your safari to bring you here."

"Don't even think of that. I'm having a paradise of a time." The duo reached the site where the wreckage had been towed and deposited and had remained for the many years since the accident. A thick column of dust had completely subdued the canvas that blanketed the vehicle to keep it from weather-related adversities and thereby prevent it from quickly falling apart. The vehicle remained the same as Tom could remember it, the front part totally burned. It seemed to have been forgotten. Wayne did his thing, Taking pictures, drawing sketches, rolling under the wreckage, testing the brakes, testing the steering efficiency, painstakingly following the brake pipes to locate any leakages, and noting every single detail in a note book as he proceeded. Two and a half hours later, Wayne was satisfied that he had covered every aspect there was to be looked into. Tom had filled him in on the details of the actual accident as it was suspected to have happened. He had also seen the police report and the Reilly and Kent report on the state of the vehicle during the accident. When it was all over, Tom was anxious to get an opinion from Wayne, but Wayne was non-committal and insisted Tom should wait for the report, which would be ready in seventy-two hours.

"And if I were you, I would keep tabs on those witnesses to the moments prior to the crash; you'll obviously need to talk to them sooner or later," was all he would part with about the exercise he had just carried out.

Those two people had been instrumental in the suicide decision the police had arrived at. The law had the requirement that the witnesses leave the particulars of their addresses, both physical and postal, with the police for a period of time, in case the need to have their testimony re-examined arose. It was therefore from these police records that Tom found the addresses to the witnesses' residences.

He was not expecting a hard time. He decided to visit Andrew Bondi's Kangemi residence first. After introducing himself, Tom asked for Andrew. The occupant responded that he did not know of any Andrew. He had lived in the very house for the last five years. The landlord who had rented the house out to him had himself occupied the place earlier.

"Can you take me to him?" Tom inquired, referring to the landlord.

"Certainly."

The landlord was a bit more informative. The man Tom was asking about had sold the house to him at a throwaway price some 19 years ago. He had lived in the house himself before letting it out.

"Did you know where he was headed and why he was doing that?" Tom asked.

"Beats logic really, the house was in tiptop condition. He seemed only interested in getting out of there as fast as he could. I could not gather where he was headed for," the landlord answered.

Tom tried the neighbours, some of whom were well in acquaintance with the case, but none of whom seemed to know about Andrew's destination. Some were very nervous and some were unreasonable when he approached them. Tom concluded that somebody must be hiding something. He left his business cards behind in case somebody changed their minds and wanted to help. He realized he had suddenly hit a brick wall. All he could do was apply some pressure and hope somebody would crack.

At Timothy Weki's Outering Estate residence, Tom was not really that surprised at what he found had happened there. Just about a year after Juve's death, Timothy had been slashed to death by burglars. They had broken into his house and gotten away with almost everything worthwhile. Tom believed he knew exactly who to heap the blame on. But as at that moment, all he had was circumstantial evidence, as the court would refer to it had he to present his suspicions before the law.

He found that the case had been transferred to the

Buruburu police station from the Jogoo Road police station on its commissioning. Tom was of the impression there was not a burglary spree in the area, since it was the only case of burglary reported from there during the week in question, according to police records.

He learnt that the police had conducted investigations and had recovered some items after a tip off from members of the public. He asked to be furnished with the list of the items recovered from the raid the police had mounted on a house they had been tipped on as a hide out of some members of a notorious killer gang. Recovered together with some of Timothy's belongings were also some items traced to a certain Johnny Mulano! Now there was a string that tied the Timothy and Johnny deaths. One gang must have conducted them! To him, the burglaries were just cover-ups. The real motive was murder. He recorded the particulars of the officer in charge of the case. He might need his testimony later on.

Andrew must have found out about Timothy's death and taken off to cheat definite 'fate' – his murder in a similar convenient burglary. Tom realized he had to find Andrew – alive.

****

Finally, Wayne's report was on his table. Wayne had gone through the trouble of posting it through speed post, though it was some two days late. With it was another package. On it were the words – TIT FOR TAT. Wayne had just learnt from his sources in America that a key suspect in one of his narcotics cases was hiding in Kenya and he wanted Tom to do a follow-up on the case.

There was a report briefing Tom on the case and the suspect's identity. There was also a photograph. The suspect's name was Salvanto Prissicalli, an Italian immigrant to the US, a leader in the Mafia circles, a seasoned drug and arms dealer, and a wildlife poaching coordinator. Tom instructed Sally to open a Salvanto file.

The report on the accident made by Wayne was almost exactly what Tom had expected it to be. It was just a further confirmation of his suspicions. The car must have been tampered with before the actual accident and still some pipes in the brake system were not burned in the front part as the rest of the vehicle and had been covered in mud which seemed deliberately done to prevent them being noticed. They must have been replaced *after* the accident! Wayne was positive the accident was by design and premeditated. Suddenly, it had now become very important for Tom to find Andrew.

He stepped up the pressure on the neighbours and still emerged empty handed. He made a 400 kilometre trip to Siaya, which he learnt was Andrew's rural home. Andrew had not been there for 22 years!

It was as Tom was about to catch some elusive sleep, wondering what to do next, that his bedside telephone brought him back. The caller, who insisted on remaining anonymous, directed Tom to a Dan Waiko, who he claimed was the Andrew that Tom was looking for.

The next morning, Tom took off to the remote village of Shago in the Rift Valley. But in Nakuru, he checked into a hotel, arranged for the car to be picked up later in the day and checked out through a private exit. He used a different car he had instructed his Nakuru helper to arrange for him. You can never be too careful with people. Somebody could be tightening the noose on him.

Shago was everything you would describe as remote. Thanks to his Nakuru helper, the four wheel drive came in handy.

Dan Waiko alias Andrew Bondi's hut was not anywhere you would describe as in sight. The villagers seemed to have strict instructions not to welcome guests to the village. It was only when Tom managed to break through the wall of hostility and explain himself severally that the villagers accepted that maybe the man himself should see the visitor.

It took some time before Andrew appeared from a corner. Accompanying him were six men of fierce muscular physique, armed to the teeth with bows and arrows, pangas, spears and clubs that had nails at their tips. The expression on their faces told of their ferocity, in a subtle but firm manner. Andrew himself was carrying an automatic pistol.

Tom realized he had to be careful. Men like this did not think with their heads but with their weapons and fists.

Tom got out of the car and slowly tossed the pistol he had carried with him for protection to the ground. He had to win Andrew's trust. He then raised his hand in submission.

"Who are you and how did you know where to find me?"

"I'm Tom Mbuke, private detective."

As if translating the tone Andrew had used to be offensive, the men surrounded Tom and somebody held a spear offensively at his neck. Tom swallowed a dry gulp as the cold sharp blade made contact with his skin.

Andrew kept away his gun and then picked Tom's pistol and toyed with it before pointing it at Tom, just inches away from his face. He set the operation lever and was just short of finishing off Tom.

"Make sure you are speaking the truth. Cause if you are not..."

"My...my top right pocket...you'll find my ID'..." Tom stammered. He was beginning to sweat. They had taught him at university to keep it cool when faced with such a situation, but they never really gave a practical demonstration.

"These papers don't say a thing. You and I know papers can be forged," Andrew said on inspecting the ID.

"Tell one of your men to get the photo album from

the car." Tom had come ready for a confrontation of this nature and hoped the album would help soften Andrew a bit to allow him to talk his way into valuable information.

There was a photograph of him attending the funeral, some high school photos, some Harvard snaps, some LAPD photos, and some current photos taken at the office.

After looking through them briefly, he raised his eyes to look directly at Tom and then back at the photos.

"I can see you were the little boy mourning the millionaire. But if I may ask what is your involvement in all this."

"I witnessed the millionaire's wife being attacked by some assailants."

"Oh, the ten-year old driver, eh. They should have given you a medal for that courageous act. But, I still don't see where Andrew comes in."

"You can remember the millionaire's daughter was kidnapped when she was just a week old?"

"Yeah, that I can remember."

"Well, I've been working on that case for some time now. I believe I know who was responsible for the kidnapping. But I need your help to nail him."

"Kidnapping? I know exactly nothing about that. You are a detective for goodness sake!"

"Not the kidnapping alone." Tom paused before continuing. He knew this was the moment when he either kissed life goodbye or made a break in the case.

"This guy seems to have been involved in the millionaire's accident. So I guess I have to take the whole case as one."

Tom watched as Andrew's expressions changed. He said something to the other men and they left. Tom realized he had done it, finally. Chances were he was going to make the breakthrough, if Andrew's reaction was anything to go by. He held his breath and hoped he was right.

"Who is this guy you are talking about?" Andrew wanted to know, as soon as the other men had left.

"Mark Lubevu." He wanted to add, 'The Wenjuve Group President.'

"You must be a damn good detective," Andrew said.

"I sure hope I am," Tom answered modestly.

He led Tom to a secluded hut in the village and beckoned him to sit, inviting him to tea and some boiled maize.

"I'll tell you the whole story," he said once they started with the dish.

"I found this village hunger stricken. I spoke to the elders and we made a pact. It's my money that buys the hybrid seeds and fertilizers and helps take their children to school and pays their hospital bills. In exchange they offered me protection. I invested heavily when I came here and the village sells its produce in return for cash. That's why you received that hostile reception."

"I can understand."

"A few days before the millionaire's accident, Mark approached me. I used to travel a lot between Siaya and Nairobi. He offered me a large sum of money to give evidence that I saw a yellow Sedan parked at a certain position. I tried to refuse the offer but he told me he had my finger prints ready for submission on an unsolved police officer's murder! Naturally, I did not believe him and he called a senior police officer, who clarified the claim. I realized I was cornered. We went to the station and there it was. The knife that had been used to kill the officer and my prints along side them!"

"What about Timothy? When did you first know about him?"

"I met him at the station, accidentally. Our friendship out of need grew. On him they had cooked up a plot to assassinate a cabinet minister. There was more than enough evidence to put him away for good. They had his prints too! A year later, Tim died under very suspicious circumstances. I wanted to walk into the police station and report everything I knew but the odds were high against me. Almost the whole police force is on Mark's payroll. That was the time I realized I had to take off."

"You said Mark approached you himself?"

"Yes. It essentially meant that should I go public, it would be my word against his. You can bet such a move would not stick on Mark. I would simply be signing my death warrant."

"Are you willing to testify to put this guy away for good?"

"You can imagine the kind of life I lead. I'm willing to do anything to get normalcy back."

"It may mean you do some time for false testimony but I believe we can arrange something."

"These guys can now do without me. They have learnt to take care of themselves and I want to go back to the life I knew. I miss my family."

"Mark does not believe in letting lose ends free. You happen to be one lose end he would give anything to clear."

"Please let me know about anything new that comes up. My life depends on it, remember." Andrew's expression had now changed to one of fear and concern.

Tom realized the dangers Andrew had to face. Mark had to be stopped.

Once back in Nairobi, Tom paid a visit to the British High Commission. This time he wanted the two Britons charged with the misleading report they had knowingly issued.

He had to build an airtight, watertight case since it involved the Wenjuve president, Mark Lubevu. Otherwise Mark would still walk free. There was no telling how many heads in the police force doubled up on Mark's payroll.

A week later, when a report from the British High Commission came that the two Britons had been apprehended, Tom booked the next flight to London.

Both positively identified Mark as the man who had engineered the false report. They named a mechanic who had worked on the car a few hours before the millionaire's accident. They also submitted another name in the Wenjuve management who worked for Mark.

"We got some one to check on," Tom announced at the Jomo Kenyatta International Airport, where Monica and Judy had arrived to welcome him, anxious to hear what he got from his English trip.

Ndomba Munaki, the mechanic, was not a complex character to crack down. Tom traced him some 24 hours after touch down.

Tom had to go through a strenuous two hours before coming face to face with the police officer he needed to see. Inspector Ponde was now a Chief Inspector and had been transferred from the Jogoo Road police station to the Buru-Buru police station.

By the time Tom was trying to trace him, Ponde had gone out abruptly and nobody seemed to know his whereabouts. He resurfaced two hours later, with another man in handcuffs.

"Hi pal. Remember Tom Mbuke?"

"The private detective, eh."

"You sure got a working memory."

"Wow, how did it go Mr. P.I.?"

"Never better, Inspector, sorry, Chief Inspector."

The two men walked the corridor into an empty room where the inspector welcomed Tom. Tom briefed him on the latest developments on the case and the reason for his visit.

Ponde called someone at the CID to help Tom obtain the search warrant he needed to storm Ndomba's apartment.

He wrote the name on a piece of paper and handed it to Tom. "The man is as clean as any angel on this earth would be and very reliable. He would find you some clean men if you need some help, too. He will be expecting you."

"Nothing leaves this room. I want this done as quietly as possible. We cannot tell who is who in Mark's payroll," Tom stressed.

"You have my solemn word. If Mark is the bad guy, then I also want to see him brought to book as much as you do."

"Thanks again, pal."

"Welcome again, P.I. And good luck."

And as surely as the chief inspector had promised, Tom found Frank 'Pure', the CID operative who people had nicknamed pure, due to his reputation as a clean, incorruptible and very reliable cop. Tom was soon armed with the search warrant and some two CID officers 'Pure' had recommended, and together with another private detective Tom had worked with in many other cases, they were off to surprise Ndomba with the Sunday morning storming of his flat. The operation was kept out of the press.

Ndomba and his female companion were caught by surprise. The exercise produced astonishing results. A consignment of cocaine, rhino horns, and an unlicensed pistol were netted.

Initially Ndomba refused to cooperate with the team. Tom told him about the dying pals of Mark and the fact that they already knew about the true nature of Juve's accident and the two Britons who had made a deal to testify against him and Mark. At that moment Ndomba realized he had to strike a deal to save himself from some very long time behind bars.

Ndomba pointed the accusing finger at Mark who he insisted was carrying out a huge drug trafficking and poaching operation and had plans in place to take over the country forcefully, shocking everyone.

After deliberations among themselves, the CID department agreed with Tom that Ndomba should be released but put under strict twenty-four hours surveillance and asked to cancel any travelling arrangements from the city. This would keep Mark from suspecting the noose was quickly tightening on him.

Ndomba agreed to fulfill his part of the deal to the letter. After all, he realized keeping a good account of himself would earn him some lenience and, ultimately fewer years behind bars. He was ready to stand against Mark in the dock.

****

Due to his experience in the case and wide knowledge on the main suspect, Mark, Tom was named the head of the top secret police operation that involved a substantial number of law enforcement officers recommended for the task for their proven diligence by none other than Frank 'Pure'.

Tom was to submit a plan within seventy-two hours for approval and implementation at the CID offices of 'Pure'.

Mark was now a threat to the nation. He had to be stopped as soon and as effectively as possible.

TWENTY SIX

With the Mark Lubevu take over, the Wenjuve Companies had slid from an empire status with over one hundred and fifty supermarket franchises around the world and six shopping paradises in Nairobi, New York, London, Paris, Buenos Aires and Riyadh, to a depleted group of companies with just five franchise supermarkets and one shopping paradise at Nairobi. Mark had even sold off the hotels at the Nairobi shopping paradise. The world was only amazed at the rate of plunge.

Mark's apparent ambitions for political superiority in Kenya were confirmed by his announcement to vie for the top job - the presidency. He insisted he was the only person in the country who belonged in the top job. He insisted that his destiny was the presidency, and nobody was going to divorce him from what was rightfully his.

Asked how sure he was about his prospects when more than a dozen people had already declared similar intentions, among them some seasoned politicians leading in opinion polls, Mark insisted it was he alone who would stand at the inauguration dais.

And as Kenyans braced themselves for the fourth multi-party elections and the build up continued to gain momentum, Mark smiled. It was a contented smile. His long held dream was finally turning to reality. With his great links and great plans, there was no way anybody was going to stop him. Or so he thought.

****

Tom put a full stop to the airtight plan Judy and Monica had helped him create. His time for submission was fast running out. He defeated the deadline by two hours. He was barely relaxed when the call from the office came in. Sally was calling to announce that the plan had already met the approval. Frank 'Pure' himself called Tom to set the ball rolling.

Monica had finally found the Lendgrade company offices in Nairobi. She noted down the particulars as the voice on the other end of the long distance telephone conversation between Nairobi and Mombasa gave them to her. Lendgrade was a subsidiary of an international Swiss bank, The Rock Solid Bank International, better known as RSB International. They were her financiers during the expansion project for transforming her kiosk into the Stardine cafeteria.

She called and asked for Mr. Martin Rodway, who had been her case manager during the expansion project. She was to learn that Martin had been transferred to Nairobi. The phone call saved her a trip to the coast and helped her trace the Skyline Towers, the building where Lendgrade's offices were located.

The next morning Monica stormed her way past the uncooperative secretary, who was insisting that she would have to come two weeks later as her boss' appointments were booked up until then. She also discovered that Mr. Rodway had been promoted to African Regional Credits Director.

Five days later, she was to receive an okay for the one-billion shillings plus financial backing for the operation. Martin himself stood as the guarantor. In matters of national security he felt he had to play his part.

Monica had finally secured the financial backing for the operation. Time to put the whole plan into action had finally come.

****

In Kenya, land grabbing and fencing off of land by some powerful, rich, politically correct and well placed individuals is a commonplace practice in every day happenings. It thus came as no surprise when the barbed wire temporary perimetre fencing came up around a school-owned land.

The land was used to generate funds for the school, as the football and rugby pitches were rented out to other institutions. The football pitch had even played host to some epic Premier League matches when a city based football club had used the pitch as their home ground pitch.

First, the City Pearl Academy's management had written a letter of protest to the country's Land Ministry and copied it to the Nairobi City Council, complaining about the fraudulent allocation.

The issue suddenly attracted the eyes of political opportunists (who happened to be many, as the country was looking forward to elections). All of a sudden it was crossfire and warnings all over the local media with each politician accusing the other of involvement. Both the Ministry and the City Commission preferred a taciturn attitude to this particular issue.

The school's management organized demonstrations around the city to protest the purported fraudulent allocation of their school's land and land grabbing in general. The land rights organizations quickly joined in the fray.

An investigative report by a weekly periodical carried an exposé on the story behind the infamous fraudulent land allocation.

A private developer, through the company Oasis, was named as the beneficiary behind the fraudulent allocation.

The company was planning a hypermarket, which was going to be the only one of its kind in the continent. The hypermarket was going to be equipped with the latest technology only available in the developed world. That piece of information threw the Wenjuve Groups into the fray.

As protests intensified and the bright idea of legal redress presented itself, the Wenjuve Groups volunteered to foot all the bills.

Personally for Mark, this was a slap in the face at his dominance of the supermarket industry in Kenya, which was almost a religion. He passed a memo to be signed by every top official at Wenjuve, declaring their support for legal redress against Oasis. For most of the signatories, this was a worthless, unfair battle, but for Mark, keeping others out was a battle worth fighting.

The historical land case quickly captured the attention of every *Kamau, Atieno*, and *Cheruyot* across the country and every John, Dick and Harry, worldwide.

From the word go, it was apparent that the plaintiffs were fighting a losing battle. By the end of two weeks of dramatic court action, defence lawyer David Mnopita had made himself a darling to the public. He had promised to prove to the world at large that the deal was 'as clean as snow' and had seemed to be on the road to achieving the fete. He supported himself with documentary evidence that the school was actually sitting on private land donated by a generous owner on a fifty-year occupancy deal. City Pearl Academy's occupancy deal had actually expired the previous year and the land had been consequently sold to Oasis. The school had put in place a completely new set of faces in the board that did not seem to understand the deal made fifty–one years ago. Mnopita had brought to the witness stand some former board members, a number of previous holders of the head teacher's office, teachers and students. His twenty-one witnesses had all unanimously declared, in their various testimonies that the land that the school was sitting on had actually automatically reverted to its owner that previous year.

The plaintiffs could not come up with any solid proof, especially faced with such overwhelming evidence. Oasis was suddenly free to develop their ultra modern hypermarket. They were in fact free to seek legal redress for the soiling of their good name!

The fourth estate were making mince meat of the plaintiffs and chasing around the victors trying to get some first-hand information on Oasis' next move. All the Oasis representatives could say was 'No comments' to the insistent questions thrown at them by the press.

"We will call the press and issue a statement after we've had a board meeting about this," were the final words by the Oasis Development Group court delegation leader as they all disappeared into their prestigious vehicles and were driven off to their various destinations.

As promised, a week later, the Oasis Development Group invited the press and Kenyans to a press conference at Hilton Hotel, Nairobi.

"We have searched through our hearts, souls and minds and all we can see is maybe there is a better way of dealing with this issue without negativity affecting the lives of so many people."

There were murmurs all over the conference room as everybody tried to speculate the next statement or digest the previous one.

"First we want you all to know we do not see the need for legal redress about the recent episodes." Murmurs pervaded the room. "We believe in forgiving," the speaker continued once the room came back to order. "We also want you to know that we have been looking and asking around and we are glad to let you know that we are in the final stages of acquiring a new site for our project."

The murmurs suddenly drowned her statement, and

for a minute, she had to wait until curious silence re-took its place in the room.

"We are sorry, we cannot reveal the locality of this site as protocol has to be complied with, but we will let you know soon where the new site will be as immediately as possible."

A coup of confused, knowledgeable and speculative noise toppled the curious silence once again.

"City Pearl Academy is no longer under the obligation to vacate the plot on which it stands as many may have expected." The spokesperson drummed the point home the moment calm returned in the conference room.

The murmur, the claps, the jubilation and the surprise all pervaded the room simultaneously. It took a long while before this eventually subsided to let the speaker continue.

"We have simply forfeited our right to that land in favour of the school. And to hammer home this point, we want to dedicate a monthly fifty thousand shillings for the upkeep of this beautiful piece of land."

Oasis had suddenly become a darling of the masses and the world at large. And the world was not getting tired of showering them with praises, awards, recognition and compliments. Theirs was a show of selflessness and self sacrifice for a noble cause, unmatched in that end of the globe.

It came as no surprise that the Oasis hypermarkets were an instant hit when they finally sprung up whichever place that was, world over.

Oasis's coincidentally came up in areas that their rival Wenjuve had their strongholds. To add salt to the wound, Oasis seemed to be out to ruin the chances of any market command the Wenjuves might have hitherto held, with their down-to-earth prices that were incomparable on their highest of quality range of goods, coupled with excellent service and customer care. Wenjuve were simply no match for the new entrants in the field of supermarket investments. Pundits quickly pointed to the fact that Oasis group seemed not to be interested in instant profit making as the pricing regime they had adopted would not sustain profit making.

And with events unfolding on those terms, it wasn't long before Wenjuve groups were cash strapped as goods remained either on shelves, or in storehouses too long and there was a marked drop in quality.

Soon, Mark was running around every corner of the globe trying to find some financial support that would keep Wenjuve afloat.

But as if predicting the downfall of the Wenjuve group in the face of competition and unwilling to put money on precarious investments, everybody shunned Mark like the plague.

Then this life saving telephone call from a stranger came through when Mark had lost all hope for help.

"Listen Mark, I can help you out. But promise you will look around for a better investment other than supermarkets. I'll only do this because Juve was a very special friend to me. I won't stand back and watch his friends and family fall apart.

The frail old man in his early seventies puffed out clouds from his expensive brand of cigars into the enormous executive office. He was dressed royally. Every inch of him was stinking rich.

Mark could swear the air around him had an odour of new crisp legal tender.

Mark was no push-over. He had always been the one to push people over. Now this bloody Oasis had pushed him to the wall. Mark had always made deals on his own terms. He knew there had to be a catch somewhere if this man was offering to help him out. But he realized no alternative existed.

His supermarkets had always provided the capital to get the poachers and drug dealers coming to him. He then sold off the wares at exorbitant prices in Europe, Asia and the Americas.

He then got weapons from these places, and sold them to coup plotters and governments of war ravaged countries. That way, he made very huge profits, which he generously lost in gambling and lavish living with girls and booze all around him. He always generously rewarded those who did his dirty work for him. His most handsome rewards went to those that ignited and fuelled wars around the world. They helped keep his business going.

However, he kept a huge fraction of the arms aside and had built several armories scattered around the country. He had already identified and recruited some five thousand men, mostly jobless youth, for his ultimate goal – take over of the country's leadership. And now he was suddenly cash strapped! He had to get back to the fold. He had no other recourse.

"I'm Ali, Ali Ombwema. But I know you have heard of Biggy."

Mark was surprised. Why would Biggy be interested in him? Mark had heard of him all right. Biggy's name was all over the press and mentioned in almost every scandal in the country. Mark had never seen him or a picture of him. It felt odd now, looking at Biggy face-to-face.

"Oh! I know what you are thinking. Not the Biggy of the scandals and political juggles. I just go by that name because I was born over weight."

"I see. And why would you wanna help me when everybody else thinks I'm some plague from space and ought to be avoided at all costs?"

"I told you Juve was a special friend to me. You didn't get to know me because I left when the missionaries first showed up at the village. We lost contact with Juve since then. Then he was called Juveninge, which was later shortened to Juve. Here is a contract I took the liberty of preparing. You sign that and we have us a deal. Fill in the figures of your choice. 500 million is the ceiling."

"I need time to think about this. I have never been in debt. It makes me helpless."

"You are not helpless, Mark. I know Juve would not approve were he here, but I don't mind if the money were to be invested in anything. And I mean *anything*"

Mark understood exactly what he meant by 'anything', be it 'clean' or 'dirty.'

"I just want you to get yourself off this crap and start being my customer at the new bank I'm setting up soon. You realize to succeed in such a competitive market I would need huge personalities like you. Once you walk out that door without leaving you signature behind, don't come crawling back to me."

So the guy needed him too, at least that made it an equal deal. He had walked the world looking for some financial help. He could not turn his back on his last chance of survival. He went through the contents of the contract, carefully. The only term was that he had to pay the full amount in six months. There were no interest charges. He filled in the maximum figure and signed. He was going to take the risk. If he was in default within six months, everything that belonged to him would become Biggy's property. He was worth some five billion at least if he included the arms and the illicit businesses. This guy thought he was clever. Mark thought he was a fool.

"You know something, Mark Lubevu, you are my first client in the new bank. I'll give you the chance to help me choose a suitable name for the enterprise. I may even give you some extra days should I be in good moods by then."

But Mark was not listening to Biggy's final statements. He took the cheque and greedily walked out of the place. He had gotten all that he wanted from Biggy. There would come that time when he would be in State House. People who ordered him around would really pay, heavily.

Time was right to order the poachers to the bushes and traffickers to their sources. He needed the money fast. 500 million would fetch him tones of cocaine, heroine, ivory and rhino horns, and, yes, arms from all over the world. He would even manage to obtain some cheetah and leopard skins. He placed his calls to his people. Then he placed one to his American Italian associate, who seemed to spin the whole world of illicit drugs, arms and poaching products – Salvanto Prissicalli.

Mark smiled. He was as good as back in the fold. He was as good as in State House. His dream was going to be realized. He was obviously one of the chosen few.

****

What Mark did not know was that Biggy too placed a call to his people.

"The meeting was successful," he announced, tossing the cigar into the dustbin. He was not a smoker. Nor was he a rich man. He was not called Biggy either, for that matter. He was not going to open any bank soon. He was called Charles Mumbe, an employee at the Stardine.

Another thing that Mark did not know was that some one else was listening in on his calls. Ndomba Munaki had placed the bug on Marks telephone as instructed.

Tom smiled. It was a satisfied smile. He had chased the case for too long. Now the end was in sight.

Judy threw her arms around him. She had no words for the gratitude she felt. Monica hopped around the room like a small kid. She could not control the triumphant feelings within. Their excitement almost drowned the breakthrough coming from the speakers of the bugging devices.

Tom placed a long distance call to the United States. Wayne was happy to hear of the news. At least Salvanto Prissicalli was in a corner. He could not find the words to thank Tom for the job well done. It was just a matter of time before a huge chunk of the underworld would be brought to book. Everybody in the room was going to be waiting - impatiently.

TWENTY SEVEN

"How's your baby."

"She's doing quite well."

"Mine too."

"Let's take 'em shopping tomorrow at eleven."

"Is 2 pm a good time?"

"That's fine with me."

There was a click sound as both phones were hung up. It was just going to be routine. Tom and his team wanted to make sure the arrest was going to be mounted only when the 'goods' were in the possession of the two drug lords. Otherwise those charges would hardly stick on either Mark or Salvanto. Tom was wondering if there was any need to put the tail on these two guys going on a shopping outing with their daughters. It would be risky if they found out they were being tailed. Such a situation as a shopping outing would easily give room for mistakes. He decided they would use the least number of men on this particular shift just to keep the tail stuck. It would be great to see those innocent daughters of the two criminals and know in his heart that saving them from their parents' life styles would be a worthy reward.

But Tom wanted to find out from Ndomba Munaki if the two really had daughters in the first place, before ordering his surveillance men to re-organize to the minimum. He was not aware that Mark was a father. But it was possible given the lifestyle he led. Tom would not be at all surprised if he learnt that Mark had many children with different mothers.

Tom easily traced Ndomba, whose answer was negative. He did not know of any daughters that those two had. Mark and Salvanto were anything but family conscious people. That was hardly like them.

"Can you come and listen in on a recorded conversation and tell me what you think those guys mean?" Tom asked Ndomba.

Ndomba translated as the tape was played back.

"Do you have the goods?"

"Yes I got them."

"Me too."

"Okay, let's exchange them at the supermarket at eleven."

"Is second supermarket fine with you?"

"Second is fine with me."

"What's the supermarket they are talking about? The Wenjuve?" Tom urgently wanted to know.

"No, not the Wenjuve. You see, Mark can't risk doing something like this in his own backyard. I tell you if I own a shop, will you go shopping there or just ask the item to be delivered to me by any of my employees? If Mark were to do this at the Wenjuve, he would be above customer regulations and that may lead to some one looking at his actions twice," Ndomba said.

"Damn! So what we have here is more than fifty supermarkets to check on. How will we know exactly where these guys are going to do this exchange by eleven tomorrow?" Tom felt cheated. They had come this far and now the chance they have been waiting for was just about to pass them!

"Ndomba, try to think back. You are the only one who could possibly know what second supermarket could be," Monica urged.

"Yeah, Ndomba, something they said or did could help us find the exact place they are going to carry out this exchange," Judy encouraged.

"Try to focus Ndomba. It would be so much easier if we could narrow this down to one supermarket since we could arrange for a welcome committee," Tom pressed.

The room fell into a pregnant silence as everyone slid

into pensiveness. If they did not come up with something fast, that would be the handicap that would give Salvanto a chance to vanish and go and regroup, a chance Tom was not willing to take.

"Wait a minute. Maybe this is it. Can I have a piece of paper and a pencil?

He got three sets of paper and pens, each from each person in the room, anxious to find a solution to the problem.

Ndomba wrote the words '*Wayo Garage*' and next to them the numerical value of twenty-three. He then wrote '*Dumno Garage*' *and* the number four next to it. He handed those to Tom.

"I can remember Mark once told me to accompany him to Dumno Garage in Eastleigh Estates, which were just 4 kilometres from the city of Nairobi. He then called Salvanto and just said '*place four garage*' on the phone. You bet Salvanto was there in the next few minutes. I also can swear I heard him mention *twenty-three* during another of their meetings and we went to a place I later came to learn is called Wayo Garage.

"That should mean that a supermarket whose name starts with a 'B' would be our second supermarket?" Tom observed.

"And most likely that would be the only supermarket whose name starts with a 'B'," Ndomba added.

"Bingo! The Badaar Supermarket, Koinange Street," Monica concluded excitedly.

"What's the time?" Tom asked abruptly.

"Twenty-five minutes to six," Judy said, puzzled at the significance of time.

"We have twenty-five minutes to get to Badaar and start making arrangements for our guests tomorrow." Tom announced.

He called *WatchAngels* and ordered 12 pieces of surveillance cameras complete with the necessary monitoring equipment and technicians to fix them. He asked them to find their way to Badaar as fast as possible and use a foodstuff delivery van to conceal the cameras. The success of the operation depended on cover. Tom had used them before in other operations and their working relationship was great. They understood his needs with the minimum of explanations.

Tom and his team needed just fifteen minutes to make it to the supermarket. Tom identified himself and asked to be shown to the manager. He was directed to a short, bulky, half-bald man. He explained the purpose of their visit. The manager was unwilling to face a risk of destruction and property loss. He proposed to remain closed for the whole of that following day. When Tom promised full compensation and the fact that the surveillance cameras would not be removed once the operation was done with, the manager was finally agreeable.

Tom placed the call to okay the *WatchAngels* technicians to proceed with the fixing. The cameras were to be concealed in all manner of places convenient for the next day's operation and would be fitted properly once the task at hand was done. The supermarket would then permanently use them. The team realized Salvanto and Mark's men might be watching the place closely, so they had to ensure no suspicion was raised. The *W&A* technicians went to work immediately and they broke the camera circuiting record time for the city.

Every formality was tackled with utmost care. The luggage box that following morning was to be manned by plain-clothed police officers. These officers were to ensure that print clean cards were handed over to the suspects to prove the exchange. The back-ups were to communicate the identity of the suspects to these officers to ensure no mix up occurred. Plain-clothed police officers would be camouflaged as supermarket employees and customers. The 50 officers on the team were to report to the supermarket at five that morning for a rehearsal to ensure no mistakes were made during the actual operation. Thirty of those would be posted in the supermarket itself and others in strategic places around the supermarket. By ten o'clock the following morning everything was in place, with officers camouflaged as anything thinkable in and around the vicinity of the supermarket.

At two minutes to eleven, a battered Nissan pulled into the supermarket parking lot. Tom did not need to see through the disguise to know who it was. His surveillance team had kept Mark under tight surveillance for the past few weeks. But anybody could easily be fooled that that was a Taxi driver.

There was another car. A blue Mercedes E200. Somebody told them on the radio that could be their other guest of honour, Salvanto, arriving in time for the ceremony. This particular car had three occupants. A huge, heavy set man in his mid-twenties got out of the rear seat of the Mercedes, which took a parking spot a few metres from the supermarket's entrance. He was carrying a huge briefcase under his arm which he gave to their query, Salvanto, who was seated in the front passenger seat, and their guest of honour walked straight into the supermarket.

Then there were two nine-seater minibuses that dropped tourists near the Badaar. There were two guys whose attire was completely same to their target's dressing, (Salvanto), and they were carrying similar bags!

Tom quickly interpreted what it meant. Salvanto was going to use them to hide his identity and avoid raising suspicion about the exchange so that the guys at the luggage compartment would not notice the peculiar exchange. He warned the team that nobody was to leave the supermarket without being screened. There could be exchange of fire as these people could be carrying weapons.

The 'taxi driver,' who had parked at an opposite parking spot, went to his luggage compartment and picked up a huge travelling bag, before walking straight to the supermarket. He passed the Mercedes without much of a glance.

The officers communicated with the men at the luggage desk. Every officer was notified about the suspect's dressing and put on high alert.

Mark and Salvanto as well as their cronies were caught flat footed. It was a bloodless operation, especially considering the fact that it was widely expected to be one of the bloodiest.

What followed was a series of arrests related to the Mark – Salvanto arrest. The five armories Mark had built around the country were stormed and some three hundred automatic assault rifles and other fighting equipment were seized and confiscated. In Kenya alone, some five hundred people were arrested and charged with cases related to Mark's situation.

Around the world, news of drug busts and arrest of traffickers, poachers, and illegal arms dealers suddenly became commonplace, as Salvanto's dens of operation were given up in interrogation rooms. The war on terror around the world had suddenly gathered momentum a notch higher. Mark and Salvanto were arming terrorist organizations around the world. Few names that had vanished from the face of the earth in the war on terror were suddenly arrested. There was talk that Abdullah Fazul Mohammed was now firmly within sight, thanks to information coming from interrogation rooms.

****

Mark was not going to face trial. He had appointed himself the judge and the accused at the same time and went on to sentence himself to death, even when put in isolation at a maximum-security cell.

Somehow, one of his men had presented himself as a priest and had gained entry into his cell and passed him some lethal tablets that he had swallowed without hesitation. The doctors were too late and Mark had achieved his aim.

For Salvanto Prissicalli, though Italians were baying for his blood for some crimes he was alleged to have committed there, the United States had arranged repatriation back to the US to face trial there.

Tom suddenly became an instant sensation for that week, as the man who had helped bring half the underworld to its knees. His photograph was the most sought after by the media fraternity. The world simply could not read and hear enough about him. He was the darling of the millions who believed in justice and the war against crime.

****

As Tom watched happenings in the press in the grip of election fever, he wondered what would happen were Mark to be involved. He feared the dreaded answer. Mark had turned out to be a greedy, calculating criminal who would stop at nothing to have his wishes granted. To him, it did not matter how many lives were wasted or what the destruction would be. And that was just an iota.

The elections seemed to have gone well, but when the results were announced and the two main contestants claimed victory. Soon, hell broke lose. By the time the two principals were signing the National Reconciliation Accord on 28th February 2008, over 1,000 people, including children, had lost lives. Brutal, gory acts of inhumanity were committed, more than 600,000 became homeless and an estimated 3,000 women brutally raped.

One name that seemed synonymous with the violence was Mark Lubevu. He was said to have been targeting a cosmopolitan constituency and the presidency. His evil game plan was hatched early in 2006 after the 2005 constitutional referendum showed that there was a latent possibility of a civil war, which would be a good excuse for a coup d'état. Inciting Information had been strategically fed into various unsuspecting political players, who were keen to make political capital, in bits and pieces shaped to fit their localized interests and designed to fuel the polarity into a break-out of violence along ethnic lines.

It was no wonder that the constituency Mark was to represent was one of the first to register cases of ethnic violence a few days before the election itself. It was also one of the worst hit. Everything would have fallen into place if Mark had not been arrested. Tom now understood what the armories were for. With all the confusion, Mark's army would come out and unexpectedly attack the government forces stretched to capacity. He knelt down and prayed. Only God could have intervened at such a timely moment.

****

From the police investigations, there emerged enough evidence that the scandals that had plunged the millionaire Juve's last days into darkness were sums of additions and minuses of Mark's premeditated intent.

A signature forgery expert with the Interpol had carefully checked the signatures on the documents that had been presented as evidence against Juve and had concluded they were fakes.

A suspect in the police swoop admitted to have been used by Mark to fake Juve's signatures. When asked to do it all over again, the suspect produced signatures that stunned even the police experts.

Another suspect had after vigorous questioning admitted that he helped Mark acquire the necessary connections for drugs and smuggled goods that included arms, months prior to the coming of the infamous Juve scandals.

It had now become an open secret that Mark had wanted Juve out of the way to gain the company's presidency and thereby a spring board into politics.

A suspect had testified that Juve's 'accident' was engineered through a small device that had been secretly installed under the sedan. It was designed to use up heat from the engine to burn the low temperature metal enablers. These enablers melted to establish contact and start up the battery operated device that cut through brake pipes, thereby inducing a total brake failure within minutes of its start up. The pipes had then been replaced by new ones and the device had been removed even before the wreckage was *discovered,* as Mark and company had all along known where it was lying battered, confirming Wayne Stelle's Version of the report.

Mark had then hired *Lorna*, the kidnapper, to take care of Kate, the heir apparent to the Wenjuve fortune.

While conducting an identification parade, a suspect's movements struck Tom as very familiar. One of his legs was slightly shorter than the other and so there was a noticeable gait to a keen eye. Tom walked over to him and asked him where else he had seen him. The suspect looked away.

While Tom and the police force were reviewing the cases, the death of Wendy Teluve came to focus as the only case he did not have much to go with. Then he remembered the suspect with a concealed gait in his walk and asked the officers to prepare the interrogation room. He was sure he had an idea where he had seen that gait before. The suspect admitted he was one of the guys who attacked Wendy while Tom watched at 10 years of age. The chemical they injected Wendy with was Arsenic. That explained all the pregnancy complications that forced the doctors to perform emergency surgery to save baby Kate, the skin complications, the heart disruptions, the brain damage and loss of resistance to infections, which allowed a small bout of pneumonia to claim her life in just under a week. It was all under Mark's orders. The suspect too had to exile himself to keep alive. Tom's childhood home-made device had found its link. It was the device that had actually procured the death of Wendy Teluve, via a press of a button that signalled the attackers to strike, just as Tom had suspected all along. It had now been confirmed by the suspect. One more suspect was apprehended after that confession while another three involved were confirmed deceased, in highly suspicious circumstances - Mark's unmistaken trademark. The police could now close the Wendy Teluve case. Tom's three cases involving the Teluve's were officially solved.

BOOK THREE – THE RE-UNION

TWENTY EIGHT

The two figures in the room could not contain within themselves what was happening to them. They had worked side by side and had not realized the attraction they had developed for each other. Each had pushed their feelings aside and concentrated on the fight against the vicious criminals.

Now the criminals had fallen and there was no where else to camouflage what they felt. Like magnets, attracted to one another by forces unknown, they were drawn towards each other. Their eyes locked in a deep passionate hold. Their arms went around each other as if life depended on it. Their lips followed, automatically, and the tongues searched relentlessly.

Their clothes dropped to the carpeted floor like tatters, as their fingers worked through the fastenings urgently. They slid to the carpet underneath and their bodies immediately assumed the rhythmic amatory motions.

"I have never felt this way about anyone all my life. If this is what they call love, then I love you so - very much Judy – Kate." Tom could not help saying when it was over. They both smiled at the sentence confusion of using 'so' and 'very' and 'Kate' and 'Judy.'

"If they call this love, then Mr. Mbuke, I love you very - so much too."

He looked at her in the eyes and said the words, "Judy, Catherine, will you accept if I asked you out on a wedding?" They laughed at the funny way he had framed it.

She looked back at him deep in the eyes and answered "Who would I be to refuse the greatest outing offer from a man I so love?" They laughed at the equally funny answer.

The date had been set for some three months later, and the count down to the Kenyan wedding of the century had begun.

****

The ownership of the Wenjuve group had to be determined by a court case that granted the financiers the company due to defaults in payment. It was on this occasion that everyone began to understand that the tycoon who had given Mark the 500 million shilling loan was in fact an employee at the Stardine cafeteria, which belonged to Monica. And in an exclusive press conference once the court victory had been secured, the biggest of all rumours was confirmed. Judy was actually the long lost Kate Teluve, the heir apparent to the Wenjuve fortune. Every newspaper that carried that interview the next day was a complete sell out worldwide.

Two weeks later Wenjuve, now under new management had made a multi-million shillings deal to buy back the twin hotels from the Swedish hotelier to whom Mark had sold them, though at very inflated prices.

For this new Wenjuve, with Judy as President, that prestige that had in the past been associated with the group had to be regained at all costs. The complete Wenjuve heaven was going to be reopened with a massive wedding reception for the Wenjuve president and her new husband.

The construction started in earnest immediately, but unpredictable weather and other delays hindered the completion of the project within the designated time frame. Tom and Judy opted to have the wedding ceremony, proceed to their honeymoon and return for the reception later, when the project was expected to be ready.

The ceremony itself was an international event and at least four television channels covered it live. The list of dignitaries from around the world was a markedly diverse list of who is who. Thousands had made the trip into Kenya, just to convey their well wishes personally.

An old, well-dressed man looked a familiar figure, but Tom could not place his finger on it. His walk, style and mannerism were not new to Tom. Tom was even surprised how he could not place it. The man wore what Kenyans commonly referred to as the *'god papa,'* a round rimmed hat that was reputed to be very expensive and dark glasses. Tom wanted to move closer to the man, but being a 'candle' in the ceremony, he could hardly manage. Then the old man suddenly vanished before Tom could move any closer.

The prolonged two month honeymoon took the newly-weds to almost every famous site they had ever heard of or came across. They drank and ate and sunbathed and disappeared into their various executive suites for most of the hours.

By the time Tom and Judy were returning to Kenya, the huge feast had already been laid in the waiting. And when they landed at the Jomo Kenyatta International Airport, they were received by a huge motorcade to take them directly to the newly restored Wenjuve shopping heaven. The ceremony would be their wedding reception and the opening ceremony of the Wenjuve heaven.

Everything proceeded as planned. First, the Wenjuve president cut through a ribbon and popped a bottle of champagne to officially open the building before the reception ceremony was to begin. The ceremony started with re-vowing, whereby the couple repeated their sacred vows. Then came prayers for the newly weds.

Cake cutting came next on the programme and was characterized by the cutting of a miniature cake impression of the complete Wenjuve Heaven.

The feasting, where all manner of varieties of foods and beverages were the main features, followed. This was quickly succeeded with dancing and merry making. Soon the master of ceremony signaled the attention of people that the newly weds were ready to receive presents.

The old man had saved himself for this particular moment. He had planned for this day for so long, and the moment had finally come. He had earlier passed the present to the man who was responsible for testing the presents for any dangerous contents such as explosives, before eventually passing it over to the couple. His had passed such tests and would be easily put near the couple.

Suddenly, it happened. The present collapsed and its contents were revealed, drawing everybody's attention.

The old man seized the microphone from the master of the ceremonies amid the confusion. The security team tried to wrestle it from him, but Tom intervened and urged them to let the man speak.

The old man waited for a long momentary pause to elapse, before beginning.

"Thanks a lot for this opportunity. I'll go straight to the point."

The murmurs were all saying in a disorderly unison, 'just another nut-case.'"

"I was driving on a lonely winding road when somebody waved me for a lift. It was already dark and I did not see why I should let him risk his life walking on such a lonely road alone at that time. I stopped and let him in. I offered to give him a lift to his place."

"The road was very clear and on one side, there was a very deep valley. You won't dream of crashing here. It would be fatal. I looked at the speedometre, and I released the accelerator pedal. There was a bend coming up. The speed was too fast for the bend."

"I pressed the brake pedal and it collapsed into the body frame. Nothing happened. I tried again and still nothing. We had no brakes. I lost control of the vehicle. It was too late to do anything more. We went crashing into the valley."

"My instincts took over. I opened the door and tried to jump. I can remember yelling at the stranger to do the same, although now I know he didn't."

"Something must have hit me hard. It was after three months that I came back from a coma. A lone doctor was looking after me in a lonely makeshift hospital."

"He asked me who I was. Then I realized I didn't know a thing about myself. The room was the only thing I knew about me. He said I had amnesia and I was suffering from total memory loss. Now I know I owe Dr. Makaza for my life, and not only once but twice."

"It took the doctor some fifteen years to find an effective formula for my amnesia. For some two years, I had to learn who I really was."

"Those files are medical records over the years, reports and tests, and police records."

He removed the hat and dark glasses for the first time for every one to see. The crowd was stunned. Judy collapsed and fainted from the shock. Tom remained transfixed and speechless before finally recovering and going through files, as the medical team worked on his wife. No wonder the old man looked familiar.

There were photographs taken over the last 18 years, a dental identity that matched perfectly, police records on prints, which were confirmed as a match from the CID department and there were some blood and other DNA tests. It was all there. Juve was alive.

It was this chronology of events that led to the naming of the Nairobi Wenjuve Shopping Heaven, the Re-union Heavens.

When Judy finally got over her initial shock and was hugging her father for the very first time ever, it formed the bulk of the following morning's headlines, worldwide.

When the book '*YEARS APART*' *hit* the stands, the publisher had to re-issue another batch after the first edition of 300,000 copies sold out in weeks.

TWENTY NINE

Myria Zombo got a copy of the *Daily Nation* from a neighbour who had managed to get a copy of that morning's newspaper that was sold out.

She read through the main story. She read twice about how Juve had picked up a stranger on the main road and proceeded to get into accident.

Her husband had disappeared that very same evening without a trace. She had made a report at the local police station and they had placed an advert in the local dailies and radio, but nothing happened. Initial investigations revealed he could have used the main road.

Anything could have happened to him in the dark. Myria had hoped that one day he would walk back into their lives, but as everyday passed she realized it was just wishful thinking. All she wanted to know was what could have happened to him.

He had been the sole breadwinner of the family at the time of his disappearance. Myria had to start from borrowing from friends. She had struggled and had finally ended up in the streets of Nairobi, hawking.

That way at least she managed to put up an iron sheet roof over the heads of her three children and fill their stomachs with some food, in their mud thatched walled hut at the Mathare Valley.

Now here comes a story of a man who had been long presumed dead and buried reappearing and saying what exactly happened on that fateful evening. Myria's heart skipped briefly. Could it be? Could her husband have been buried in the name of somebody else?

She had to find out. She owed it to herself, her husband, whether dead or still alive somewhere, and their children.

She looked for a directory. When she found the numbers she wanted she found a phone booth and tried to dial. The lines were busy. What would anyone expect from people whose story alone could put bread and butter on millions of tables?

She borrowed the *Daily Nation,* dressed up in her best outfit and proceeded to *Nation* house.

The next morning when the paper followed up on its previous day's story and carried her version of the story, the Wenjuve group responded and asked the woman to go to the group's premises personally.

When Juve saw the picture of her husband, he responded affirmative. It was that man he had offered a lift to. She had finally found her husband and maybe unexpected benefits with it after all.

As a token of their sorrow and apology for what had happened, the Wenjuve group set up the widow and her three children in Nairobi's posh Kileleswa Estates, and promised to take care of her and her children for the rest of their lives. The children were enrolled into prestigious schools, and suddenly she became a proud owner of a posh car. It was funny how fate works sometimes.

****

Wenjuve groups of companies were quickly returning to take their rightful place on the world stage as one of the most successful giants in the supermarkets field. The Wenjuve supermarkets sprung up at every other corner of the globe and the Wenjuve Heavens were also growing in numbers.

For Monica, the over 30 million dollar loan she had secured was quickly serviced and everything was flowing smoothly.

For the newly weds, Tom and Judy, there could never have been a better wedding present. For the first time in her life, Judy had somebody she could call father.

Interpol had quickly moved in to establish Tom as a regional chief detective. His once semi-executive office was now a well-equipped investigation centre, complete with latest forensic and ballistic divisions, and dozens of experts at his disposal.

Doctor Fexwell Makaza had been nominated for the Nobel Prize for chemistry, and had quickly moved to take his place in the medical circles.

EPILOGUE

The song *'Here comes the bride'* pervaded through the church air, coming from the choir. The bride walked slowly and purposefully, through the isle towards the altar.

Her long, pink, expensive designer wedding dress laden with ribbons, laces, and jewels, moved harmoniously and rhythmically with her every step. The flickering of cameras disturbed the cool air in the church.

To one end of the church was a section reserved for the fourth estate in the otherwise packed ceremony where every member of the congregation was a special guest, short listed from the millions who wanted to attend and the thousands who had a real chance to be there. Here, you could count almost every international and national media organization. Nobody was ready to miss out on this.

After the vows and the rings had been exchanged, the priest made the commonplace declaration, "I now pronounce you Juve and you Monica husband and wife. You may kiss the bride," he said to the groom.

The cameras went wild and the rest of the congregation cheered, as the symbolic, brief, customary kiss was exchanged. Juve had finally gone beyond his tribulations and had found someone to share his ripe age with. Monica had at last found a man she could trust. It had almost taken her a lifetime, but she had at last met Mr. Right.

The reception at the Wenjuve Heaven was memorable and sumptuous. It was at the time that Juve removed a paper from the inner breast pocket of his suit.

"My wife and I have been discussing this matter for some time now."

It was the sort of statement that every journalist and camera man knew to mean their attention was needed.

Once the media was ready Juve continued. "Edmund Burke once said, 'When bad men combine, the good must associate; or else they will fall one by one, an unpitied sacrifice in a contemptible struggle'."

"He also said, 'All that is necessary for the triumph of evil is that good men do nothing'."

"When I travelled to Spain once to inspect the site for a Wenjuve Heaven in Barcelona, I remember a Spanish partner telling me, 'a wise man changes his mind and a fool does not'."

"I led my life as a business man and shunned politics. But the events of early this year have made me realize that I made a mistake. I stayed away when my country needed me most."

The cameras, recorders and pens became energized. Was Juve Teluve going to jump into the murky waters of politics? Or maybe Monica was throwing her hat into politics. It was going to be the story for days, weeks, months or even years.

"When over 1300 people lost their lives and millions of other lives got disrupted, I began to ask myself if my decision to keep off was the right decision. Today I'm convinced it was not the right decision. I'm convinced it was a selfish self preservation mechanism. I realize I'm probably too old to get embroiled in a political campaign. I however want to ask my sons and daughters not to follow me into the mistake of allowing this nation to reach these kinds of alarming levels. I want to confirm that we will help not just them but anyone whose intention is to clean up our politics."

Suddenly the questions came in their threes and fours - which party? What constituency? Are you going for the presidency? Have you taken cognizance of the effect politics will have on your reputation and company? What about the Wenjuve group? Who in Wenjuve is going for the presidency, Judy? Tom? It was a market place. Juve cleared his throat to indicate there was more. He signaled his wife to continue.

"For these reasons...' Monica waited for the noise to die down. "For these reasons Wenjuve Group of Companies has decided to create the Change the Game Foundation. We hope to work with like-minded individuals and organizations to fund, assist, award and reward any person or persons, or organizations in Kenya that will come up with initiatives that will push for betterment of the political culture in this great country. The modalities and other spheres of the initiative will be announced in due course. God Bless Kenya"

The roar of the market returned, this time it was deafening loud. Every journalist wanted more information and wanted their questions answered. The couple's only response was "We've got a honeymoon to enjoy right now" as they were whisked away into the waiting vehicle to the private jet that flew them to a hidden destination for their honeymoon.

ENDS